"So I decided to take m~~~~~~~~~~ to take matters into my own hands.

Miss Danby sat up straighter and gave a brisk nod, as if to encourage herself. "I decided to look around me and to attempt to judge the character of gentlemen and make my own choices. I noticed you, Your Grace. I saw you were courteous, that you took the trouble to ask wallflowers to dance and to converse with the elderly ladies. I never once saw you treat staff with discourtesy, nor overheard you speak crudely or with disrespect of anyone."

She paused for another of those deep breaths and Alex swallowed hard. Surely she was not going to—

"And I heard that you are not a rich man—the rumors say that you are looking to the Marriage Mart to provide you with a well-dowered bride this Season. So I thought I would...I would ask you. In case you had not realized that I would be suitable. To marry. Because I think I am," she finished in a rush and closed her eyes, her face suffused with a blush.

Hell's teeth. I have just been proposed to.

Author Note

Regency young ladies are supposed to wait modestly for gentlemen to propose to them. Regency dukes are strong, silent types not given to romantic daydreams... Or perhaps not. I wondered what would happen if my heroine decided that she would do the proposing. But, unfortunately for her, as she and I discovered, my hero is a true romantic who is looking for love, not just a very tempting dowry. There is liking there, even friendship, but not love. And then he realizes that he really does need that dowry.

How is a romance going to flower with a start like that? I hope you enjoy finding out as much as I did, although here's a spoiler—it all ends in flowers in a riotous London May Day celebration.

How Not to Propose to a Duke

LOUISE ALLEN

Recycling programs
for this product may
not exist in your area.

ISBN-13: 978-1-335-59612-3

How Not to Propose to a Duke

Harlequin Enterprises ULC
22 Adelaide St. West, 41st Floor
Toronto, Ontario M5H 4E3, Canada
www.Harlequin.com

Printed in U.S.A.

Louise Allen has been immersing herself in history for as long as she can remember, finding that landscapes and places evoke powerful images of the past. Venice, Burgundy and the Greek islands are favorites. Louise lives on the Norfolk coast and spends her spare time gardening, researching family history or traveling. Please visit Louise's website, www.louiseallenregency.com, her blog, www.janeaustenslondon.com, or find her on Twitter @louiseregency and on Facebook.

Books by Louise Allen

Harlequin Historical

Marrying His Cinderella Countess
The Earl's Practical Marriage
A Lady in Need of an Heir
"The Viscount's Yuletide Betrothal"
in *Convenient Christmas Brides*
"Snowed in with the Rake"
in *Snowbound Surrender*
Contracted as His Countess
The Duke's Counterfeit Wife
The Earl's Mysterious Lady
His Convenient Duchess
A Rogue for the Dutiful Duchess
Becoming the Earl's Convenient Wife

Liberated Ladies

Least Likely to Marry a Duke
The Earl's Marriage Bargain
A Marquis in Want of a Wife
The Earl's Reluctant Proposal
A Proposal to Risk Their Friendship

Visit the Author Profile page
at Harlequin.com for more titles.

For AJH—the very best of pit crew

Chapter One

London—10th February, 1816

Just knock. And remember to breathe.

Miss Jessica Danby nodded, a sharp, decisive jerk of her head, and Alfred, her footman, trod up the remaining steps and gave a brisk tattoo with the heavy brass knocker.

Beside her Trotter, her maid, made a sound like a faint whimper. Jessica ignored it. Ignored, too, the ferocious Medusa head glaring at them as if in resentment at Alfred's finger-marks. She would not allow anything to shake her resolve.

Through the fine mesh of her veil she saw the door open to reveal the black-clad form of a butler.

'Miss Danby to call upon His Grace,' Alfred said and produced her calling card.

The butler blinked, just once. His eyes flickered from Alfred in immaculate livery to Jessica's veiled figure in its highly fashionable walking dress, then to Trotter beside her. Jessica defied even the most rigid dowager not to find Trotter a model of decorum and respectability.

'If you would care to step inside, madam. I will ascertain whether His Grace is receiving.'

He spoke with admirable calm, Jessica thought. The

most experienced butler would be forgiven for being disconcerted by the unannounced arrival of a respectable unmarried lady on a bachelor duke's doorstep at eleven in the morning.

She inclined her head in thanks and mounted the steps. *Remember to breathe. What can possibly go wrong? Everything.*

Alexander Francis Demeral, Seventh Duke of Malvern, slumped in the vast carved chair behind his desk and stared at the toes of his boots which were currently propped on the blotter.

They were very worn toes, because the boots were old, much repaired and comfortable, which was fortunate, because the latest in the line of the Pinchpenny Dukes had no more in the way of funds than his ancestors had.

King Charles II had created the obscure Viscount Demeral a duke as an apology of sorts for the short-lived regal *affaire* with Lady Demeral but, distracted by the calamitous events of the year 1660, had omitted to do anything about lands to support the honour. The plague and the Great Fire of London were enough to distract anyone and had proved a drain on the already constrained royal purse.

The King had, however, left a lasting legacy in the looks of the son born to Lady Demeral some months later. Even now, one hundred and fifty years on, the resemblance of the Duke to a young Charles Stuart was startling: the lean height, the black hair, the dark eyes under heavy lids and the assertive nose. All that was missing was the wig of tumbling black curls, the world-weary gaze and the procession of buxom mistresses.

Alex was contemplating his options for repairing the

houses of the tenants on his Hereford estate. It was not a pleasant topic. His choices seemed to boil down to two: sell yet another tranche of unentailed land—not that there was much of that left—or marry an heiress. The view of his boots was not providing any easy answers.

It was February, the Season was getting into its stride, marriage was the sensible option and this was the best possible time of year to find a bride. Marriage was also the prudent solution to his troubles as it would be the means of securing an heir, a necessity for a man whose nearest male relative was a somewhat vague rural dean. The Reverend Hector Demeral lived in genteel poverty with a brood of unruly sons, most of whom Alex predicted would end up on the gallows before much longer.

The problem was… The problem was entirely due to his own character, he admitted to himself after a short struggle. He was a romantic and he always had been. He wanted to fall in love. He *needed* to fall in love. There was a tradition that Demerals all married for love—after that one regal infidelity.

In that respect he was a true Demeral, growing up in a household where the two things that were never in short supply were love and affection. The problem with that was that Demeral men always seemed to fall for ladies as well-bred and impoverished as themselves, fathering yet another Pinchpenny Duke in the process.

Which meant that, in addition to finding his true love, she had to be a healthy, well-bred, intelligent young lady with a large endowment whose parents were willing to part with both daughter and dowry in return for the title.

He ought to have a clearer, stronger, sense of duty and break with tradition. He ought not to yearn for a relationship such as his parents and grandparents had enjoyed. It was, he acknowledged, a failing in himself. His peers would laugh themselves sick at the thought of a duke yearning for a love match.

He ought, in short, to be the last of the Pinchpenny Dukes and the first of the Comfortably Wealthy Dukes. The ones who made sensible marriages, expanded the estates, housed their tenants decently, repaired Demeral Castle and sired sons and daughters who would go forth and marry into the great families of the land, all of whom would bring honour, lands and influence with them. And yet... Something in him refused to give up hope that he would look across a crowded room—and there she would be. The One.

He had attended numerous balls, musicales, Venetian breakfasts and masquerades this Season already. Enough, surely, to have met most of the young ladies making their come-outs or embarking on a second or even third Season. There had been rich ones, beautiful ones, witty and amusing ones, along with many who possessed perfectly pleasant characters and countenances. But none of them had stirred anything within him that might be called love, or a desire to know them very much better.

Perhaps he had better sell the marsh grazing down near the Bristol Channel. A pity, because the sheep fed on the salt grass produced wonderful mutton. But the tenants' roofs were leaking, a new bore hole should be made for a well so it was not so far for them to collect fresh water and something must be done with the castle's east turret before it fell on the Great Hall. He would give it another month, he thought. And then—

'A Miss Danby to see you, Your Grace.'

Alex swung his booted feet down off the desk, sat up straight and stared at his butler, who appeared to have parted company with his senses. 'Who? I am not expecting any callers, let alone ladies.'

'Her card, Your Grace.' Pitwick offered a somewhat worn silver salver in the middle of which reposed a calling card, gilt edged and handsomely engraved on heavy stock.

Miss Danby
Adam Street

'Who the devil is Miss Danby?' Alex demanded. The address was good enough, one of the streets off the Strand around the Royal Adelphi Terrace, the handsome creation of the Adam brothers. Her neighbours would be wealthy and socially acceptable, if not of the highest *ton*.

'I regret to say I have no idea, Your Grace. She is accompanied by a liveried footman and her abigail appears to be a most respectable woman. Her attire is both of the mode and, I would judge, of high quality.'

'In other words, a lady. Not a…'

'A high-flyer, Your Grace?' Pitwick suggested with a discreet cough. 'Oh, no, most definitely not a person of that type. Quite a young lady, too, I would judge, although she is veiled.'

'You had best show her into the drawing room, Pitwick. Tea, do you think?'

'Yes, Your Grace. There is something reassuringly respectable about tea.'

There was much to be said for a butler with a sense of humour, Alex thought as he got to his feet and went to squint at his own reflection in the tarnished old mirror above the fireplace.

He straightened his neckcloth and ran one hand through his hair. He kept it cropped short, not so much to be in the fashion as to remove all possible resemblance to Charles Stuart's mass of black curls. It didn't make much difference—with his dark colouring and long nose he still looked like the young prince about to put on his wig.

As he crossed the hall he passed a man standing to attention, all six feet of him clad in dark blue livery heavily encrusted with silver lace. He was the very model of the perfect London footman, right down to his well-moulded calves in silk stockings. Beside him on one of the hard hall chairs sat a maid, again one who looked as though she had been selected from a catalogue of ideal servants. She stood as she saw him, eyes down, and bobbed a curtsy as he passed.

Interesting that she had not accompanied her mistress into the drawing room, he thought, warily leaving the door open by a good foot as he entered.

The figure standing gazing up at a portrait of his parents was of average height for a woman, her slenderness well displayed in a dark green walking dress. She turned at the sound of his tread and dropped into a curtsy. He registered curves and a youthful suppleness.

'Your Grace.'

'Miss Danby?'

'Thank you for receiving me, Your Grace.'

There was something vaguely familiar about her as she stood composedly regarding him. She had put back the heavy veil from her bonnet—he was relieved to see that she had at least the sense to arrive in decent anonymity—

and she returned his stare with a level, blue-eyed gaze. Honey-blonde hair, an oval face, freckles. An open, intelligent, expression without a hint of coquetry. A pleasant-looking young lady, if not a great beauty.

'Will you not be seated, Miss Danby? Tea is on its way.'

'Thank you.' She sank down gracefully on to the nearest chair and Alex took the one opposite, the low tea table between them.

'This is most unconventional, I realise that,' she said and for the first time he saw signs of agitation in her clasped hands and the slight shake in her voice. Her accent was educated and the tone would, he judged, be pleasant when she was not so tense.

'Perhaps if you were to tell me in what way I may be of service to you?' he suggested. Where was Pitwick and that confounded tea tray? And why hadn't he simply said he was not at home? Curiosity, he supposed. That could be dangerous—he was very aware of just how compromising this could be. It simply was not done for a man to be alone and unchaperoned with an unmarried lady of, at least, the gentry class.

'If you will allow me, I should tell you something of my circumstances,' she said, then fell silent as Pitwick entered, accompanied by James, one of the footmen, who was bearing the tea tray.

The butler gestured to the low table. 'There, James. Will you pour, Miss Danby, or shall I?'

'Thank you, I will,' she told him with a flash of a smile and proceeded to do so. Clearly she had received the typical upbringing of a lady. 'Sugar, Your Grace? Lemon or milk?'

Alex was conscious of his staff leaving, although the

slight draught on his nape reassured him that the door remained open.

'Lemon, thank you.' He took the cup, waiting until she had taken a sip from her own. 'You were about to tell me of your circumstances, I believe.'

'Yes. We have met before, You Grace. Twice you have honoured me with a dance, but, no, I do not expect you to recall me,' she added when he began to speak. 'London is full of young ladies, most of them far more memorable than I. But my father is Broughton Danby, an ironmaster. A very wealthy man. You will excuse the vulgarity of my mentioning the fact, but it is relevant to my purpose.'

'I have heard of Mr Danby, of course.' Who had not? Like a handful of other self-made industrialists who bestrode their worlds of iron and coal, steam, pottery and textiles, his name was familiar to any gentleman who took an interest in the economic affairs of the country.

'Papa is not in the best of health and has retired from the day-to-day running of the company which is now in the hands of my two brothers,' Miss Danby said. She set her cup and saucer down with a slight rattle. 'Papa and I have moved to London for a while. He wished me to make my come-out, to do the Season. To find a husband.' She drew a visibly deep breath.

'Again, I beg you to forgive my frankness, but my dowry is large. Exceedingly so. Papa wishes to ensure that I secure a husband of rank. Since the death of my mother it has become his passionate desire and the energy he is expending on that is all, I fear, that maintains his well-being now he no longer has the company to run.'

Alex, unable to think of anything to say other than platitudes, murmured that he was sorry to hear about Mr Danby's ill health. He was conscious of a distinct sense of alarm. Dowry? He should never have admitted her.

'Naturally, I wish to oblige Papa in all things,' this startling female continued composedly. 'I love him dearly and hope that I am a dutiful daughter. However, I find myself, on the one hand, courted by fortune hunters for whom I can feel no liking or admiration and, on the other, snubbed for my lack of breeding, for my association with industry.'

Miss Danby's deportment and accent were impeccable—no doubt the result of no expense being spared on her upbringing and schooling—and her taste in dress was without the slightest vulgarity, but of course that would not stop the whispers and sneers about Cits, about the 'stink of the factory chimneys'. The *ton* knew their *Peerage* and its pedigrees as well as they knew their own countenances in the mirror.

'I can imagine,' he said. Where the devil was this going?

'I feel I owe it to myself to marry someone with whom I could share affection and respect. So I decided to take more control, to take matters into my own hands.' Miss Danby sat up straighter and gave a brisk nod, as if to encourage herself. 'I decided to look around me and to attempt to judge the character of gentlemen and make my own choices. I noticed you, Your Grace. I saw you were courteous, that you took the trouble to ask wallflowers to dance and to converse with the elderly ladies. I never once saw you treat staff with discourtesy, nor overheard you speak crudely or with disrespect of anyone.'

She paused for another of those deep breaths and Alex swallowed hard. Surely she was not going to—

'And I heard that you are not a rich man—the rumours say that you are looking to the Marriage Mart to provide you with a well-dowered bride this Season. So I thought, I would... I would ask you. In case you had not realised that I would be suitable. To marry. Because I think I am,' she concluded all of a rush and closed her eyes, her face suffused with a blush.

Hell's teeth. I have just been proposed to.

Chapter Two

Alex put down his cup and saucer and realised he was braced to spring to his feet and escape.

'Miss Danby.' How the devil was he to turn her down? There were no precedents for such a situation as far as he was aware and all of his instincts were telling him that he was in a highly precarious position. How would she react to the rejection of her outrageous proposal? By making a scene and screaming that he had assaulted her? By rushing back to her father to say Alex had compromised her?

'Miss Danby, you honour me with your estimation of my character, but I must decline your most flattering suggestion. I have… I have hardly begun my search for a suitable duchess.' He took a steadying breath and decided that only honesty would do, even if she laughed in his face at the idea of him being such a romantic.

'I do not know whether there is, somewhere, the lady for whom I might cherish warmer feelings than merely liking. I will confess that it is my ardent hope that I will, that I will recognise her when I find her. To commit myself to a betrothal with someone I do not know and who, however observant, does not truly know me…that would seem to me to be imprudent. On both our parts. It could only lead to future unhappiness.'

He went over that speech in his head. Had it been tactful? Suitably kind yet definite? Miss Danby must have been racked with nerves, coming here. He had to let her down gently, but without leaving the slightest hope that he would change his mind. He thought he had done that and now he had to get her out of the house. Fast.

'Yes,' she replied after a moment and opened her eyes. 'I see. Of course. I quite understand. I had expected your reply to be in the negative,' she said, her voice tight with an emotion that she was rigidly controlling. 'But I felt I ought to try. In case you thought we might suit.' She stood up and Alex shot to his feet. 'Thank you for your consideration.'

'You may be assured of my discretion,' he said. Was it his imagination or could he feel the cold sweat rolling down his spine? 'You have come in your own carriage?'

At least, as her father was a commoner, it would not be emblazoned with a coat of arms on the door, he realised with relief.

'It is waiting around the corner,' she said as she lifted her veil and settled it to hide her face again as Alex tugged on the bell pull.

'Pitwick. Please show Miss…the lady out. Good day, ma'am.'

'Good day, Your Grace.' She dropped that neat little curtsy again and went out of the door the butler was now holding wide open.

Alex went to the window. By great good fortune Hill Street seemed clear of promenading fashionables, passing carriages containing Patronesses of Almack's or anyone likely to rush to the scandal sheets with the intelligence that a heavily veiled lady was leaving the Duke of Malvern's town house at a most unconventional hour. Given

that the street ran between the fashionable haunts of Berke-
ley Square and South Audley Street this was a minor miracle and he duly gave thanks to whatever guardian angel
watched over impoverished dukes.

Alex strode across the hall as the front door closed behind Miss Danby and her retinue and fell into the chair
behind his desk with the sensations of a fox that had somehow eluded the hounds.

He should have refused to see her, of course. Whatever
had he been thinking? He had been taken by surprise, he
supposed, and then good manners made it impossible to
simply insist that she leave the moment it became clear
what her purpose was.

At least he hadn't been in two minds in the moments before he turned Miss Danby down. He had not been tempted
to agree by the promise of her dowry. That would have
been fatal, because he was certain any hesitation would
have shown on his face somehow and she might have been
emboldened to try persuasion. That could only have been
deeply embarrassing for them both.

Only, now that he was alone and could think more
clearly, Alex realised that he *was* tempted and it had only
been the shock of being proposed to by a lady that had
stopped him considering it. Danby was a very rich man
and Alex could well imagine that he would stop at nothing, baulk at no expense, to maintain his daughter in true
ducal style if she married him.

An ironmaster's fortune would secure what Alex already owned, enable him to purchase more land, create
a great estate befitting a duke. It would repair the castle,
provide the tenants with homes fit to live in. Perhaps even
build a new model village with a school.

And Miss Danby, although no great beauty, was clearly intelligent, well-educated and the possessor of good taste—if not of the desirable maidenly virtues of modesty, discretion and reticence.

Such a match would cause titters and nudges, but then his ancestors had always been known as the Pinchpenny Dukes, so probably there would also be a great deal of admiration for him having caught such a prize. After all, dukes had married actresses before now. A respectable iron founder's daughter was a considerable social improvement on that.

But. But he would despise himself for it, he knew. He had accepted that he must marry a lady with a respectable dowry at the very least. And at the same time he had been determined to wed someone for whom he could feel the warmest emotions. Love. And he did not love Miss Jessica Danby. He had apparently danced with her without feeling the slightest glimmer of attraction and, on seeing her again, had noticed only a vague awareness of having met her before. Whereas she had learned of his title, had observed enough to feel confident of his character and had then made her proposal.

A prudent man would go out now, present himself before Mr Danby and request the honour of his daughter's hand and he would be accepted, he had no doubt of that. But Miss Danby would then know that he had cold-bloodedly assessed her likely fortune and had decided it outweighed the excuses he had made to her about warm feelings and affection. She would know him not only as motivated by the desire for wealth, which she accepted, but a hypocrite to boot. She would never be able to trust anything he said to her again.

He had burned his boats to a cinder because if he had only been resolute about abandoning his search for love and had been even vaguely aware of her dowry and that she found him tolerable, then he could have sought her out, established some relationship between them, assessed whether or not it might be a match both of them could commit to.

'Hell and damnation, you fool,' Alex said as the door opened.

'I beg your pardon, Your Grace.'

'Not you, Pitwick. Me. I should have done my research before launching myself on to the Marriage Mart and now I have lost what might be the biggest prize in it.' There was no point in trying to hide his circumstances from his butler, or his valet, come to that. They knew the financial situation as well as he did. And they probably knew as well as he did why he was being so stubborn about doing the right thing and ruthlessly finding an heiress. If only he could shrug off that conviction that somewhere there was his true love.

'Tsk,' Pitwick said, conveying in that one sound regret, sympathy and the assurance that he hadn't the faintest idea what his employer was talking about. He rather spoilt the effect by adding, 'And will you be launching yourself upon the choppy waters of the Marriage Mart again tonight, Your Grace?'

'I suppose I had better, Pitwick. Kindly tell Cook that I will be dining off the refreshments at Almack's this evening. That will save the cost of one dinner, at least.'

His butler looked sympathetic, as well he might. Lemonade and slightly dry seedcake was no meal for any man.

* * *

The earth had not opened up and conveniently swallowed her, embarrassment, blushes and all, Jessica thought grimly. Which meant that she had best grit her teeth and prepare for another excruciating evening at Almack's. It was a Wednesday, one of the nights the Assembly Rooms were open to those fortunate enough to possess the precious vouchers of admission.

'The blue silk gown, I think, Trotter,' she said. She had worn dark green that morning and instinct urged her to another colour, as though that would somehow shield her from the Duke's gaze.

The Duke had been all that was considerate, she thought for the hundredth time. He had been polite and thoughtful in producing a reason to turn her down that in no way reflected upon her. He could have refused to receive her—which would have been wise of him—or he could have recoiled from her unmaidenly proposal, snubbed her viciously for the source of her wealth and her humble antecedents. Instead he had been kind and tactful.

Which was why she had selected him in the first place, of course, she thought, sitting still while Trotter did something complicated with her hair. At least her judgement of his character had not been at fault.

'Are you well, Miss Jessica?' Trotter asked. 'You are a trifle pale, if I may say so.'

'Perfectly well, thank you, Trotter. I am merely a little tired.'

And, really, there was no need to fret about seeing the Duke again. He had danced with her twice before and had not even remembered her this morning. He would simply ignore her when he encountered her again and she could hardly blame him for that. 'The pearl and sapphire earrings, I think, with this gown.'

Jessica, accompanied by her chaperon, Lady Cassington, arrived at the Assembly Rooms in King Street at nine. At the start of the Season her father had engaged the services of her escort, a baronet's widow who was possessed of impeccable breeding, but very little funds, and who maintained the polite fiction that she was merely doing dear Miss Danby a favour by introducing her into polite society.

Almeria Cassington had proved to be an inspired choice because, as a cousin of Lady Cowper, one of the Patronesses, she had been able to persuade her amiable relative to grant Jessica one of the precious vouchers of admission to Almack's. It had required her to pay an afternoon call on the Countess, which had been terrifying, but the verdict was that she was a nicely behaved young lady who showed impeccable taste in her attire and conversation.

'One would never know about her background,' Lady Cowper had remarked, not quite quietly enough for Jessica to miss. 'She might do for poor Austin.'

Fortunately, Jessica had managed to contain herself until they were safely in the carriage. 'And who is "poor Austin" for whom I "might do"?'

'One of her godsons. No money and some very regrettable, er, habits. We can do much better for you, my dear Miss Danby. But I suspected that the prospect of your dowry would be enough to prise a voucher from her and I was correct.'

It was the first of numerous humiliations, some mere pinpricks, others that left her smarting, but Jessica had schooled herself to appear never to notice them. And Lady

Cassington was certainly assiduous in her promotion of Jessica's interests. She suspected that her chaperon had been promised a sizeable bounty if she secured a marriage proposal. It was probably on a sliding scale, knowing Papa, and would depend on how high up the aristocratic tree she could be boosted. A baronet or a baron would be a grave disappointment, they were both well aware.

Now, standing on the threshold of the Assembly Rooms, Jessica could see that the main chamber was filling fast. It might well hold more than five hundred before the end of supper at eleven o'clock when the doors were closed, regardless of who might arrive a minute late.

Jessica looked around for the group she thought of as her special friends, the group she had mentally labelled the Exotic Wallflowers.

There were the usual drab little group of everyday wall-flowers, of course: the desperately shy for whom this was a ritual torture and the plain girls without outgoing wit to make them sparkle, or helpfully large dowries to counterbalance their looks. The judgement of the fashionable elite was quite unforgiving to those who fell short of its standards.

Jessica's wallflowers had wit and spirit in plenty, but those were coupled with handicaps that separated them from the flock of other desirable young ladies who had the expected combination of prettiness, modestly simpering manners, excellent bloodlines and respectable dowries.

Her friends all appeared to be present in their usual alcove. Lady Anthea Mulrose, the bluest of bluestockings who had no time for any gentleman who was not interested in natural sciences, found the Classical authors fascinating and was *au fait* with the latest theories about the formation of the earth; Miss Belinda Newlyn, of genteel birth and modest endowments and who was pretty and witty, but walked with a severe limp; Lady Lucinda Herrick whose grandfather, an East India Company nabob, had married an Indian princess in the days before attitudes to those who were not Christian and European had hardened into intolerance and Miss Jane Beech, whose head of ginger hair was considered positively vulgar, as though she could do anything about it. Her pleasantly plain face was a mass of freckles and that combination, along with a very modest dowry, was enough to condemn her to oblivion.

Jessica liked them all in their own ways and had soon been absorbed into their little circle. They were rarely disturbed, except when a gentleman who had a better-developed sense of his duty, such as the Duke of Malvern, asked one of them for a dance, or a determined chaperon dragged along a reluctant young gentleman who was compelled to stand up with an equally unwilling partner. Or, of course, when a fortune hunter managed to track down Miss Danby.

She took a seat next to Miss Beech as Lady Cassington swept off on her endless search for an eligible partner for her.

'Did you manage to find a suitable paint box at Ackermann's?' she asked. Miss Beech was an accomplished water colourist and had decided to invest in better equipment than she had been using.

'Oh, yes. Thank you for recommending them. Their shop in the Strand is quite marvellous and I could have spent my entire quarter's allowance there.' She launched into a description of the range of choices she had been faced with. On her other side Miss Newlyn and Lady Lucinda were discussing the horrors of being fitted for Court dress—'I declare I look like a candle snuffer in those dreadful hoops!'—and Lady Anthea was, as usual, absorbed in a small pamphlet she had produced from her reticule.

Jessica became aware of the prickling sensation of being watched. Please, not the Duke, she thought, discreetly scanning the immediate area from behind the shelter of her fan.

A small group of young men were standing nearby, sniggering in the irritating manner of immature bores who think they are great wits. They were nudging each other and, Jessica realised, they were staring not at her, but at Jane Beech, as though egging each other on to do something daring.

She lowered her fan and gave them a discouraging frown, but they were intent on her companion. Three of them sauntered up.

'I say, it's Miss Beech, isn't it?' one of them said. They were very young, Jessica thought. Very young, very silly.

'Yes,' Jane said uneasily.

'We was wondering, don't you know, if you're keen on hunting.'

'No. Not at all.'

'Hah, told you so,' the youth said to his friends. 'You wouldn't be, of course,' he added, turning back, 'seeing as your mama was frightened by a fox when she was expecting! Hah, ha!'

Jane turned scarlet. Jessica opened her mouth to utter a savage set-down and a voice said calmly, 'Good evening, ladies. Miss Beech, my dance, I believe.'

Chapter Three

'My dance, I believe.'

It was the Duke of Malvern. Jane stared at him, blinking away the tears that had gathered visibly on her lashes. Jessica, who had half risen from her seat, sat down again with a bump and the Duke turned a cold look on the three young men.

'Are you by any chance annoying my partner?' he enquired. 'I find myself constantly amazed at the riff-raff that somehow manages to obtain vouchers for Almack's these days,' he added, turning back to the ladies. 'I must have a word with the Patronesses.'

Jane, without a word, took the hand that was extended to her and was led into the set that was forming nearest to them.

'That was the Duke of Malvern,' Lady Anthea said. 'What on earth is he doing? I know for a fact that dear Jane's card is quite without partners.'

'Coming to her rescue,' Jessica said, fanning herself. Really, she felt quite…quite breathless. That had been so smoothly done and with such authority. Across the dance floor she could just make out the backs of the three young men as they made for the door. They would not be sniggering now.

'But why would he trouble himself?' Anthea persisted. 'He doesn't know any of us. It was most gentlemanly of him, but so fast! I was about to give them a set-down myself, but I had hardly taken breath to do so.'

'I had a hairpin ready.' Lady Lucinda slid a jewelled spike back into her sleek black hair and turned to Belinda Newlyn, who was jotting something on the back of her blank dance card. 'What are you doing?'

'Writing a description. I intend to find out who they were,' she said tightly. 'I keep a little list of people I intend never to forgive. One day I will have my revenge.'

'The Duke must have been standing very near to us,' Jessica said, answering Anthea. 'Perhaps he had encountered those young men before, was expecting trouble and was keeping an eye on them.'

Or on me.

She had not been aware of him watching them, but then the room was very crowded. Through the whirling dancers she could see the Duke and Jane talking as they waited their turn to go down the line. Jane's furious blush had faded and she looked positively happy.

'Jane is a very good dancer,' Lady Lucinda observed as the pair sidestepped under the raised arms of the other couples in their set. 'But then she is musical and that no doubt helps.'

When the set had finally come to an end they expected Jane to return, breathless and in need of reassurance after her adventure, but all Jessica could see were occasional glimpses of red hair on the other side of the room.

'My goodness, he has introduced her to another partner,' gasped Belinda. 'Oh, do look, it is Mr Locksley.'

And, sure enough, Jane was making her curtsy to the only other person in the room whose hair was a match for hers. Mr Locksley, tall and bespectacled, was beaming at his new partner and Jane was smiling back up at him.

'And he is quite well off, I believe,' Lucinda remarked. 'A very nice estate in Warwickshire and his godmother is a cousin of the Bishop of Somerley.'

'It is only a dance,' Jessica protested. 'Not a betrothal.' But she could see other people were watching the couple and their smiles were kind, not mocking. Two redheads apparently cancelled each other out, or perhaps it was simply that Mr Locksley was well known and liked.

'How clever of the Duke,' Anthea said. 'And how thoughtful.'

'I believe him to be both,' Jessica said, a little stiffly. 'From what little I have seen of him,' she added before anyone could ask her how she knew.

'Well, in that case, perhaps he can find us all suitable partners,' Belinda said. 'He is doing far better than Jane's aunt has managed in a whole month. Now, if we can order up a university professor for Anthea, a horse-breeder for me, a connoisseur of the arts for Lucinda and a—what kind of a gentleman would you like, Jessica?'

A hard-up duke, please.

'Oh, the richest man in England,' she said with a laugh. 'Then he will not care about my dowry and is at liberty to fall madly in love with my elegant eyebrows and my exquisite earlobes.'

There was no sign of the Duke: clearly both her eyebrows and her earlobes had failed to make an impression.

* * *

Eventually Mr Locksley returned Jane to them and enquired if she would favour him with the supper dance.

To her friends' amazement Jane replied with tolerable composure, and much blushing, that she would be delighted and he bowed and left them.

'What was it like dancing with the Duke?' Lucinda demanded.

'Oh, I was ready to drop with embarrassment.' Jane fanned herself vigorously. 'But he was so kind and so matter of fact. He said it was a depressing fact about the immature men that they often could not recognise the true beauty of unusual things because of their lack of sophistication. Their insecurity, he said, made them clumsy and offensive. And I just gawped at him like a perfect airhead, because I couldn't believe that he meant my hair was beautiful, and he said that I should never be shy about accepting compliments about it.

'And then we just danced and chatted about ordinary things and I didn't fall over my feet once, as I'd feared because, really—a duke!' she said happily. 'And then he introduced me to Mr Locksley. And he was lovely, too.'

Jessica sat silently while the others demanded every detail about lovely Mr Locksley. Even Anthea put away her pamphlet.

Where *was* the Duke? She scanned the throng that was now hot, noisy and, if truth be told, becoming rather less than fragrant.

There, over in the far corner near the entrance to the refreshment room. There was no mistaking the dark head topping most of the men in the vicinity.

'Excuse me for a moment,' she said. The others, heads

together, acknowledged her departure with vague smiles before they returned to their analysis of Jane's sudden success.

Jessica skirted around the room, acknowledging a few greetings and ignoring several cuts from those who thought that daughters of industry had no place in Almack's Assembly Rooms.

The Duke was standing talking to a group of other gentlemen of about his own age. They were discussing racehorses, she thought, catching a few words as she passed slowly in front of them.

Long odds…soft going…too short in the back…

She caught the Duke's eye and, without stopping, inclined her head. *Thank you,* she mouthed silently and walked on.

That, she hoped, would be that. He had, perhaps, intervened because he felt uncomfortable about having refused her proposition. Whatever his motives, she had thanked him and there would be no need for their paths to cross again.

Jessica saw that she had walked around half of the ballroom, reaching the ladies' retiring room without noticing it. She might as well go in and make certain her hair was still in order and take a few moments in the relative cool and quiet.

When she emerged five minutes later a tall figure moved away from the wall and fell into step beside her.

'You wished to speak to me?' he asked.

'No! I mean, no, I merely wished to thank you for intervening just now, Your Grace. Those wretched young men were a moment away from having their ears boxed, being stabbed with a hairpin and beaten over the head with a pamphlet on the true age of the earth. It would have created a most unfortunate scene and probably lost us our vouchers. Not that any of us would be devastated by that.'

Almack's, a bulwark of respectability, was not provided with any little alcoves where couples could escape for a private conversation—or something more intimate—but the Duke steered her neatly into the shelter of a group of tall potted plants.

'There is no need to keep saying *Your Grace*, you know,' he said. 'Call me *Demeral*. Or *Duke*. Or *Malvern* if you feel uncomfortable with that in company.'

In company?

When am I likely to be having conversations with you in company? Jessica wondered.

But she managed to say, with a reasonable degree of composure, 'Thank you, Demeral.' She should go now. Return to her friends. But her curiosity got the better of her.

'Why *did* you intervene?' she asked before she could stop the question.

'Because I dislike bullies,' he said simply.

'I had not realised you were there.'

'I happened to be passing.'

'And there was no obligation to find Miss Beech another partner.'

'It was too tempting to see whether they got on together or clashed—literally or figuratively. But I happen to know that Locksley endured considerable bullying as a young man because of his colouring, so I felt certain that your friend was in sympathetic company.'

'So sympathetic that he is taking her in to supper.' Demeral smiled, clearly delighted that his stratagem had been successful and, off guard, she said, 'The rest of the Exotics joked that you should find us all our ideal partners.'

'The Exotics?'

'Oh, that is just my silly name for our little group. We are all wallflowers, but the reasons for that are somewhat unusual in each case.'

'Miss Beech's hair, your father's occupation. Yes, I see. Will you not take a chair, Miss Danby, and tell me about your other friends?'

She should return to the others and not risk being seen talking intimately with the Duke—with Demeral—behind the potted palms. If Lady Cassington saw her she would be reporting back to her father in great glee and he would be leaping to conclusions—conclusions that could only end in disappointment for him. On the other hand, she was not visible from the chaperons' corner and it seemed discourteous to hurry away when he had performed such a service for Jane.

Jessica sat down, perched on one of the uncomfortable little white and gilt chairs that seemed expressly designed to prevent one from lounging. 'Lady Anthea is highly intelligent and a bluestocking. She has a mind above all this—' she waved her hand in the direction of the dance floor '—and, although not exactly *against* marriage, despairs of finding a gentleman of equal intellect. She becomes very easily bored and they resent that.' From Demeral's expression she could tell he had some sympathy with the gentlemen in question. Certainly, keeping up with Anthea was a strain sometimes, even for her friends.

'Lady Lucinda's grandmother was an Indian princess. The fact that the East India Company positively encouraged their employees to make marriages with the local rulers at that time seems to carry no weight these days, now attitudes have changed so much. Apparently the fact that

Lucinda has inherited her grandmother's exquisite taste and deep interest in art is not enough to change the opinion of unpleasant people who whisper about "natives". And Miss Newlyn limps. It was the way she was born. She is a wonderful rider, however. You should see her when we go out together to Rotten Row. I must go back.'

She stood and Demeral rose with her.

'Now you know all about us.' She hesitated, then blurted out the question that had been puzzling her all day. 'Why did you not refuse to receive me this morning? Why are you being so…so *pleasant* when I must have been such a grave embarrassment to you?'

'I received you out of perfectly vulgar curiosity and the fact that I was half asleep, if you must know the truth. Then, once I had heard what you had to say, I admired your courage in going after what you wanted. And now I admire your loyalty to your friends.' He glanced around. 'Perhaps, for discretion, you should leave the cover of our little woodland first. I will wait a while.'

Jessica glanced back when she was halfway to her seat. There was no sign of the tall figure.

'Where have you been? It is time for supper and we are all faint with hunger,' Belinda said. 'Jane has already been claimed by Mr Locksley.'

'Then we will go and indulge ourselves in rather dry cake and insipid lemonade and pretend we are not watching them,' Jessica said and the four of them made their way around the edge of the dance floor to the refreshment room.

What a very strange day, Jessica thought as she sat at her dressing table once more, unhooking her earrings as Trotter removed all the pins from her hair and began to give it a firm one hundred strokes of the brush.

She had behaved like a complete hoyden and had somehow emerged with her reputation, if not her nerves, intact. She appeared to have gained the friendship of a duke, even if he was a most unusual one, and she very much feared that she had developed a mild *tendre* for the man, on top of the liking that had led her to make her outrageous proposal.

The sooner you forget that, my girl, the better it will be for you, she told herself, wincing slightly at the vigorous brushing.

Demeral had made it very clear that he was looking for a love match and that she was not what he was seeking in a wife.

She was going to have to make up her mind—tell Papa that she had met nobody so far that she could tolerate as a husband and give up this whole excruciating Season, or fix a smile on her lips, ignore the snubs and try to find a good man among the fortune hunters. *Another* good man.

'That was a big sigh, Miss Jessica.'

'It was rather a trying evening, Trotter. That is all it is.'

Chapter Four

Perhaps his decision to see Miss Danby yesterday morning had not been so wrong after all, Alex mused as he ate his breakfast the next morning.

She was sensible and tactful. She was also a loyal friend, as he had discovered last night. And one with a sense of humour. The Exotic Wallflowers, indeed! They had sounded an interesting, and intelligent, group of young women and he wondered whether one of them might be the right person for him. He had certainly disregarded them before, hardly aware of their presence.

He poured himself another cup of coffee and wondered how to get to know them better. In a formal social setting they were clearly ill at ease, clustering together for protection and company, but away from the ballrooms and drawing rooms they might be more relaxed and allow him to see the real women behind the careful smiles and calculated reserve.

Miss Danby had mentioned Rotten Row. Now that would be an excellent place to meet young ladies: very fashionable, but far more relaxed than an evening event. But it would not do to appear too obvious.

Carrying his coffee cup with him, Alex went through to his study and began to write notes. Safety in numbers.

* * *

Dusk came quickly at that time of year so, although the most fashionable time for riding and driving in Hyde Park was impossible in February, on a pleasant day the Row was still thronged in the early afternoon.

Alex kept his bay gelding to a walk as he made his way down through the park towards Rotten Row on its southern edge. Around him he had a group of friends: Major Percy Rowlands, riding his old grey cavalry charger, a survivor of Waterloo, Sir Harry Eynsham on his new chestnut mare that was proving something of a handful and Viscount Oakham, mounted on a handsome black gelding with perfect manners.

'That mare needs schooling, Eynsham,' Oakham remarked as the chestnut skittered nervily across the track. 'Pretty enough, but she'll have you off if she's spooked.'

'My brother-in-law bought her for my sister, the fool. He is no judge of horseflesh and she was besotted with this creature's looks,' the baronet said. 'No, there are no tigers behind that bush, you idiotic beast.' He halted the mare's sideways progress away from the threatening foliage. 'Susan can't manage her, so I bought her off him before she broke her neck, thought I'd see what I can do with her, but I think she needs work on a lunge rein in the paddock for a month or two before I bring her out in a crowd again.'

'Now that is what I call a handsome animal,' Oakham remarked, gesturing with his whip in the direction of the Row. 'And a rider who knows what she's doing.'

Alex did not recognise the rider of the dapple grey who was wearing a dark blue habit, a low-crowned hat and a veil, but he did know the driver of the phaeton she was riding beside.

Who was it that Miss Danby had said was an excellent rider? Miss Newlyn, that was it.

'A Miss Newlyn, I believe,' he said as they converged on the group.

Now they were closer he could see Lady Anthea Melrose sitting next to Miss Danby. She appeared to be reading a book, totally ignoring the crowds around her. Miss Newlyn, mounted on the fine long-tailed grey, was talking to a tall young woman on a bay mare and behind them were two riders deep in conversation too. Alex had no difficulty in recognising Locksley's red head as he doffed his hat to the occupants of a passing carriage. It must be Miss Beech beside him, her own fiery locks subdued in a snood with a hat and veil on top. That left the bay's rider as Lady Lucinda Herrick.

A full set of the Exotics.

Alex rode forward and raised his hat. Miss Danby reined in her pair and drew in to the side of the carriage drive. 'Good afternoon, Duke.'

'Ma'am. May I compliment you on your handling of that pair. Hanover bays, if I am not mistaken.'

'They are indeed. Aren't they fine? They would look even smarter drawing a high-perch phaeton, but I am afraid I have yet to convince my father that I would not overturn it.'

'I imagine there would be no danger of that,' he said, noting how calm she kept the high-bred pair and how steady her tan-gloved hands were on the reins. 'May I make known to you my friends, Miss Danby? Lord Oakham, Sir Harry Eynsham, Major Rowlands. Gentlemen, Miss Danby.'

'And I should introduce my companions,' she said as the gentlemen began raising their hats. 'Lady Anthea Melrose,

Lady Lucinda Herrick, Miss Newlyn and, behind us, Miss Beech. I am sure you all know Mr Locksley.'

There was a general exchange of bows and greetings. Even Lady Anthea tucked her book to the side of her seat and regarded them from under rather straight dark brows.

'Major Rowlands? Not the author of *Some Observations on the Inhabitants of the Pyrenees*?'

'Yes, ma'am.' Percy looked somewhat startled at the recognition. 'It is merely some jottings I made when I was serving in the Peninsula during the late hostilities and was prevailed upon to publish.'

'Rather more than jottings,' Lady Anthea said severely. 'You should not make light of intellectual endeavours. Now, I am interested in what you had to say about the difference between the folk customs of the Spanish and French sides of the mountain range. Do you consider them to be influenced by the differences in the climate and therefore the agricultural practices?'

To a man, his friends rode around to the other side of the phaeton, abandoning Percy to be interrogated, although, Alex saw, once he had recovered from his surprise, he seemed to be holding his own.

Miss Beech and Locksley rode up to join the group and Alex talked to Miss Danby about her bays while he covertly watched his friends and hers.

John Wilbraham, Viscount Oakham, had brought his gelding alongside the tall rider who, now he was closer, Alex recognised for certain as Lady Lucinda. She really was a very beautiful young woman with dark eyes and black hair that must be the legacy of her grandmother. Oakham appeared to be doing most of the talking and he wondered whether she was shy, reserved or braced for some insensitive remark about her heritage.

Miss Newlyn, on the other hand, was already laughing at something Harry had said and Percy was talking intently with Lady Anthea who showed every sign of thoroughly enjoying the argument.

'Whatever are you about, Demeral?' Miss Danby said with a severity that was at odds with the smile in her eyes. 'You descend on my little party of ladies with your battalion and have captured every one.'

So much for his bright idea of finding a bride for himself from among them: his friends were already showing their interest.

'Are you setting up as a matchmaker or simply carried away with enthusiasm after introducing Jane to Mr Locksley?' Miss Danby persisted.

'I deny it,' he said, mentally crossing his fingers. 'Locksley and your friend do appear to be getting along very well though, do they not?'

'Apparently he was on her doorstep at ten this morning with roses, sent them in with a request to know when he might call and was told to find her in the Park this afternoon. She does seem very taken with him, but whether it will endure closer acquaintance, I have no idea,' she said, keeping her voice low.

'He is of good character, or I would not have introduced them,' Alex answered as quietly. He decided that a white lie was called for. 'But as for the rest of them, it is mere coincidence that we happened to be riding out. Sir Harry appears as entranced by Miss Newlyn's grey as its rider. A fine animal.'

'Yes, I think I said she was an expert horsewoman. Her

family have a long tradition of breeding superb animals and that grey is possibly the best they have produced in many years. You would not think so to look at it, but it is a very spirited animal.'

'Then she is a most capable rider. As you are a whip, Miss Danby. Those bays are a strong pair that many ladies might hesitate to drive.'

'Why, thank you.'

He liked the way she accepted his compliment without false modesty or blushes.

'I wish Papa would allow me a perch phaeton, but he is convinced I would have an accident. He does not drive himself, so he finds it difficult to judge the dangers, I think.'

'How is his health? You mentioned the other day that it was not robust. He is not finding London too much for him, I trust?'

'He is rather improved, I think. I suspect the planning and the arrangements and the journey down and so forth were a strain—his heart is not strong—but now we are settled he seems much better. And he has been accepted into the Ironmongers' Guild which pleases him and gives him an occupation with their meetings and social gatherings.'

She smiled. 'It is not the same as the iron founders' association he belongs to at home, of course, but it stops him fretting about what my brothers Ethan and Joshua are doing with the business. He cannot accept they are thirty and twenty-seven now. They have been involved since they were hardly out of leading reins. It was impossible to keep them away from the forges as they grew up and now they are very confident in what they are about.'

'I know little about the guilds, I must confess,' Alex said.

Truth be told, he had little interest in them either, but he wanted to keep Miss Danby talking—his friends seemed to be enjoying their own conversations.

The bays moved uneasily as a noisy group of riders swept past them and Miss Danby collected them without fuss. 'The guilds maintain the standards of the craft and manage apprenticeships,' she explained. 'And there is a great deal of charitable work—widows and orphans, schools and so forth. And dining, of course. That is very important! I believe the Master has asked Papa to become involved in something to do with the charitable work—at breakfast time he said he wanted to ask my advice and it can hardly be about the fees charged for apprenticeships.' Her mouth curved into that warm smile again. 'It does him good to keep his mind active.'

Two carriages passed them and Miss Danby looked around. 'I think I should move along, before we cause an obstruction. It was pleasant to have the opportunity to converse again, Demeral.'

She brought the bays up to their bits and turned to her passenger. 'I believe we should continue on our way, Anthea.'

'We must? Oh, very well. Major Rowlands, here is my card. Please call, I feel there is a great deal to discuss about the links between modern religion in the Pyrenees and ancient pagan custom.'

Alex thought his friend looked slightly alarmed at the prospect, but he took the card and said, 'I look forward to it, Lady Anthea,' with a fair assumption of enthusiasm.

The phaeton moved off and with it the little group of three ladies and Mr Locksley who greeted the other men as he passed, but showed no sign of wanting to leave Miss Beech's side.

'An interesting collection of ladies,' Harry remarked. 'Originals! Wherever did you make their acquaintance, Demeral?'

'I hardly know them, but I have danced with Miss Danby on a couple of occasions.'

So she tells me.

How could he have forgotten her? She must have subdued all that intelligence and directness under a dull mask of propriety.

'Well, I am glad to have made Miss Newlyn's acquaintance. She tells me her father has some young colts that sound promising.'

'Happy to have been of help,' Alex said. 'And Percy found a fellow antiquarian, I think.'

'The poor fellow looks stunned,' Harry said cheerfully. 'I think Lady Anthea turned his brain inside out and gave it a good shaking.'

Jessica drove along the Row and then turned off on to one of the quieter grassy drives. Belinda and Lucinda promptly moved forward, one each side of the phaeton's seat, although Jane and her companion lagged behind.

'Was that meeting by arrangement, you sly thing?' Belinda asked. 'Fancy being able to produce a duke and three interesting gentlemen, just like that.'

'It was pure happenstance,' Jessica protested. 'I had made no rendezvous, I assure you.'

Although I had mentioned that we rode and drove in the Park. But surely he did not seek me out deliberately? And accompanied by three friends who had proved so compatible with my companions...

'Sir Harry appeared very impressed with Moonlight,'

she remarked to Belinda. 'How did you find Lord Oakham, Lucinda?'

'Interested in art—and he actually knows what he is talking about, instead of merely chatting about the latest fashionable show he has attended. I found him easy to talk to.'

That, from Lucinda, was high praise indeed.

'Perhaps we will encounter them again at Almack's or some of the events we are attending and you can continue your conversations,' Jessica said lightly. 'Shall we leave now? It is beginning to get quite chilly and the light will be going soon.'

Chapter Five

'What is all this I hear about a duke?' her father enquired at breakfast the next morning.

'Dukes?' Jessica took a hasty gulp of coffee. She was not feeling very awake after a late night at a stuffy, and not very entertaining, musicale.

'Lady Cassington tells me you have attracted the interest of the Duke of Malvern.'

Oh, dear. Quite the wrong way around.

'His Grace very kindly intervened when some rather obnoxious young men were making a nuisance of themselves at Almack's the other evening. Miss Beech was much embarrassed by them, but he handled the incident with great tact. Possibly Lady Cassington observed me thanking him.'

Her father's face fell. 'So you have no news for me?'

'I am afraid not, Papa,' Jessica said demurely. 'But we did meet him again in Hyde Park yesterday afternoon, riding with several of his friends. A viscount and a baronet among them.'

That cheered Papa up. Jessica felt a pang at deceiving him into thinking those two might be potential suitors, but at least their failure to propose wouldn't be as much of a disappointment as her not securing the interest of a duke.

'You were going to tell me about the Ironmongers' Guild activities, Papa,' she said, passing him the mustard.

'Ah, yes. They are good fellows. Not the same as iron *founders*, of course, but the best we can hope for down here in the south and they welcomed me with open arms, you know. Mind you,' he observed with a shrewd look, 'they probably know the advantages of being on the good side of a man with access to as much iron as I have.'

Jessica waited patiently while her father speculated on the opportunities for securing some advantageous contracts and then prompted, 'And this activity they asked you to manage? A charitable event, I assume.'

'May Day.' Her father appeared to think that was all that needed to be said and addressed himself to the sirloin steak on his plate.

Jessica finished her omelette before saying, 'May Day? But we are not in the country.'

'Apparently it is as much a festivity in the City as it is at home. No maypoles, I believe, but processions and wreaths and music.' He passed her his coffee cup to be refilled. 'And we need milkmaids.'

'Milkmaids? Whatever for? But that should not be a problem, surely? There are milk cows in Green Park and I believe I saw some in Lincoln's Inn Fields. There must be dozens of milkmaids around when you think of the demand for fresh milk in London.'

'They are all engaged. This is the first time the Ironmongers have participated and the other guilds have been using the same girls for years.'

'What else might be a problem?' Jessica was prepared to believe that her father knew everything there was to know about iron, but a more unlikely person to be organising a May Day festivity she could not imagine.

'We need lads.'

'The Guild can find many apprentices, I imagine.'

'And maidens.'

Would the apprentices be safe with the maidens? Or vice versa? How literally were they expected to interpret 'maiden'?

'Is it the kind of festivity that respectable young ladies might take part in? Perhaps you could enquire.' The daughters of the Guild members might do, provided it was not too much of a romp. 'What else?'

'Horse-drawn floats, garland makers, musicians. Chimney sweeps.' He frowned. 'Or perhaps I am mistaken about that. It seems improbable.'

It was beginning to sound like a formidable list, even without the sweeps. 'Never mind, we have more than two months to assemble all of those elements,' she said encouragingly. 'Do we need the cows to go with the milkmaids?'

'Fortunately, no.'

'I think we need more information, Papa. Timing and how long the procession route is to be and a map of where it will go and how many of the different kind of participants we will need. And what they are expected to do.' She pondered it over her next cup of coffee and realised that she could go to the newspaper offices and ask to see their accounts of the previous year's parades. The newspapers were all located to the east, in Fleet Street, as far as she could recall.

Papa would probably consider that area a den of iniquity. She knew that ladies did not walk about the City without a male escort and even then only with a very good reason, such as visiting her lawyer or banker to sign documents.

'May I involve my friends in this? I am certain they would find it interesting, discovering all about the festivities.'

'As you wish. I must confess, I would be glad of the assistance. It seems far more of a female endeavour to my mind.'

After breakfast Jessica went to her desk and made a list of the things her father had remembered would be required and then one of things to do. Then she wrote notes to her friends. Would they be interested in helping her?

Footmen were dispatched to deliver the notes and Jessica sat and thought about milkmaids. If London's milkmaids were already spoken for, where would one find others?

On great estates, of course. A duke must employ a number of milkmaids and his friends would also need them. Perhaps there were enough near London to supply a suitable number.

The first thing she must do was to visit the newspapers and see the reports, because, for the life of her, she could not imagine how the congested, dirty, utterly urban streets of the City of London could be transformed into a celebration of the arrival of May.

Jessica went upstairs, telling Henry, the first footman she encountered, to be ready to accompany her in half an hour and to order the carriage. She rang for her maid when she reached her bedchamber.

'I hope we are not calling on any more gentlemen, Miss Jessica,' Trotter said severely when she was asked to find a simple walking dress and a bonnet with a veil.

'We are not. Instead we are visiting newspaper offices and I am reliably informed they are not the place to find *gentlemen*. Quite the contrary.' Trotter did not appear to find that amusing, but Jessica kept talking. 'I am looking for reports of last year's May Day festivities as I am helping Papa with the Guild's efforts this year, so you may be easy in your mind.'

'Easy in my mind? With you gallivanting about the City? You know quite well, Miss, ladies don't visit the City, any more than they go calling on gentlemen.'

'Absolutely no gallivanting will be involved, Trotter. And no dukes. I can assure you. No dukes at all.'

It was not far to Fleet Street from Adam Street. Along the Strand, past Somerset House and they were there. The problem was, Jessica discovered as she sat in the carriage turning the pages of the *Directory* she had borrowed from Papa's study, the offices were certainly in the Fleet Street area, but not they were not all lined up neatly on the street itself. She was going to have to be more adventurous in her travels.

She selected two that she had heard of as reliable—*The Times*, which was in Printing House Square, just south of Ludgate Hill, and the *Morning Herald*, in Catherine Street, off the Strand. She had just passed that turning, she realised.

'Pull the check string, please, Trotter.'

The carriage drew up at the kerb amid much shouted abuse from passing carters and hackney coach drivers and Henry jumped down for instructions.

'Printing House Square off New Bridge Street first and then we will return to Catherine Street off the Strand if necessary.'

'Very good, Miss Jessica.'

They set off again to renewed shouts and catcalls. Trotter jerked up the window strap, her cheeks red.

Printing House Square proved to be difficult to find. Jessica traced their path as best she could on the map in front of the *Directory*. Down New Bridge Street, into Earl Street, immediately up Water Lane—and then into Playhouse Yard to turn around, because George the coachman had missed the narrow turning into Printing House Lane.

Jessica was beginning to feel a trifle flustered by the time Henry opened the carriage door and let down the steps for her, but she adjusted her veil and, flanked by Trotter and Henry, walked into the offices as confidently as she could.

It was noisy, dusty and seemed full of people, many of them shouting. A man looked up from a desk flanked by rows of pigeon holes. 'Yes? Advertisement, is it?'

'No, I wanted—'

'Only ladies with veils, it's usually an advertisement of some kind.' The slight leer on his face made Jessica feel exceedingly naive. What on earth could he mean?

'No, I do not wish to place an advertisement. I wish to see the reports in this paper of last year's May Day celebrations,' she said firmly.

'That's a new one. Patrick!'

A skinny youth trotted up in response to the summons.

'Take this lady to see Mr Baggley, then get your lazy ar—' Henry cleared his throat loudly and the man glanced at Jessica. 'Your lazy *self* back here.'

Mr Baggley proved to be an elderly and very dusty gentleman with a bald head balanced by vast side-whiskers. He presided over what Jessica assumed must be the newspaper's archives and, to her relief, not only knew where to find what he wanted, but gave her a seat at a relatively clean table to sit and take notes.

'I think I have all I need,' she said with some relief when she had thanked Mr Baggley and emerged from the depths of the building. 'We do not need to go to Catherine Street, George,' she told the coachman. 'But it occurs to me that while I am here, we could call at Rundell, Bridge & Rundell to collect the necklace they were repairing for me. Papa took it to them two weeks ago, so it might be ready by now. When we get there, Henry, please go in and enquire.'

'Thirty-Two Ludgate Hill, Miss Jessica,' the coachman said, nodding. 'I know the place. I reckon if I go down that lane there and cut through the back we'll be virtually on the doorstep.'

To her surprise they emerged on to Ludgate Hill without any further problem. George drew in to the kerb and Henry jumped down to push a brake shoe under a rear wheel against the slope of the road. It was even more crowded and chaotic than the Strand and Trotter put her hands over her ears at some of the language as a stagecoach made its way past coming from the Belle Sauvage Inn further down towards the valley of the River Fleet, the horses labouring as they took the steep incline up to St Paul's Cathedral.

Jessica looked out of the window, enjoying the colourful scene and trying to ignore the language. She caught the eye of a small boy who clutched his hoop and fidgeted with boredom, while his parents stood looking in the jeweller's window. The woman was pointing something out and the man was shaking his head. As Rundell, Bridge &

Rundell held the Royal warrant, the display in the window was especially lavish and glittering and priced accordingly, no doubt.

Henry was being a very long time and it was not only the small boy who was growing impatient. Jessica opened the door, ignored Trotter's protest, stepped down to the pavement and went to look in the window, too.

As she did so the lad gave the hoop an experimental twirl, got a sharp word from his father, pouted and then, as soon as the man's attention was back on the window, did it again. This time it spun out of his hand and went bowling across the pavement past Jessica, bounded into the air when it hit the kerb and then rolled into the road, its owner scampering after it.

'No! Look out!' Jessica cried.

A carriage wheel crushed the hoop, the boy stopped dead in the middle of the road and burst into tears and the blast of a horn signalled the approach of another coach, this one forcing its way down the hill.

Jessica ran, dodging a cart, a horseman and a tilbury, caught hold of the child by the arm and whirled around, looking for a safe way out to the opposite pavement. There wasn't one. The stagecoach driver reined in hard, the horses skidding on the cobbles as the wheelers went down on their haunches as they'd been trained in an effort to brake the coach on the hill.

It was too late, they'd be under those hooves in seconds. Jessica braced herself to jump under the heavy dray in front of her. If she could just avoid the wheels—

Alex folded the bank draft and slipped it into his breast pocket. The quite hideous diamond and emerald parure had fetched considerably more than he had expected when he took it in to the jewellers. He had found it quite by chance in the back of an elaborate chest of drawers that had stood in his grandmother's long-unused dressing room. How long it had been there he had no idea, but it was completely out of fashion now. Perhaps one of her rumoured lovers had given it to her decades before her death and she had hidden it away from her husband's suspicious eye—it certainly was not on the inventory of entailed family gems, which meant he might dispose of it with a clear conscience.

He could tell that the manager had been interested, despite pointing out how dirty it was and how out of the mode. Alex had shrugged and said he would take it elsewhere. No doubt, he said, it would be a simple job to clean and the stones could be recut and reset, at which point they began some serious bargaining.

Now he felt positively light-hearted as he opened the shop doorway. He would take the draft to his bank while he was in the City—his banker would be almost as pleased to see it as he had been. It wouldn't solve many of his problems, but he would be able to get the new well dug and that was desperately needed by the villagers.

The tinkle of the shop bell as he closed the door and emerged on to the pavement was lost in the noise of Ludgate Hill. Then the quality of the racket struck him— shouting, the screams of passengers on top of the stage-coach that was coming to a sliding halt, the shriek from the window of the carriage standing just up the hill from where he stood.

'Miss Jessica!'

Chapter Six

There in the middle of the traffic, frantically clutching a small child to her, was Jessica Danby. Her only hope of escape was to dive under a slow-moving wagon and Alex saw her realise it at the same moment he did.

Alex was already running before he completed the thought. He crashed into her, wrapped his arms around both of them and leapt for the wagon, rolling under it and then digging in everything—heels, elbows, his one free hand—to keep them there safe from its great wheels.

They were in a little bubble of silence in the middle of a torrent of sound. Alex found he had stopped breathing. And then the child began to cry and he heard Jessica murmuring something soothing. They were all alive then.

The wagon had stopped, people were reaching for them. Cautiously Alex untangled himself from the others and looked down. 'Are you all right?' he asked urgently.

'Arthur! Arthur!'

The child scrambled free and scooted under the wagon into the arms of the woman kneeling on the pavement, regardless of the dust and worse that coated the stone.

'The boy seems to be,' Jessica said, her voice shaky. 'And I do not think that I have broken anything.'

'Let's get out from here.' Alex slid out and reached for

her, realising as he did so that the index finger on his left hand was at a strange angle. And, now he saw it, it hurt like the devil.

Jessica took one look at his hand and scrambled out unaided, only to be fallen upon by the child's mother who burst into tears. Behind her, her husband, little Arthur in his arms, was repeating over and over, 'Thank you, thank you.'

'I suggest you take your son to see your physician as soon as possible,' Alex said, getting to his feet and helping Jessica untangle herself from the grateful woman. 'Miss Danby, is that your carriage over there?' As her maid was clinging to the half-open door sobbing in relief, it seemed a reasonable assumption.

'Yes, indeed. I will drive you to a physician.' They crossed the street with little trouble as most of the traffic had come to a halt now, drivers and riders gawping at the scene. 'Now, Trotter, stop that noise at once, I am quite all right. George, please drive us to—could you tell us the direction of your physician, Demeral?'

'Thank you.' He told George the address and climbed into the carriage after Jessica. *Miss Danby,* he reminded himself as he sat, carefully holding his left hand away from his body. The shock of the last few moments was the only excuse for thinking of her by her first name. That and the lingering memory of her, soft and vulnerable, crushed between the hard road and his body. 'But should we not go first to your own physician?'

'I do not have one. Papa has engaged the services of a Dr Frazier, but I do not place much hope of him doing anything but bleeding me, and giving me something for my "nerves". All ladies suffer from nerves, apparently. I do not feel that a tonic would be helpful.'

'Not for bruises, no,' Alex agreed. 'In that case you might like to ask my doctor's wife, Mrs Chandler, to tend to you. Robert Chandler was an army surgeon and his wife followed the drum with him, even assisting him on the battlefield. You may be sure she will miss no injury that needs attention.'

He watched her as she sat back against the squabs and closed her eyes. Her bonnet was a crushed and dirty wreck on the seat beside Trotter, her hair was coming loose, her face was filthy and she must be aching all over from a mass of bruises. But she was not weeping, not complaining, not even impatient with her maid who was trying to thrust a smelling bottle under her nose and fan her with a handkerchief.

A rare young woman, Miss Danby. He found himself having to resist the urge to reach over and touch her cheek, as much to reassure himself as her. Life was so very fragile.

'What happened?' he asked.

'The family were looking in the jeweller's window. The child was bored and wanted to play with his hoop,' she said without opening her eyes. 'It is matchwood now, I fear.'

The carriage came to a halt and the footman opened the door. 'Should we go and tell Mr Danby what has occurred, Miss Jessica?' He was looking anxious and well he might be, Alex thought. The ironmaster would expect the strapping footmen he employed to keep his daughter safe from as much as a jostle on the pavement, let alone a close encounter with the iron-shod hooves of a stagecoach team and the foot-wide wheels of a heavy dray.

'No, it is perfectly all right, Henry. And it was not your fault. After all, I sent you into the shop. You cannot be in two places at once.'

The young man looked a little relieved at that and helped her down, closely followed by the agitated maid, then ran up the steps to knock. The front door opened and Alex followed them, trying not to wince as he moved.

It took a few minutes for Jessica to properly realise where she was. The drama on Ludgate Hill had shaken her more than she had realised and her body was beginning to feel every point where she had hit the road. And every point where Demeral had lain over her.

She was aware of him talking to another man, one with a deep, reassuring voice, of being seated on a hard hall chair and then of women's voices, of a firm but gentle hand under her arm and of being helped to climb a flight of stairs.

'Where—?'

'I am Anna Chandler and this is my maid, Morris, and this must be your own maid, I assume. Now let us take off these clothes and loosen your stays and we can see if you have done any damage. That's right, do not try to help, just let us work and then you can lie down and everything will feel much better...' The voice faded away and so did the blurred image of the room.

The faint cannot have lasted many minutes, Jessica thought as she began to make sense of what was happening around her. She was lying on something soft and the pressure of stays and lacing had gone. When she opened her eyes she saw she was dressed only in her shift with a sheet over her and an unknown woman had folded it back so that she could examine her right leg.

'Ah, good, you are back with us, Miss Danby. Please can you wriggle your toes for me? Excellent. And bend your knee up. And down again. Turn the foot to the side. Does this hurt? And this?'

The examination went on methodically, one limb after another. Then her chest, her shoulders and neck, her head. She was rolled over, prodded some more and then rolled back.

'There is a lot of bruising and it will be very painful as it works out. I can give you a salve for it and I would recommend hot baths at least twice a day. Take willow bark tea for the pain; I would prefer it if you did not take anything stronger and certainly not any quack medicines.'

Jessica wriggled up a little against the pillows. 'Mrs Chandler? Is that correct? Are you a doctor?'

'No.' Her smile was rueful. 'But I have learned battlefield medicine and surgery by both assisting with it and performing it. You appear to have been ridden over by a troop of cavalry, so your injuries are quite familiar to me, Miss Danby.'

'It was almost a stagecoach, but the Duke landed on top of me and rolled me to safety.' As her head cleared she remembered how he had looked: tough, dirty, pale under the grime and with an injury to his hand that he was ignoring. 'How badly is he hurt?'

'A dislocated finger, I suspect, rather than a break, and probably a fine collection of bruises, although perhaps less than you, as he landed on top of you.' She turned from the basin where she had been washing her hands and picked up a towel. 'But do not worry about Alex, he is hardier than the average society gentleman.'

'You know him well, Mrs Chandler?' Jessica managed to sit up a little further, very curious now.

'Anna, please. Yes, Alex is an old friend. We all grew

up together. He lived at the castle, my father was the vicar and Robert was the doctor's son. We played as children, he and Robert shared the same tutor and I would slide in to the schoolroom and listen and learn. I grew up thinking I would marry Alex—that was my firm intention from the age of five—but then when Robert came back from his studies and said he was going into the army as a surgeon I realised who it was I truly loved.'

'You have lived an adventurous life.'

'It was.' She smiled faintly. 'And hard. But only five years of it were with the Army. Robert always intended to set up his practice in London.'

She was about Demeral's age, Jessica thought, past her mid-twenties but not yet thirty. Anna was tall, brisk and handsome rather than pretty, with dark hair coiled at the nape of her neck.

'Do you wish you could practice medicine or surgery in your own right?' she asked, curious about another woman with such skills.

'Yes, of course. Perhaps one day women can be admitted to the medical schools and be accepted as physicians. As it is, I have my own practice of sorts—many women come to see me, even if their fathers or husbands receive a bill for my services in Robert's name. Now...' she tossed the towel aside '... I suggest we get you dressed, without your stays, and you return home. Alex tells me that your father is likely to become agitated if you are away for a long time.'

It was painful, but eventually Jessica was dressed again, her clothes brushed and sponged by Trotter and Anna Chandler's maid. Not all the buttons would do up without the stays tightly compressing her waist, but she was decently covered, at least.

'Tell me,' she said, when the other women had left the room and Anna was helping her with her shoes, 'what was Demeral like as a boy?'

Anna chuckled. 'A little devil. We all were, I suppose. But he was the worst. He was always getting into scrapes, always inventing new games or adventures. He has a wonderful imagination. If he had his way, he would have been a knight, or an explorer.'

'That sounds as though he was a romantic.'

'Very. Or do you mean as a young man in relation to women? Oh, most definitely that. It was how I managed to run away with Robert. Alex saw we were in love and helped us in every way he could—he lent us money, even though he had little himself, he pretended he had seen me in the town when I was three hours down the turnpike road in the opposite direction heading for London, then he led everyone on a wild goose chase suggesting that I must be lost in the hills. He said that one day he would fall in love, too, and he hoped that then someone would help him.'

So, it had not been an excuse to spare her feelings when she had made that impossible proposal. Alex Demeral really was looking for his true love and she was not that woman. He had made that quite clear.

'Keep it strapped up for a day or two until the swelling goes down and then exercise it gently.' Robert Chandler tied off the bandage bracing Alex's little finger to the one next to it. 'A brave young woman, that Miss Danby,' he added casually.

Alex was not deceived. 'An original, and a very wealthy

one,' he said, equally casually. 'The daughter of Danby the ironmaster.'

Robert whistled as he began to pack away his instruments. 'Her papa will be very grateful for your rescue, then. Unless you were her escort, in which case he'll probably have something in mind for you involving blast furnaces, or heavy hammers, for allowing her to stray into danger.'

'I had no idea that she was in the area. I came out of Rundell, Bridge & Rundell and there she was in the middle of Ludgate Hill with this child in her arms and a stagecoach bearing down on her.'

'So you were the hero of the hour.'

'No, that was Miss Danby. The child would have been killed if it were not for her. All I did was arrive late on the scene and push them under a passing wagon.'

'But you were acquainted with her before this?' Robert leaned against his desk and began slowly re-rolling what was left of the bandage.

'What is this? An interrogation? I had met her two or three times at social events and once in Hyde Park.'

'And the size of her dowry has not convinced you that you have fallen in love?' Robert was having trouble suppressing a grin, curse him.

'No, it has not,' Alex said, trying to look mildly amused and not at all defensive. That was the trouble with old friends, they knew you too well. Damn it, he liked Jessica Danby and he admired her courage, but he was quite easy in his mind regarding his feelings for her.

'How is the practice shaping up?' he asked, firmly changing the subject. 'Are you building a good list of patients?'

'I am and so is Anna. Quite a number of ladies who have

met her as chaperon when consulting me have switched their allegiance to her. We have to be careful—it would cause me a lot of trouble if she was accused of trying to practice as a doctor. But we are certainly very comfortable now.'

'That is good.' Alex tried not to feel jealous of his friend's happiness. Robert had a wife whom he loved, a career that was fulfilling and one which apparently maintained him in some comfort.

He would find the same for himself, he told himself firmly. The wife for him must be out there somewhere. They would meet and fall for each other. He had the title, she would have the wealth and together they would make the estate prosper and raise a brood of happy, healthy children.

He gave a firm nod, encouraging himself, and then felt a fool as he saw the amused expression on Jessica's face. She was standing in the doorway, probably wondering what on earth he was grimacing about.

What was it about this young woman that made him feel so self-conscious?

Chapter Seven

'I did not hear you come in, Miss Danby. You look much recovered,' Alex added truthfully. The dirt had gone, she had regained some colour and, thankfully, she had incurred no damage to her face. He tried not to think of the bruises she had suffered on the rest of her body. In fact, he tried not to imagine her body at all, although he couldn't help but notice that her curves were rather more natural than before, which meant Anna had removed her stays. He was definitely not going to think about that. His body reminded him about how she had felt beneath him and he tried to flex the injured finger until the pain drove those thoughts out of his head.

'I am, thanks to Anna's skill,' she said, smiling at him as he held open the consulting room door for her. 'How is your hand? Is it very painful? I hope you did not break any bones.'

'A dislocated finger, that is all.' He held up his bandaged hand to show her. 'It will be perfectly all right in a few days.'

'I am so glad. Now, may I offer you a place in my carriage? If you give my driver your direction, we can easily make any detour necessary.' She drew on her dirt-streaked gloves as she spoke, perfectly composed.

Why the devil was he feeling quite the opposite? Delayed shock, or, more likely, his imagination conjuring up the image of pale curves disfigured by the black and purple marks of cobblestones.

'Thank you but, no. I was on my way to my bankers and I should return there. It is in quite the opposite direction, so I will take a hackney.' Now he was talking too much. He turned back to his friends. 'Thank you for this, Robert.' He held up his bandaged hand and then turned to kiss Anna on the cheek. 'You must both come to dinner very soon.'

He escaped into the hall and took his hat and gloves from the maid who was waiting patiently with them, then went briskly out and down the steps, stuffing his now shredded gloves in his pocket and hailing a passing hackney as he went. Once again after an encounter with Jessica Danby he had the sensation of having escaped. But from what?

Alex pulled the bank draft out of his pocket and read it again. At least there was no mystery about that, only thoroughly good news.

'May I settle my account now?' Jessica asked as the door closed behind the Duke. 'Only I would prefer not to worry my father with the realisation that I had to seek medical attention.'

'There is nothing to settle,' Anna said. 'Not for a friend of Alex's.' She gave Jessica a quizzical look. 'You *are* a friend of his, are you not?'

'I believe so,' Jessica said coolly. 'I have much to thank him for. And thank you so much, Mrs Chandler. Mr Chandler. Trotter, it is time we returned home, please go and summon George.'

'He's just outside, Miss Danby,' Trotter said, tight-lipped.

Miss Danby, not Miss Jessica. Now what was the matter with her? It soon became clear when they were seated in the carriage.

'You have no bonnet, Miss Jessica. What are people going to think?'

'What people?'

'Whoever sees you arriving home, of course. No lady goes out without a hat.'

'I did not go out without it,' Jessica pointed out. 'But I can hardly put on the dirty, crushed object that it has become. And if anyone sees me between the carriage and my front door in such a shocking state of undress, they may think what they like. Now, do not go alarming Papa with exaggerated tales of what took place on Ludgate Hill. And there is absolutely no need to mention it to any of the staff either. Henry and George will not, I am certain.'

'Because they would be in trouble for not looking after you better, Miss Jessica, that's why,' Trotter said smugly.

'They are no more to blame than you are. You did not try to stop me getting out of the carriage,' Jessica said, rather unfairly, and saw that sink in. 'It is best for all of us if we do not worry my father with this.'

Jessica had spent two days endeavouring to move about as little as possible when her father was present. The bruises had made themselves painfully apparent and she had been hard put to it not to hobble and wince.

By the third day she was feeling better. There was no word from the Duke, for which, of course, she was very grateful, so she caught up with her correspondence and completed a chart from her notes at the newspaper office.

'Here you are, Papa,' she said, carrying it into his study

after luncheon. 'I have listed all the parts of the various Guild parades last year—the number of floats, what they portrayed, all the different groups of people involved, how they collected money and so forth.

'I believe the first thing is for you to establish what theme, if any, the Guild wishes to represent and what the budget is. Then we can make firmer plans. And several of my friends say they would be interested in helping me.'

'Excellent, my dear. What a support you are to me.' He scanned her notes and nodded. 'Yes, I will be off to the Guild this afternoon and find out about all these points.'

He got to his feet and enveloped her in an affectionate hug that almost had her yelping with pain—it seemed the bruises were not as improved as she had thought. Perhaps she would not attend the ball this evening and plead a head-ache. Squeaking with discomfort every time she raised her arms would not be the behaviour expected of a young lady.

It took a week before the worst of the aches and pains subsided. Jessica had resumed her social activities sooner than she really wanted so as not to worry her father and she could not help be glad when he announced at luncheon that he was going out. But the prospect of an uninterrupted afternoon of rest with the latest three-volume novel from the circulating library was shattered—no sooner had the front door closed behind her father than there was the sharp rap of the knocker.

'Miss Beech has called, Miss Jessica. Are you receiving?' the butler enquired.

'Yes, certainly. Have tea sent in, please, Markham.' Although whether Jane would want it so soon after luncheon was doubtful.

What Jane did need, however, was a supply of handkerchiefs. The tears she was holding in check burst free the moment the door closed behind Markham.

'Whatever is the matter?' Jessica sat her on the sofa and put her arm around the shaking shoulders.

'It's Sydney,' Jane sobbed into her handkerchief.

'Sydney? Who is he? Oh, Mr Locksley, I suppose. What has happened? He is not ill, is he?'

Or dead... This degree of distress...

'He came to ask Papa for my hand in marriage,' Jane said.

'But that is excellent news.' Jessica reached into her sewing basket and found the handkerchief she had been hemming. 'Here, take this and try to speak more calmly, I can hardly understand you. Mr Beech did not refuse him, did he?'

Jane managed a snuffle, a nod and a gulp. 'Yes, he did. He was *horrible.*'

'What on earth has your father against the match? Mr Locksley has land and very eligible connections, has he not?'

That produced even more sobs, but eventually Jessica managed to get her friend calm enough to declare, 'Sydney wants to enter Parliament.'

'But that is good, surely? I thought that your father was deeply involved in politics and is thinking of standing for Parliament himself.'

'But Sydney is a *Whig.*'

'Oh. I understand the problem now.' Mr Beech was a Tory of the old school and Jessica had once had the misfortune to have to listen to him declaiming about the evils of the Whig party for a full half-hour. To him Whigs were disloyal to the Crown, would bring down the country by giving votes to the residents of the industrial towns—who were little more than rabble who would bring in revolution and the guillotine given half a chance—and attack the Church of England by extending rights to non-conformists.

'Sydney must have told him his plans to stand for election, because the next thing I knew—I was waiting in the little parlour—was that Papa was shouting for the footmen to throw Sydney out and declaring that he would see me a lifelong spinster rather than marry a Whig. I ran down the backstairs and out of the door into the yard and managed to catch Sydney before he could hail a hackney and we went to talk in the garden of the square.'

Jane blew her nose and took a gulp of her cooling tea. 'Sydney says he can never renounce his principles, although he would give up his Parliamentary ambitions for me. But that would be no better, Papa would still object to him now he knows his allegiance. And besides, how could I stand in the way of Sydney's ambitions? I could never forgive myself.'

'What does Mr Locksley propose doing?'

'He says we must wait until I am of age because we can marry then without Papa's permission. But that is two years!'

'Not so very long,' Jessica soothed.

'Papa knows this gentleman, Sir Willoughby Grafton, who is a political ally of his and he thinks he would be the ideal match for me. But Sir Willoughby is almost forty and takes snuff and has a damp handshake and I hate the way he looks at me. Papa says he will have me despite my hair,' she concluded miserably.

'Then you must just keep saying *no*.' Jessica was brisk.

'This is not the Middle Ages…your father cannot force you to the altar.'

'That is what Sydney says.' Jane dried her eyes and sat up straighter. 'But I am such a mouse, I know I am. I cannot bear anyone shouting at me. If only I had the courage to *do* something.'

'What are Mr Locksley's intensions for this evening, do you know? Perhaps if he is at a gathering that I am attending I can have a word with him, see if we can come up with a plan to change your father's mind.'

'He is going to his club this evening, he said. I was too upset to ask him about every day this week, but I know he is going to a masquerade at the Pantheon with a party of friends in three days' time because he told me yesterday. I wanted to go, too, but he said it was quite unsuitable for a young lady. Apparently it is attended by anyone who can afford the price of a ticket and some quite…er…loose, women will be there. I said in that case I was surprised he would go to such a place, but he says some of his friends who are supporting his candidacy will be in the party and he does not wish to offend them.'

'So what does Mr Locksley propose you do now?'

'He said we should meet in the Park tomorrow, but I think it will rain and Papa will find it very strange if I want to go out in that. And I began to cry and then Sydney became cross and said I was not helping by being over-emotional. So I told him he was being a beast and to go away because I never wanted to see him again.'

'Then you shall come for a drive with me in a closed carriage tomorrow and we will tell your father we are going shopping. An outing will do you good and I am sure Mr Locksley will apologise very soon and you can have a sensible, calm discussion about what is best to do. Now, don't you think you had best go home now and show Mr Beech a calm face? We do not want him guessing you are planning to disobey him, do we?'

'I need to do *something*…anything. Talking will do no good,' Jane said mutinously, but she left with a kiss for Jessica, a vague promise about shopping and a murmur of thanks for her support.

The encounter had left Jessica feeling decidedly unsettled. She spent the rest of the day brooding over what she could do to help Jane and not coming to any sensible conclusions, other than to try to strengthen her resolve to wait for two years. Later she would be attending a party at the home of Lady Archibald, who had secured the services of a leading soprano to give a recital during the course of the evening. Perhaps her other friends would be there, too, and they could put their heads together and come up with some ideas on how to help Jane, or at least lift her spirits.

It had given her an uneasy feeling to hear Jane speak so wildly. Jessica shook her head at her own fancies: Jane herself had said she was too much of a mouse to do anything. Even so, it was difficult to settle to Walter Scott's *Guy Mannering*, the hero's convoluted adventures doing nothing more than confuse her thoughts further.

Three days later Jessica had begun to relax and decide that her friend was not going to do anything foolish. Then, at half past nine, as Trotter was fastening her evening cloak for a soirée, Henry tapped on the door.

'What is it, Trotter?' Jessica asked impatiently. She was already late because between them they had dropped her jewellery box and everything had spilt out, some of the earrings vanishing under the bed and the dresser and having to be searched for on hands and knees.

Trotter came back with a decidedly sour expression on her face. 'That red-headed friend of yours has done something rash by the sound of it and her maid is downstairs asking to speak to you. I wouldn't get involved with it if I were you, Miss Jessica. You can do without other people's scandals.'

So her forebodings that afternoon were not so foolish after all. 'Henry, please bring her up,' Jessica called, ignoring Trotter's tut of disapproval.

Jane's abigail was much younger than Trotter and very agitated. Her bonnet was askew on her head and her coat buttoned wrongly. 'Oh, Miss Danby, thank you for seeing me, only I don't know what to do for the best, I don't truly. I'm scared to go to the master, but what if Miss Jane's in danger?'

'Take a deep breath, calm down and tell me what your name is.'

'I'm Rigby, Miss.'

'Now, what has happened?'

'Miss Jane has gone to the masquerade, all by herself,' the girl gabbled, wringing her hands together.

'The masquerade at the Pantheon?'

'Yes, Miss, that's the one. And she shouldn't go there, I'm sure. I've heard they are dreadful romps, not fit for any decent lady.'

'When did she leave, Rigby? Was she by herself?'

'About nine it was, Miss. I think she must have had an invitation she hadn't told me about, because she's been in such a strange mood all day. I thought she was staying in for the evening, but then she rang for me and told me to find her an evening dress and a domino and a mask. I asked her what time the carriage was ordered for and she said a friend was collecting her. But when she went out she hailed a hackney carriage and Peter—that's our foot-man—said she asked for the Pantheon. But that's not at all respectable, is it?'

'I should say not indeed,' Trotter said. 'A den of iniquity. Ruined she'll be. Ruined.'

Chapter Eight

'Trotter, be quiet and let me think,' Jessica said, holding up a hand to stem the flow. Jane must have decided to rebel against her father and show Locksley that she was an independent woman—always assuming she had applied any rational thought at all to the matter and had not been simply acting out of frustration and pique.

The best outcome would be that Jane found Sydney Locksley at once, that her mask and the hood of the domino concealed her identity and he was able to get her home and back into the house undetected.

What was far more likely was that she would become lost in the throng at the masquerade and would be recognised or, even worse, was assaulted. Or both.

'We have to get her away from there,' she said out loud.

'*We*, Miss Jessica? I hope you are not thinking that you or I are going to involve ourselves with this fiasco,' Trotter stated flatly.

Jessica could not delude herself that she was capable of finding and removing Jane by herself, or even with Trotter. Without help she would be as vulnerable as her friend. There was only one person that she could think of who could help her, although whether he would put himself in such a compromising position she had no way of telling.

'Trotter, I need the simplest of my evening gowns, the black domino and a mask.' The maid opened her mouth, refusal written plain on her face. 'Unless you want me to tell Papa that you wish to return home to Shropshire? If that is the case, then Rigby can help me dress. I am going to write to the Duke and ask for his help. I will be quite safe with him.'

As she turned to her little writing desk she saw the sudden calculation cross Trotter's face. If Jessica was compromised with the Duke, then that would be a very satisfactory outcome in Trotter's opinion—and in her father's, too. The maid began to shake out a gown with considerable enthusiasm.

Jessica scribbled a hurried note, not disguising how serious she thought the situation was and ending.

I know you have no reason to assist me but, for the sake of a young lady too innocent to realise what danger she is in, I beg you to come. J.D.

'Trotter, find Henry.'

She sealed the note, wrote the Duke's name and address on the wrapper and thrust it into the footman's hand. 'Henry, deliver this as fast as you can. If the Duke is not at home, find where he has gone and follow him. It is very urgent. If he agrees to return with you, do not bring him into the house. Ask him to remain in the carriage and come and fetch me.'

'Yes, Miss Jessica.' He turned and she heard his shoes clattering down the back stairs.

Now all she could do was change her clothes, wait and hope.

* * *

'I found the Duke at home, Miss Jessica,' Henry announced half an hour later, breathless after running back up the stairs again. 'He says of course he will help and he's waiting in his carriage outside. Oh, and he says to bring a maid with you.'

'So I should hope,' Trotter said with a sniff. 'I'll get my bonnet.'

'I think it had better be you, Rigby, if you are willing.' Jessica was already wearing the concealing domino over her gown, with no jewellery at all. She picked up the plain black silk mask that would conceal the upper half of her face.

'Oh, thank you, Miss Danby. I'd be easier in my mind if I was doing something and that's a fact.'

'Come along then, Rigby. Trotter, if anyone asks for me, simply reply that I was engaged to go to Lady Dreyscourt's entertainment, which is the complete truth.'

'Yes, Miss Danby.' It was clearly going to take a lot to soothe Trotter's ruffled feathers tomorrow, but for now Jessica had other things to think about.

Henry hurried to open the door of the carriage standing outside, its side panels covered, presumably to hide the ducal crest. Demeral was inside and half rose as they entered. He, too, was masked and wearing a domino, its hood thrown back.

'Miss Danby, good evening. This is not Trotter, I think?' He rapped on the roof and the carriage moved away immediately.

'No, this is Rigby, Miss Beech's abigail.'

Rigby, clearly finding the entire evening almost too much, gave a faint squeak of agreement.

'What was your mistress wearing, Rigby?' Demeral asked.

The girl gulped, but managed to speak clearly. 'A white silk evening gown—quite a plain one, because of the domino, sir. I mean, Your Grace. And a dark red domino and a half-mask with the face of a cat—white with black whiskers.'

'At least it is not another black domino,' Demeral said. 'That is something. Miss Beech's hair is very distinctive. Did she attempt to disguise that?'

'No, Your Grace. It was quite a simple arrangement though. I don't think much of it would show when the hood was up.'

'Then all we have to do is find her in a throng of several hundred people, most of whom will be drunk and all of whom will be bent on having a wildly good time which will not include respecting women. Rigby, you had best stay in the carriage. My driver and groom will be with you the whole time. Miss Danby, you and I will brave the masquerade.' He looked at her, no amusement in his expression at all. 'Do not, even for a moment, leave my side.'

'I will take hold of your domino and not let go,' Jessica said earnestly. 'I promise you.'

The eastern end of Oxford Street was not somewhere Jessica would usually have reason to visit and certainly not at night. She looked out of the carriage window and confessed to herself that, even if she had been foolhardy enough to come in pursuit of Jane by herself, she would have turned tail and fled when she saw the scene outside.

They were on the opposite side of the street to the Pantheon and she was surprised their driver had managed to get so close. The road leading west out of London was a busy highway at the best of times, but now it was chaos, with throngs of revellers on their way to the theatres, the inns and the more dubious pleasures of Soho, mingling with those who were arriving at the Pantheon and the crowds who had gathered to watch the spectacle.

The frontage of the building, with a portico and four Classical pillars, was clearly designed to look imposing, but the effect was somewhat spoilt by the position, crammed between narrow houses and shops on either side and opening directly on to the pavement. The milling crowd in front, most of whom were clearly not of the *haut ton,* did not help in raising the tone either.

Hawkers with baskets of pastries and oranges slung around their necks wove though the throng and others with barrows added their cries to the racket. Someone appeared to be selling meat for dogs, of all things.

'Are those…er…courtesans?' she asked as a flock of bejewelled women passed them. Their gowns appeared designed to reveal, or hint at, considerably more than they covered. In fact, Jessica thought they all looked as though they had come out forgetting at least one layer. Their hairstyles were wildly extravagant and their voices shrill with laughter.

'I think you are giving them a status in their profession that is more elevated than the reality,' Demeral said drily. 'A courtesan will be in the keeping of a gentleman with her own apartment and maid. Those girls will be going home to an entirely different kind of establishment, or to some squalid room. Not that I should be telling you any of that. Rigby, you stay here. Keep the blinds down, do not open the door except to me or the driver and groom.

'Come, Miss Danby. On with your mask. The sooner we find your friend, the better. And do not let go of me for a second.' Demeral adjusted his mask, a simple band of black silk with eyeholes, raised his hood and lifted her down to the pavement. He put his arm through a slit in the side of his domino and she did the same, tucking her hand firmly under his elbow. It felt strange to be so close to a man, to feel the warmth of him against her side, to grip the muscles that flexed slightly under her hand. Strange and rather exciting.

They crossed the street and Demeral forged a path to the door, paid for admission and led her inside. The noise was tremendous, echoing around the space which resembled nothing more to her eyes than a theatre without the seating. Music was being played loudly from the stage at the far end, dancers in every kind of fancy dress were energetically cavorting in the main body of the hall and the tiers of boxes lining the walls each seemed to be the venue for a private party of the wildest sort, with participants leaning over at dangerous angles, wine bottles being waved and—goodness! Jessica hastily averted her eyes from the nearest ground-level box where a man appeared to be undressing his fair companion.

'I thought there was a dome,' Jessica said, looking ceiling-wards in the hope things were less embarrassing higher up.

'There was, that is why the original building was called the Pantheon, like the original in Rome. But that version burned down. Now, we will start searching at this level and work our way up to the boxes if we have to. Look out for Locksley's hair, he'll have no reason to disguise it. He'll be easier to find than one girl in a dark red domino.'

* * *

It was a slow business and Jessica was beginning to panic, convinced they would never find Jane. There seemed to be an improbable number of red-headed men present and Jessica clung to Demeral as they criss-crossed the floor, getting close enough to study each one they saw.

Fortunately, despite Demeral's prediction, dark red dominos were not as common as red-headed men, it seemed, and most of the women present were not troubling with them at all, relying on their masks to conceal their identities. Or perhaps not… Jessica's attention was caught by a group of laughing young women, none of whom was wearing more of a mask than a tiny arrangement of feathers and lace. It was simply an aid to flirtation, she realised.

A large man, worse the wear for drink, jostled them and Demeral pushed him away with his free hand.

'This is getting rough. If we do not find her in a few minutes, I am going to take you back to the carriage.'

'Over there—look, another red-headed man.'

He was sitting on the low padded edge of one of the boxes at ground-floor level. There were little doors to allow the occupants to step out, but all along the row men were simply climbing over on to the dance floor and swinging their partners across, too. Demeral pushed a path to the box and the man looked around. It was Sydney Locksley. His mask had gone and he was gingerly touching a red mark across one cheek.

'Found you at last, Locksley.' The Duke pushed back his hood.

'Who the devil are you?' Locksley narrowed his eyes, wincing. 'Demeral?' He shook off the hand of one of the scantily clad girls who was pawing at his coat for attention. 'Let go of me, you've done enough damage already tonight.'

Jessica could see the entire box now. There were three other young gentlemen and two pretty girls draped across their laps and a table with bottles and glasses.

'Where is…?' She dropped her voice and whispered, 'Jane?'

'I don't know.' Locksley seemed dazed.

'Pull yourself together,' Demeral snapped. 'I don't care how drunk you are and I don't care what I have to do to sober you up. I want to know where the young lady is and I want to know now.'

'I tell you, I don't know. We'd settled in the box and were joined by these…ladies. There were four of them, but I told them to go away, that wasn't what we were here for. One left—she flounced off—but one sat on my knee, and then Jane appeared. I have no idea how she found me. She called me all kinds of names and before I could explain we hadn't invited the girls she slapped my face and it caught me off balance. The chair tipped, I fell off and hit my head. Knocked me out for a moment, I think. When I came round she had gone.'

He looked around, blinking as though he expected to see Jane still standing there. Jessica realised he must still be befuddled from the blow to his head.

'How long ago was this?' Demeral demanded.

One of the other men shrugged. 'Ten minutes? Less, perhaps.'

'We have to find her,' Jessica said to them. 'You go that way and you, that.' She pointed towards two corners of the room. 'We will search this way. That dark red domino with a cat mask must be an unusual combination.'

They hesitated, clearly unused to being told what to do by young women, but Demeral jerked his head and they climbed over the edge of the box and disappeared into the crowd. Jessica let herself into the box, climbed on to a chair and then on to the table, uncaring that she was showing her ankles or that several young bucks turned and stared.

'Get down from there.' Demeral raised his hands to lift her.

'No, I can see better up here.' She turned slowly, the little table rocking beneath her. Demeral took hold and steadied it. 'Look, over there under that big chandelier—a dark red hood. Oh, and something is happening.'

Chapter Nine

'Locksley, you stay here and get your wits back. Jane may return.' Demeral grasped Jessica around the waist and lifted her off the table and over the edge of the box. At that level there was no glimpse of the red domino, but he headed confidently into the crowd, forcing his way through. Jessica clung to his cloak.

Even above the noise all around them they heard the shrill voice as they came closer. 'No, I will not take off my mask! Let me go, I want to leave, you horrible man!'

Three young men, their clothing respectable rather than costly and fashionable, had surrounded the red-cloaked figure and were making playful snatches at her cat mask while one held her arm. Whether it was Jane or not, this young woman needed help, Jessica thought as she took a firm grip on the strings of her reticule. It was a fashionable one, stiffened with card to hold its geometrical shape and sharp angles.

'Let her go this minute,' she said, poking her finger into the ribs of the nearest man.

He turned with a snarl and she hit him with the reticule, squarely on the nose. He retreated, howling. Demeral had the arm of the man holding the girl.

'The lady told you to let her go,' he said.

He was answered with a few short words of abuse that broke off in a gasp of pain. 'You've broken my bloody arm!'

'Excellent. Do your friends want to see what else I can break?' Demeral enquired of the man's remaining companion.

He took one look at his friends—one clutching his arm, the other with a handkerchief clamped to his bloody nose—and retreated back into the crowd.

The young woman gave a cry of 'Jessica!' and reached out for her.

'Jane, are you hurt?' Jessica demanded, pulling her friend close. The whiskers of the pretty cat mask were bent and below it there were tear tracks on Jane's cheeks. Her hair was coming down and her domino had been pulled crooked.

'No, not really, though my arm is bruised, I think. This is a horrible place. *Horrible*. I want to go home.'

'And so you shall. We will just go and collect Mr Locksley first.'

'I am never going to speak to him again! He is a libertine.'

'No, he is not,' Demeral said calmly as he started to guide them both back towards the box. 'Those women will go from box to box, uninvited, hoping to have drinks bought for them and to be paid for their company. They are devilish difficult to get rid of. There he is and he appears to have recovered from your assault. You knocked him out, you know.'

'Good. I hope it hurt,' Jane said, but she did not sound as though she meant it. When Locksley vaulted over the barrier and took her in his arms she went into the embrace with a sob and hugged him tightly. There was no sign of his companions,

'Have you got a carriage?' Demeral asked as the two men started towards the entrance, Jessica and Jane sheltered between them.

'No, we came in a hackney.'

'We have Miss Beech's woman in mine. I suggest you take it and escort her home in that. If the worst happens and you are discovered trying to get her inside, then at least you'll have been in a respectable carriage with the maid. We will find a hackney.'

But when they stepped back from the kerb as Demeral's carriage set off, containing a weeping Jane and a very grateful Locksley, there wasn't a hackney in sight.

'There never is when you want one,' Demeral said. 'At least it isn't raining. If we walk west a little, towards Mayfair, we should find one.'

'We could walk all the way,' Jessica said. 'It cannot be more than a mile, can it? And I put on very sensible shoes because I had no idea what we would have to do.'

'You put on sensible shoes.' Demeral said flatly, then looked down at her and grinned. 'Has anyone ever told you that you are a very remarkable woman, Miss Danby?'

'No,' she said, suddenly feeling very cheerful and full of energy. 'Shall we go? And call me Jessica, please. We can't be formal if we are having an adventure.'

'Jessica, then. And I am Alex and if we begin our adventure by going that way, eastwards, for a couple of turnings we will find Wardour Street. That will take us down to Leicester Square. Then we will cut across the bottom of that and work our way down to the Strand. Let me know if you become tired and I will find a hackney.'

'Very well.' She slipped her hand into the crook of his elbow and they walked briskly away from the crowds around the Pantheon, passed two streets on the right and then took the third, heading south.

'This is Soho. It is not an area a respectable lady would ever dream of going, so keep you mask on and, if there is any trouble, get behind me.'

'But it all seems very busy, and well lit,' Jessica said, looking around with interest. It was not at all what she might imagine a notorious district to look like. There were small houses, probably divided up into apartments, she thought. There were shops, too, each only a few feet wide, their doors open to spill light into the street and business going on briskly inside. She saw one had the three golden balls that signified a pawnbroker hanging crookedly from its frontage. That was doing particularly good trade.

The smell of meat pies and ale wafted from several places and on one corner a man was playing the fiddle, his black and white dog carrying a battered cap around the onlookers. Someone tossed in a small coin and the dog put down the cap, barked a thank you and picked it up again to general laughter. A woman, middle aged, buxom and wearing what looked like several layers of tattered skirts, took the arm of a man and swung him into a dance. Someone was passing around a stoneware flagon and both men and women were taking swigs from it.

'Gin,' Alex said.

Jessica did not feel at all intimidated by what she had seen so far, even if this was one of London's more louche areas, but that was probably because she was on the arm of a man who had already demonstrated that he was very effective in dealing with trouble. She felt a little frisson of excitement, although whether it was at the thought of the possible dangers or the closeness of the Duke, she was not sure. *Alex*. She was very aware again of those muscles under her hand.

'It all feels good natured,' she ventured. 'Although perhaps that will not last long if everyone is drinking gin like that.'

'Yes, we are fortunate it is this early.' He sounded relaxed, but she could sense his alertness, the slight shift of balance, the turn of his head, at each movement in the shadows, each unexpected sound. 'In the small hours I wouldn't dream of bringing you down here.'

'Are you armed?' It was a very long street, not wide and with many side turnings and dark entrances. She suppressed a gasp as two figures staggered out of one alleyway, singing and passing a bottle between them, and then vanished into another. Their tuneless song echoed back, distorted by echoes.

'A pocket pistol and a knife,' he admitted. 'And I have no hesitation in fighting in a most ungentlemanly manner if that is required. But it will not be, never fear.'

'I don't. I feel quite safe.'

With you.

A young woman came out of the shadows and smiled at Alex. 'You can do better than that with me, luv. Or she can join in if she likes. I'm not fussy.' Her dress looked fine in the poor light, then Jessica saw the hem was ragged and the woman was not young beneath the paint, her smile gap-toothed.

'I do not share,' Jessica said firmly, returning a smile just as false. Her imagination reeled. What on earth was she proposing? 'So sorry.'

Alex chuckled and guided her on, giving the street walker a wide berth.

'Don't laugh. The poor soul,' she chided as they passed on down Wardour Street. 'Imagine having to make your living in such a way.'

'And there are many of her sisters out on the streets. It doesn't take much for a woman to fall from safe respectability into that kind of life,' Alex said. 'At least it isn't raining or bitterly cold tonight.'

They walked in silence for a few steps then, Jessica said, 'Alex suits you. Why did your parents choose it, do you think? Alexander the Great? The Czar? It means warrior, I believe.'

'I am named for one of my godfathers. The richer of the two,' he added drily. 'Not that the flattery did much good. He left me a pocket watch, a collection of very dry volumes from his library and fifty pounds. And Jessica? Were your parents Shakespeare enthusiasts?'

'I am certain they were not. But Mama read somewhere that it means gift in Hebrew and she and Papa had wanted a daughter, so that is what they called me when I finally arrived after two large, noisy sons.'

'Are they still large and noisy?'

'Goodness, yes. They fill a room just by entering it. So much energy and self-assurance and such loud voices. I am finding London quite restful in comparison,' she said with some feeling. 'Do you have siblings?'

'I had a brother and sister. Twins. But they never thrived and died very young.'

He must have spent a lonely childhood, she thought, unless his parents took pains to prevent that—perhaps he'd had good friends. Ethan and Joshua were exhausting, but they were good brothers and she had never felt alone or isolated as the only girl. But she did not know the Duke—*Alex,* she reminded herself—well enough to ask about his childhood. She suspected he would resent probing questions.

'This does not seem quite real, does it?' she said instead.

'What doesn't?' Despite her hood she was aware of him turning his head to look down at her.

'Walking through the streets of London after dark. Catching glimpses of other people's lives. It is magical, somehow.'

That provoked a snort of amusement. 'Magical? Drunks and drabs and the stench wafting from dark, dangerous alleyways?'

'I mean out of this world. Out of my world, anyway. I feel…free.'

'And you do not feel free normally?' he asked, sounding puzzled.

'Try being a woman for a while and you would not ask that,' she said tartly. 'Especially being a respectable, unmarried lady. You may never be alone, you may never act on impulse. Every action, every word must be guarded, be correct, or you are labelled fast and ill bred. Perhaps being a widow is best for a woman. A rich widow, of course.'

'To be a widow you would have to be a wife first,' Alex pointed out.

'I know.' She gave an exaggerated sigh. 'Depressing, isn't it?'

'You, Miss Danby, are an original, I think.'

'I know what that means,' Jessica retorted. 'Indefinably odd, but everyone is too polite to say *eccentric*.'

'It is *not* what I mean,' Alex said, no longer sounding amused. 'You are a refreshing change from young ladies who have been schooled to hide whatever wits or originality they have, who have been trained to throw themselves squeaking in alarm into the arms of the nearest gentleman at the slightest provocation—a mouse, a loud noise—and who must never, ever disagree with a man.'

That was a compliment indeed and it made Jessica feel uncomfortably flustered. 'The impulse to throw oneself into the arms of a man because of spiders, mice or any other trivial alarm is soon shaken out of any girl with brothers,' she said. 'And Papa said that as I would have money then I must learn to look after it, so perhaps some of the lessons I shared with my brothers would surprise you. Then, when Mama died five years ago, I had to start learning how to manage the household. It would have been chaotic if I had pretended to have less wits than hair.'

'I imagine it would have been. We have just passed Lisle Street, so we will be in Leicester Square very soon. You are not tired?'

'No, not at all. Have you been to Mr Barker's Panorama?' Jessica asked, deciding it was time to move away from personal revelations. It was dangerous to become too friendly with this man, she told herself. He was the perfect gentleman, of course, but her unruly feelings were already a little bruised. 'It is just along here, I think. I hear it is exceedingly interesting.'

'I confess I have not.' He sounded rather short. Perhaps he thought she was angling for an invitation, which was embarrassing. 'Now, which would be the best way to Adam Street, I wonder? I think we will cut across the bottom of the Square towards Chandos Street and then down Bedford Street to the Strand. That keeps to the wider streets, but avoids you walking along the Strand for any distance.'

'I am hardly likely to be recognised, am I?' Jessica pointed out. 'But I suppose, so close to home, it would be sensible. If we go into Salisbury Street, just past Adam Street, then we can get to the back entrance of the house. I do have a key.'

'Sensible woman,' Alex said, sounding less distant again. Perhaps he was feeling the responsibility of allowing her whim to walk through the dark streets.

It was not so much fun now, she realised. The magic had gone out of the evening as the lights of the Strand grew closer. Now it was a question of negotiating the broad, busy thoroughfare, of worrying about getting into the house unseen.

'I hope Jane has returned home safely and that she has made it up with Mr Locksley,' she ventured as they made it safely to the southern side of the Strand and Alex tossed a coin to the crossing sweeper. 'And I do hope it will force them into some kind of decision about their future. They have to make a plan, not simply mope about.'

'You are a great believer in plans, are you not, Jessica? Down here, you say? Yes, I see. Which is the back gate to your house?'

'That one.' Had that remark about plans been a jibe over her scheme to propose marriage to him? 'I do try to form strategies, yes. I have been brought up to be businesslike. Sometimes they do not work out as I had intended, I suppose,' she added, trying to sound cool and not defensive.

'Jessica.' Alex stopped, just outside the tall gate leading into their small back garden.

'Yes?' She looked up at him. He was very close, a dark shadow in his black domino. The silence seemed to stretch on, full of a strange tension, and to break it she slid her hand from under his arm.

'No.' He caught her hand, held it, then lifted it to his lips.

Chapter Ten

'No, do not be offended. I was not criticising you,' Alex said and dropped a light kiss on her knuckles.

Jessica was wearing gloves, of course, but the tissue-thin kid of evening gloves was no barrier against the warmth of lips, even in such a fleeting brush.

'There is no need to apologise,' she said and found her voice husky.

He released her hand. 'Where is your key?'

'Here.' She found it in her now somewhat battered reticule. Alex unlocked the gate and eased it open. 'What about the back door?'

'I have that, too.'

They walked quietly across the back garden, fitfully illuminated by a lamp that had been left burning in a first-floor window. A cat shot out of the shadows with an angry hiss, sending Jessica rocking back on her heels.

Alex caught her, steadied her and she turned in the circle of his arms, some instinct making her lift her hands to his shoulders, one of them sliding across to the back of his neck.

He bent his head, his lips so close she could feel his breath, taste the faintest hint of the brandy he must have been drinking when her note reached him. 'Jessica?'

The magic had returned to the night and with it a strangeness, the sensation of being out of her world, of leaving convention and common sense behind. She went up on tiptoe and their lips met, a fleeting touch, the merest sensation of warm flesh meeting an answering heat, then she was back firmly on both feet and Alex was a step away.

You fool, what have you done?

'That was a thank-you and a goodnight kiss combined,' Jessica managed to whisper with the lightest of laughs that she hoped did not sound as forced as it felt. He would never know how it had affected her, would he? 'You really have saved the day for Jane.'

'I hope so. Now, back inside, quickly, before anyone hears us.'

There—Alex did not sound shocked to the core that some idiotically impulsive female had just kissed him. It was probably simply her own lack of sophistication and experience that made that small touch seem such a significant thing. He probably kissed women goodnight on a regular basis.

'No, you must leave first so I can lock the gate behind you.'

He nodded and went out, a silent shadow among the alleyway's deeper shade. She thought he raised his hand in farewell as the gate closed behind him, but she could not be certain.

Jessica turned the key, then returned to the back door. It opened with the faintest of creaks as she crept inside, closed and locked it. The bolts at top and bottom had been barely opened—Trotter must have slipped down and done that after Markham, their butler, had made his rounds before retiring—so she slid those home, wincing at the scrape of metal through the hasps.

There was the dull glow from the banked-down range to guide her across the kitchen floor, then the dark of the passageway to negotiate before she found the foot of the servants' stairs where there was a perceptible lightening of the darkness. When she reached the first landing the light grew stronger and she found the lantern had had been left on the sill of the narrow window. She blew it out, then turned to open the door which led on to the first floor. Now she only had to creep past Papa's bedchamber and she was safe.

There, I have done it.

Trotter, dozing in the armchair in front of the fire, sat up with a jerk. 'Miss Jessica. I've been that worried,' she whispered.

'No need. We found Miss Beech and she will be home by now, although whether she has got in safely without being discovered, I have no idea.'

'That young lady deserves a good spanking, if you ask me, Miss Jessica,' Trotter muttered, but her fingers were busy with the fastenings of Jessica's gown and she added, almost grudgingly, 'You're a good friend, I'll say that.'

As the lock snicked closed Alex backed across the narrow alleyway so he could see the faint light in the upstairs window. If that vanished and no others were lit, then Jessica would have made it to her bedchamber undetected.

He told himself to stop thinking about bedchambers, but that fleeting, innocent, kiss had been powerfully arousing. Jessica meant nothing by it, of course. She was naturally warm and friendly, they had just shared an adventure that had been highly unconventional, slightly dangerous and, as Jessica had said, magical. A mere brush of the lips at the end of that meant nothing.

All his feelings proved, he decided, was that he was missing intimate female contact. It had not felt right, somehow, to set up a mistress at the same time as courting a wife, so in the New Year he had parted on good terms with the goldsmith's widow in the nearby town who had welcomed the *company*, as she put it, but by no means expected any permanent arrangement.

The light at the window flickered and was gone. He would wait another few minutes, just to make certain there wasn't a sudden uproar signalling her discovery, although what good he could do if that occurred, he couldn't imagine. The presence of a man would only make things worse.

Or would it? As he turned to make his way back to the Strand it occurred to Alex that if they had been discovered in the garden they would have been thoroughly compromised and then he would have had to marry Jessica. He would have secured his wealthy wife and Mr Danby would have captured his noble son-in-law.

Was that a twinge of regret he was feeling? Alex gave himself a sharp mental shake. He liked Jessica, he admired her and he found her stimulating company, but he was not in love with her. And she, although apparently liking him well enough at the start to suggest marriage, clearly considered him now in the light of a friend. From what he had observed, young ladies in love with a gentleman were incapable of behaving in an open, relaxed and friendly way around him. They blushed, they were shy, or they hung breathless on his every word. There was giggling. Much giggling. He had never heard Jessica giggle.

Laugh, yes, She had an attractive range of laughs from a throaty little chuckle to a clear, musical, peal.

What he needed was a drink. Alex turned and made his way towards the Coal Hole Tavern, haunt of actors and the location of the Wolf Club drinking society, founded by actor-manager Edmund Kean, for the benefit of, as he said, gentlemen whose wives would not let them sing in the bath.

The story always made Alex smile and he was in the mood for rowdy, cheerful and uncomplicated company. Women were, most definitely, not uncomplicated.

Jessica woke the next morning with a mixture of sensations. There was a general feeling of uneasiness, a flicker of panic and a warm glow of something indefinable. She blinked herself awake in the chilly February light and sat up to sip her cup of hot chocolate while Trotter supervised the maid who was setting the fire.

The panic was anxiety about Jane, she decided, the warm glow was satisfaction over having found her last night and hopefully settled the rift with Sydney Locksley. The uneasiness she explored, tentatively, much as one probed an aching tooth with the tip of the tongue.

Last night she had kissed Alex. Kissed the Duke of Malvern. He had not kissed her—except her hand—*she* had been the one to take the liberty.

Now what would he think of her? That she was wanton? Or perhaps that she was still trying to lure him into marriage? Or perhaps he would realise the truth, that she had been giddy with excitement after their adventure and had acted without thought or intention.

That was the best she could hope for, although she had no idea now what had possessed her, there in the dark. She finished the chocolate and found she was smiling. It might have been immodest and reckless, but she had enjoyed it.

Such memories from a fleeting moment of contact. Warmth, that faint hint of brandy, a taste she could not quite describe, but supposed must have simply been Alex, the sensation of his lips, soft and yet firm, and the slight prickle of masculine hair.

What now? It would not be discreet to send Alex a note to thank him for last night and besides, she had probably already done more thanking than she should have done. On the other hand, she had to find out whether Jane had reached her own bed safely or she would perish from curiosity. She would go after breakfast, far too early for a normal social call, but nothing out of the ordinary between young ladies and their friends.

At breakfast her father looked up from the pile of post he had been reading as she entered and she thought how much improved his health seemed to be. Perhaps it was the realisation that leaving her brothers in charge of the business had not resulted in the immediate collapse of the company, she mused with an inward smile.

'Good morning, Papa.'

'Good morning, my dear. And how was your party last night?'

'I am afraid it made absolutely no impression upon me at all,' she confessed truthfully, pouring him another cup of coffee before sitting down and thanking the footman for the pot of tea he placed beside her. 'Is there anything I can help you with today, Papa? I had thought of visiting Jane Beech this morning, but it should not take me long.'

'No, nothing, my dear. I am going to the Ironmongers'

Guild to attempt to shake some answers out of them about this May Day affair. I could not find anyone with much idea when I called the other day. It seems to me that they decided to take part because most of the other guilds do and then did nothing about planning it. They have no concept how they wish to represent the guild. It is no way to go about a business,' he said with a sorrowful shake of his head.

'I expect they all run their individual businesses very efficiently,' Jessica said, undecided over which jam to choose for her toast. 'But put them together and they lose focus. Because you are not an ironmonger yourself, you will be able to take a dispassionate view. I am sure you will guide them firmly, Papa.'

He preened slightly at her praise, his chest seeming to swell under the green brocade of his waistcoat. 'You may well be right, my dear. I shall be firm, but tactful. I have to thank them for taking an ironmaster from Shropshire into their company, after all.'

Jessica arrived at Jane's doorstep in Conduit Street on the stroke of ten. 'Good day, Fitton,' she greeted the butler. 'Is Miss Jane at home?'

'Good morning, Miss Danby. Miss Jane is in her sitting room. I will show you up.'

'Please don't trouble, Fitton, I know my way.' She ran up to the first floor where Jane had a small room with her writing desk and some comfortable chairs where she could entertain friends without disturbing her parents. Mrs Beech, who possessed the reputation of enjoying exquisitely sensitive nerves, much preferred to keep her drawing room free to entertain her own acquaintances.

The door had hardly closed behind the butler when Jane leapt up and ran to embrace Jessica. 'Oh, you've come! Thank you, I was going to send a note, but it is so difficult to think what I could safely write.'

'Tell me what happened,' Jessica said, disentangling herself and sitting down. 'You got back safely, obviously,' she added, keeping her voice low. It was a mistake to assume that servants never listened at doors, even in the best-run households.

'Rigby was wonderful—she had thought to bring the back door key with her and she had asked one of the other maids, who thought Rigby was slipping out to go courting, to open the bolts for her after Fitton had locked up. I have given her a very nice present of money, because if she had not warned you, I do not know what would have happened.'

'What on earth possessed you?' Jessica asked bluntly. She had a very good idea of what would have happened, even if Jane had not.

'I thought Sydney had simply given up and didn't care enough about me. Which was so unfair, because he was unhappy, too, which is why he went out with his friends. I thought I would be dashing and decisive and do something—and then when I got there, it was horrible and those girls who were with them were so pretty... And poor Sydney, I hit him and he banged his head. I don't know why he has forgiven me.'

'He loves you.'

Jessica's woebegone face broke into a smile. 'Oh, yes, he must do. He was so sweet in the carriage coming back. He said that we should elope because he could not think of any way to change my father's opinion, but I said, no, because it would blight Sydney's chances if there was a scandal.'

'I am not so sure about that,' Jessica said thoughtfully. 'As a young man Lord Eldon, the Lord Chancellor, eloped. I remember reading about it. His sweetheart climbed down a ladder from a window in her house in Newcastle in the dead of night and they were married over the Border. I'm sure I read that both his father and hers forgave them after a while and you can hardly say that *his* chances were blighted! He was made a baron and has been Lord Chancellor for simply years.'

Jane stared at her. 'The Lord Chancellor eloped? My goodness, how wonderful. Perhaps I am wrong to worry about Sydney's career. After all, it is not as though Papa is a well-known public figure and, although he may have many friends and have influence among the Tories, his opinion will not hold any sway with the Whigs.'

'That's the spirit,' Jessica encouraged. 'If you are certain that Locksley is the one for you, then you will have to do something drastic or face the future with someone who is second best. Has he any money?'

'He has a doting godmother who gives him an allowance and he has been offered a post as secretary to Lord Wantage.' She frowned in thought. 'He needs to make certain both his godmother and Lord Wantage would not disapprove, but if they will support him then we would have enough to live on modestly, even if Papa cuts me off without a penny.'

'There, you have a plan. Now all you have to do is talk to your Sydney and he has to consult his patrons. Now I had better go, because I need to help Papa with this May Day planning for the Guild and he is visiting them today to press for some decisions.' It was an excuse because her father would not return for some time, but she wanted to encourage Jane to do some hard thinking for herself.

They kissed cheeks and Jessica, mentally crossing all her fingers for the couple, collected Trotter from where she had been waiting in the hallway and emerged on to Conduit Street. They had walked because the day was dry with a little weak sunshine breaking through the clouds, but now, as the wind freshened, she was glad of the warm pelisse she was wearing.

'Where now, Miss Jessica?'

'Home, I think, Trotter,' she said, wondering why the maid was staring over her shoulder with a decidedly odd expression on her face.

'Good day, Miss Danby.'

It was the Duke, driving a high-perch phaeton drawn by a fine pair of matched bays.

'Would you care to take a turn around the Park?'

Chapter Eleven

'Drive with you?' Jessica said, then collected her scattered wits and bobbed a slight curtsy. 'I mean, good morning, Demeral. Thank you, but I am not certain—'

I am not certain of what I am not certain! she thought, almost ready to laugh at herself for being in such a fluster.

And over what? An innocuous invitation from a gentleman to drive in an open carriage.

'As you see, I have my groom up behind, so we would be perfectly respectable, although I regret there is no room for Trotter to accompany you.' Alex was keeping a perfectly straight face, although she strongly suspected from the twinkle in his eyes that he, too, was amused by her confusion.

'Thank you, Demeral, I should be delighted. Trotter, His Grace will return me home, so there is no need for you to wait.' She opened her reticule. 'Here is the fare if you would prefer to take a hackney carriage.'

'Thank you, I'm sure, Miss Danby.' Trotter had her sucking lemons' expression back. 'What shall I tell Mr Danby should he enquire as to your whereabouts?'

'That I am driving with a friend in the park, of course. Papa is a busy man, Trotter. There is no need to disturb him with tittle-tattle about my doings.'

'No, Miss Danby. You will be back in time for luncheon?'

'Of course. Thank you.' That was to the groom who had jumped down from his perch to assist her up to the high seat that balanced precariously over the front axle of the carriage. 'Goodness, what a long way up! I am already changing my mind about asking Papa for such a carriage.'

'This one will be on the market soon,' Alex said with a grimace as the groom ran round to climb up behind. 'Both the carriage and the bays. They are an extravagance to maintain. I won them at cards last year, but I should content myself with my curricle and greys.'

That was frank speaking, Jessica thought. Most gentlemen would avoid any suggestion that they could not afford their blood horses or their sporting vehicles and would cheerfully run up large debts if that was what it took to maintain them. She liked it in Alex that he would tell her so candidly; it argued that he had little false pride and also that he trusted her as a friend.

'A curricle must be equally stimulating to drive,' she suggested. It was also rather more dashing than a phaeton in her opinion, if not as showy for parading about in the park.

'That is true. Do you have a taste for speed, Jes—' He broke off and she was suddenly conscious of the groom behind them. 'Miss Danby?'

'I fear so. At home in Shropshire I have a gig and I am always in trouble with Papa for dashing about the countryside. But I would not dare attempt anything more than a sedate trot in London. It would be considered fast for a lady to do so, would it not?'

'I fear so, but if you go out to Richmond Park, for example, you could enjoy more freedom. Would your father object if you were to drive me there with your own groom in attendance?'

Jessica shot him a startled glance. 'No, he would not object in the slightest.' She dropped her voice. 'But he would leap to a quite incorrect conclusion if we were to do so. In any case, I think you should be driving other young ladies about, in search of your kindred spirit, not spend your time with me, a mere friend.'

The bays checked as though Alex's hands had tightened involuntarily on the reins, but he answered her lightly enough, 'Never *mere*, Miss Danby. Tell me, have you news of our mutual friends and their adventures?'

'She arrived safely home, I am glad to say. I have spoken to her and suggested that concerns about his career if they take drastic action might be pessimistic. I told her about Lord Eldon and his youthful elopement and that seems to have stiffened my friend's resolve to take action, or, at least to discuss tactics calmly with the gentleman.'

'Excellent. Let me know if I can assist. I am sure I can lay my hands on a rope ladder if required.'

That made Jessica laugh. 'I really cannot imagine anything as foolish as leaving a house that way—although that is how Lord Eldon managed it, I understand, and from a window at the front of the house on quite a busy street by Newcastle's riverside. Perhaps it was an ordinary ladder, though. Just think, with a rope one it would be swaying about, the lady clinging on for dear life and probably squeaking in terror. And down below the gentleman trying to keep his horses quiet and reassure his love at the same time. If that was not enough to wake the household, nothing would.

'No, if I were to elope I would do it in the morning, announcing that I was going to my dressmaker for a lengthy fitting and then planning on taking luncheon with a friend and spending the afternoon shopping. I would have smuggled out the necessities for the journey over several days and I would take enough money with me for things I had forgotten—tooth powder, for example. You cannot expect gentlemen to remember such things. As a result there would be no drama and no one taking alarm at my absence for hours.'

'Very practical, but not very romantic. You leave little scope for the lover to display his courage in confrontations with footmen or in frantic races for the Border,' Alex said as they turned through the reservoir gate into Green Park. It sounded as though he was trying not to laugh. 'Tell me, would you care to take the reins once we are past the reservoir? The rides towards the Queen's House look quiet to me.'

'I would, thank you,' she said eagerly, watching as Alex eased the bays past the more crowded area around the long reservoir, always a favourite area for nursemaids to allow their small charges to scream with excitement as they chased the unfortunate ducks, or threw them crusts of bread. There were several ladies walking small dogs on leashes, most of which stopped to yap shrilly at the passing phaeton. The bays, well-schooled, loftily ignored them, although Jessica felt herself tense each time.

'There now, a nice quiet track ahead of us,' Alex said once they were well past the water. He handed her the reins and then the whip. 'The angle will seem strange at first, being higher and further forward than you are used to. Relax your wrist and hold them just here. That's right.'

The bays stood obediently while Jessica's heartbeat

speeded up strangely. Two pairs of gloved hands meeting, that was all it was, she told herself severely. And she should be concentrating on the instructions Alex was giving her, not on how close he was.

'I think I have got it,' she said, hoping the slight squeak in her voice could be mistaken for nerves over driving the swaying carriage.

'Then off we go,' Alex said sitting back.

Help, she thought, resisting the urge to thrust the reins back into his hands, then relaxed her grip, made an encouraging clicking sound to the pair and let out a breath as they walked placidly forward.

'It is easier than I had feared,' she confessed after a few minutes of sedate walking. 'But I do not think I want to trot yet.'

'Take your time,' Alex said comfortably. 'Neither the bays nor I are in any haste.'

'But surely you were going somewhere when we met?'

'I was on my way to visit the other party in last night's excitements,' he explained. 'But my mind is now at rest, although I suppose I had better call at some point today and offer my support for whatever scheme he has come up with. I will pass on your views on rope ladders and discourage him from any attempts at escape in the small hours.'

That made Jessica laugh and relax her hands and the bays broke into a trot. She resisted the urge to rein them in and let them continue, pretending she had intended the increase in speed all along.

Alex, who seemed as relaxed as his horses about her driving, glanced towards another grass ride converging with theirs. 'That's Percy Rowlands driving his curricle. I wonder who—can that be your friend Lady Anthea?'

Jessica risked a look. 'It is and without a book in her hands, which is a minor miracle. They seem to be deep in conversation. You don't think—surely not?'

'To be frank, my mind is having problems with the thought of the two of them driving together, let alone anything more…personal. Do you want to stop and talk when we reach them?'

'No, not really,' Jessica confessed, reining in the bays to a walk. 'They seem very engrossed in each other.' Besides, she did not welcome an intrusion into her companionable drive with Alex.

'Then let us stop here and take a stroll through that grove of trees. The ground looks dry enough.' He twisted around on his seat. 'Will, when we stop, take the reins and bring them around to meet us on the other side of that clump.'

'Yes, Your Grace.'

Jessica brought the bays to a halt and tried to feel confident when Alex jumped down leaving her alone in the vehicle. But it was only for a moment before the groom climbed up to take the reins from her and then Alex was reaching for her.

For a giddy moment she was in the air, his hands firm around her waist, and then she was on the ground. 'Thank you.'

Alex did not move, his hands still holding her lightly, and she found she did not want to stir either, because she was looking into his dark eyes and reading things there that made her catch her breath. Then the carriage moved slightly as the bays fidgeted and the moment, whatever it had been, had gone.

Imagination, Jessica told herself. Dark eyes like Alex's always seem soulful. But she could still feel the warmth of his fingers at her waist, the sensation of exhilaration as she was held in mid-air and the confidence that she was safe with this man holding her. All dangerous thoughts. She set off briskly towards the trees along a path trodden through the grass.

'We are very fortunate with the weather for the time of year,' she observed with the firm resolve of keeping the conversation strictly impersonal. It was bad enough to feel as she did about the man, without entertaining ideas about the way he looked at her. Or allowing him to see how he affected her.

'We are indeed.' Alex caught up with her. 'Would you like to discuss the King's health or the latest exhibition at the Society of Watercolourists? We could compare our thoughts on the latest novels, perhaps?'

That surprised an unladylike snort of laughter from her. 'I was attempting the conventional conversation expected of a young lady walking in the park with a gentleman.'

'But you are not conventional, Jessica,' he pointed out. 'So why should—? Oh, Lord. Now they've stopped. Quick, stand behind this tree.'

'Why?' Jessica demanded, flustered at being unceremoniously bundled into cover. 'And it isn't a tree, it's a prickly bush. A *very* prickly holly bush, in fact.' She glanced up from freeing her skirts from the spiky leaves. 'My goodness!'

Major Percy had brought his horse to a stop and, apparently feeling they were adequately screened by trees, had taken Lady Anthea firmly in his arms and was kissing her. And Anthea, far from boxing his ears as Jessica would have expected, was returning the embrace with considerable fervour.

'Whatever has come over them?' she whispered.

'I would have thought that was obvious and I do not know why you are whispering. I cannot imagine that they would hear us if we were accompanied by the band of the Household Cavalry,' Alex said, somewhat tartly.

'Don't you approve? Of them as a couple, I mean, not of them kissing in a public park.'

'I have no right to approve or disapprove, but Percy is an intelligent fellow. If he has decided to fall for a ferocious bluestocking, then I imagine he will somehow make it work. She is not likely to be trifling with his affections, is she?'

'I should not think that Anthea has ever trifled with anything in her life, let alone a man's affections,' Jessica said, making herself stare at the glossy green leaves of the holly bush and not at the couple in the curricle or the man next to her. What if he were infected by his friend's mood and wanted to kiss her? That would be…

'That is two of my acquaintance now,' Alex said, jolting her thoughts away from improper musings.

'What do you mean?'

'Falling in love at first sight—Locksley and Miss Beech share a couple of dances and two weeks later are contemplating elopement. Percy encounters Lady Anthea and, if he is not planning marriage now, then he is not the gentleman I always took him for. It seems that I am not the only man foolish enough to be a romantic.'

'You believe that is the only way to find true love—to be struck by the emotion on first acquaintance? You do not think it can develop more slowly as people get to know each other, discover each other's true character?'

'That is friendship,' Alex said. 'It could grow into love

of a sort, I suppose. But it is not as I imagine true, deep, romantic love to be. That is a case of finding one's soul-mate, not simply a congenial partner.' He half turned and looked down at her quizzically. 'Do you think that makes me unmanly, talking of romantic love, seeking for it?'

'Not at all. It makes you the kind of romantic hero that Sir Walter Scott writes about. You have high ideals and only the right lady will meet them.'

And that is not me, obviously.

'They have driven off now, thank goodness,' Alex said.

'Yes, that is a relief.' Jessica rather wished she had a fan to hand, she really was becoming rather heated despite the cool breeze. 'Shall we walk on?'

Chapter Twelve

Alex fell in beside her and they strolled together under the bare branches of the elms until they were clear of the copse. In the distance they could see William, the groom, driving the phaeton at walking pace away from them, which was a relief. There seemed to be too many thoughts jostling for attention in her head to be able to concentrate on driving a valuable pair.

Jane and Anthea, two of the Exotic Wallflowers, young ladies who had no expectation of making happy marriages, if of any marriage at all—and there they were, apparently head over heels in love with two perfectly eligible and pleasant gentlemen. Who might be next? Not her, of course. The only gentleman she felt the slightest inclination to marry was strolling next to her and showing no signs of regarding her as anything except a friend.

A congenial companion, she thought, wrinkling her nose.

Perhaps if she were to dress up in flowing robes and don a pointed headdress with veils it might arouse some knightly passion in his breast, but Jessica rather doubted it. Alex expected to walk into some crowded room, look across it and have his eyes alight upon a lady who would look back directly at him, alerted to his presence by some mysterious element in the air. Their gazes would interlock as they experienced a mutual jolt of powerful recognition as killing as a lightning strike. She sighed.

'What is wrong?'

'Sometimes I think that it is women who are the sensible sex, grounded in reality, and men are the fanciful ones, holding on to dreams and illusions.'

'And becoming romantics?' he said. 'You may well be right. Men are certainly the hypocritical ones. We pretend to believe that women are frail and simple and need protecting and sheltering, when all along that suits us very well. My mother was certainly the one in that marriage who ensured that we did not slip from being merely the Pinchpenny Dukes to becoming the penniless ones.'

'How long ago did you lose your parents?' she asked.

'Four years past. It was an epidemic of the influenza. The entire village seemed to be infected and we lost perhaps a dozen souls altogether. I had it, too, but not badly, which was a good thing—there was a great deal to be managed once I had recovered.'

'And you must have been young for such a huge responsibility,' Jessica said. No wonder Alex clung to his romantic dreams as some sort of relief from what must be, for a conscientious man, the enormous responsibility of estates and tenants. It would be a weight of obligation that would never leave him.

She did not make the mistake of thinking that his feelings made him any less strong and determined than men with a more cynical or ruthless temperament. Never once on that strange night-time walk had she felt anything but safe and protected. The only danger she had been in was from her own emotions.

'I was twenty-two,' he said. 'Old enough. It was hardly as though the state of the estates came as any surprise. My father had done his best, but he had become depressed and, I think, had somehow given up. I will not do that. The tenants deserve better, the land does, too.'

'And the family name, I suppose,' she said.

The family name?

Alex gave a short laugh. 'You would think that, for a self-confessed romantic, I might find something attractive about how we became dukes, but I have to say that the elevation of the family owes everything to the amatory skills of my ancestress and nothing to any merits of the Demerals. There are no acts of chivalry or valour, no gallant knights or battles fought in our history, despite what I dreamed of as a boy. The only consolation is that we never had wealth in the first place, so it has not been frittered away, or lost in gambling. All my predecessors appear to have done their best.'

They were so close as they walked along a narrow path cut through the grass that he felt Jessica's shrug beside him. 'There is no virtue in relying upon the deeds of one's ancestors,' she said. 'You have a good name, Alex, one you made for yourself. I have never heard anyone speak sneeringly of the Pinchpenny Duke, even if they might use the nickname.

'I have no patience with members of the *ton* who appear to think that their title is everything, that they have merit and entitlements above others simply by an accident of birth and they need do nothing to earn the respect of the world except simply exist.'

'And yet you proposed to a duke,' he said and this time

Jessica stiffened so that the sleeve that had brushed his was drawn away, leaving him oddly bereft of the slight contact.

'I proposed to a gentleman who appeared to have the makings of a tolerable husband, as I must have one, it seems,' she said. 'My father's dearest wish is for an aristocratic son-in-law. If he had desired that I marry a red-headed man with political ambitions, perhaps I would have sought out Mr Locksley and embarrassed *him* with my boldness.'

Damn.

'Now I have offended you. I had no intention of doing so and I apologise for my clumsiness. I spoke without thought.' He realised that he sounded as stiff as she. 'And you did not embarrass me.'

'Now that is an untruth,' Jessica said. 'You know perfectly well you were furious with yourself for not denying me in the first place.'

He did not contradict her. Refusing to admit Miss Danby would have been absolutely the correct thing to have done. 'I admit, I should have done just that. But I was half awake when Pitwick announced you. I was brooding on economies, if you must know.'

And what had Pitwick been about, even enquiring if he would receive an unaccompanied lady? Any other butler would have politely informed her that the Duke was not at home. Yet Pitwick was a very experienced upper servant…

'You know, that was strange,' he said, thinking aloud, 'Pitwick ought to have refused you and yet he did not. He looked at your card and… Confound it, the man knew who your father was! Now my servants are matchmaking for me. Presumably in the hope of an increase in wages,' he added bitterly.

'Oh, goodness. He must be furious that you acted in such an honest and gentlemanly fashion.' Jessica was laughing now, all the irritation of their tiff completely gone.

'Old family retainers are the worst,' she said confidingly. 'Our butler at home, Chesterfield, looks as though butter wouldn't melt in his mouth, he seems so chilly, but he is always nudging us in the direction he thinks we ought to go. *"Oh, Mr Danby, sir, I'll send that new coat back to the tailor's, shall I? I know you are too kind-hearted to let your valet know he advised you ill on that colour."* And, of course, he knows Papa chose it himself. Or, *"Miss Jessica, I wouldn't be attending the Wilkinsons' picnic, if I were you. I hear they obtain their lobsters from a very dubious source"*—said with the clear implication that the entire family is second-rate. In truth, Markham runs the household and our lives. I doubt we have a single secret from him.'

Alex opened his mouth to say that a trusted retainer in a family was different to a bachelor duke's butler and closed it again. He must pay more attention to Pitkin in future; the man was more devious than he had imagined and he did not appreciate being managed. But at least the *froideur* that had developed between Jessica and himself had thawed.

Jessica was still looking up at him, a little smile on her face as she watched him absorb her words.

'Be careful, the ground is rather rutted here.'

'Where?' She turned her head sharply, but too late. 'Oh!'

As Jessica tripped he reached out and caught her arm, spinning her around. She flailed for balance with her free arm, ending up flattened against his chest.And the breath left his lungs.

Jessica clung to his lapel with her free hand and Alex put his arm around her.

Just to steady her, he told himself.

But the tightness in his chest did not ease and he found himself staring down at the brim of her blue velvet hat with the intensity of a man seeing a great work of art for the very first time.

His breath came back with a gasp. What the devil had just happened? He realised that he was aroused and had the fleeting thought that it was fortunate he was wearing comfortable old breeches and not fashionably skin-tight inexpressibles. But physical desire was not all that was making his heart race and keeping Jessica's hand wrapped tight in his.

Then it dawned on him that she was making faint sounds of distress and released his hold as though her fingers were hot iron. 'I am sorry, I hurt you.'

'No, no, you didn't. You stopped me falling.' She reached for his arm and steadied herself, sending his pulse racing again. 'I turned my ankle in a rut. So foolish. I should have been looking where I was going.'

And so should I. I have just walked into something I do not understand.

But Jessica was hurt. This was no time to stand around grappling with his feelings. 'Do not put any weight on that foot. William has turned and is driving back towards us. I'll soon have you in the carriage.'

He took off his hat, waved it and saw the groom urge the pair into a brisk trot. 'We'll have you home in no time at all.'

'I am certain it is not a serious strain, please do not worry.' Jessica spoke as though she was trying to reassure him and Alex wondered if he was sounding strange to her ears. What the devil was wrong with him?

'Even so, you should have your doctor look at it for you. I will take a message once I have taken you to Adam Street.'

'I would rather see your friend Mrs Chandler. I am sure she will strap it up for me without any nonsense about bleeding me, or nasty-tasting doses of medicine.'

'Very well, but then I will take you straight home,' Alex said firmly as the groom drew the bays to a halt beside them. 'William, get down and hold them steady, Miss Danby has suffered a slight injury.' At least he had not mentioned anything as improper as a lady's ankle, he thought with a returning flicker of humour.

A high-perch phaeton was not the easiest vehicle to lift a lady into, but he took Jessica by the waist and lifted her until she could put her sound foot on to the step and then twist to lower herself to the seat. She did not appear to be in any great pain and managed it without a grimace, which was reassuring.

'Should I remove your half-boot, do you think?' he asked, sincerely hoping the answer would be, *No*. The thought of such a personal touch was unsettling. Lifting her had been bad enough. Jessica accepted him as a friend now; she would be appalled if he let her glimpse this new physical attraction he was feeling for her. That was all it was, surely?

'I do not think so. I cannot feel it swelling. In fact, I feel something of a fraud now. Perhaps I should simply go home and rest it for a while.'

'And then find it is worse than you thought? You have a busy social round, you cannot afford to be limping around the dance floor.'

She laughed a little at that, sending a strange tingle down his spine. 'I am certainly finding myself with more partners now. The effect of a dance with a duke on a wallflower's desirability is clear. I find myself actually enjoying balls now and I never thought I would say that of ones in London.'

It struck him that he knew nothing of Jessica's life before she had come to London. 'You enjoyed a varied social scene at home?' he asked as he took the reins and brought the pair up to the bit.

'There is no lack of society, even if it is not exactly Society with a capital S as the *ton* in London would recognise. Shrewsbury is our nearest large town, but Wolverhampton has more assembly rooms. Bridgnorth is also pleasant, if rather quieter.' After a pause she added, so softly he hardly heard her, 'I would have been quite content to remain there.'

'But your father has ambitions for you.'

'Yes,' she agreed, rather coolly, he thought. 'And also, it seemed a good idea to have Papa away from the business while my brothers found their feet running it. He truly wants them to succeed, but he finds it very hard to let go of the reins.'

'So did you reluctantly leave any beaux behind you in Shropshire?' Alex asked, with the sensation of prodding an injury to see if it was as bad as he thought—irresistible, even though he knew it would be painful.

'One or two.' Yes, Jessica was definitely cool now, although she answered him readily enough. 'But reluctantly? No. I think some distance is always wise. Familiarity can blind one to characteristics one would find…tiresome in marriage.'

Alex reminded himself that Jessica had been equally dispassionate in assessing his character before she proposed to him. She took the question of marriage very seriously, but she also seemed to regard it in the same way as her father might approach a business proposition. How very different from the other young ladies launched on to the marriage mart, schooled only to think of attracting the 'right' gentleman with their looks and their pretty manner and their complete lack of any characteristic that was unconventional or threatening to male sensibilities.

Jessica saw people very clearly, even those she loved, like her own father. It was an uncomfortable realisation for a man who did not want his own thoughts probed too deeply just now.

Chapter Thirteen

'And any proposals, if I might venture to ask?' Alex recognised that reckless need to probe again.

'Six,' Jessica said with composure. 'One ridiculous, one all too obviously mercenary and four that were—' She made a rocking gesture with one hand. 'Four that aroused no emotions in me whatsoever. Papa says I am now expending too much thought on the plans for May Day festivities and not enough on finding a husband.'

'And how are the plans for the Guild's procession progressing?'

'Surprisingly well. Having established that the world will not end if the milkmaids are not the genuine article, I find that many friends have young female servants who would love to dress up and take part. Our coachman is finding float-makers and hirers of dray horses so we can have them committed early, even though the Guild members are dithering about what exactly they want depicted on the floats.'

'So what else is needed?'

'Flower garlands, musicians and whatever the themes of the floats require, but I am feeling much more optimistic about it all now.' She sounded warm and relaxed and Alex felt himself relax, too, now the coolness had gone from her voice. He should take care not to probe into her personal affairs again. They were, after all, none of his concern, unless someone upset her when, as a friend, he would deal with them. As a friend.

He realised that they were at the Chandlers' front door and he must have driven there without any recollection of the journey. William jumped down to knock.

'Your friends are going to think me ridiculously accident-prone,' Jessica said as the groom returned to hold the horses and Alex could climb down to help her descend.

'You are somewhat prone to accidents,' Anna Chandler said as soon as they were alone.

'I was just thinking you would conclude that I am very clumsy,' Jessica confessed. 'And I am feeling something of a fraud now. My ankle gave me a very painful twinge when I turned it, but now it barely aches. Demeral would not hear of taking me directly home without it being examined, however.'

'A stubborn man, especially when he is looking after someone,' Anna said. 'Can you remove your half-boot yourself or shall I help you?'

'No, I can manage, thank you.' She eased off the shoe, relieved to see no swelling. 'Demeral has a strong protective instinct, I think.'

'Certainly, with anyone or anything he feels responsible for,' Anna agreed. 'Now, just put your foot on the stool. I do not think we need to have your stocking off.' She bent over Jessica's foot, peering closely, then took hold of it and began to move it gently back and forth. 'Say if it hurts.'

'That is fine. Ow, just there.'

'Wriggle your toes, please. Many landowners who are short of money would raise their tenants' rents, but not

Alex. Instead he tries to improve their living conditions, which is admirable, but means his are not much better, for all that he lives in a castle.'

'Is it a real castle?' That would be enough to give any impressionable boy romantic daydreams.

'Yes, a real medieval one, not a sham built in the last century. It is quite small and in very poor repair, but it has all the right features—battlements and turrets, arrow slits and a drawbridge, plus a rather green and smelly moat, I'm afraid.'

Anna settled back on her heels. 'I do not think you have done more than give it a slight twist. I will strap it up just to support it, but you can take the bandage off tomorrow. Try to use that foot as normal.'

'Thank you. And this time I really do insist on you charging me for my treatment.' She took a card from her reticule. 'Please send the accounting to this address. I will tell my father that Dr Chandler was recommended to me by a friend and I will confess to turning my ankle. Then, in future, if I do need a doctor, Papa will not think it strange if I consult you—in the guise of your husband, of course.'

'Very well.' Anna stood up and took the card. 'Perhaps it would be best if we send you home in our carriage.' She hesitated, half turned to the door. 'Do be careful of Alex, won't you?'

'But I feel perfectly safe with him,' Jessica protested.

'It was not your safety I was concerned for,' Anna said wryly and opened the door. 'Ah, Alex. I am sending Miss Danby home in our carriage. Morris, tell John Coachman we need it at once.'

Jessica walked in to the drawing room and found to her relief that her strained ankle hardly ached at all. Perhaps it was Anna Chandler's skill, or perhaps it had not been such a wrench after all. Perhaps, she thought uncomfortably, she had made a fuss about it to distract both her and Alex from the surprise of finding themselves in each other's arms again.

It had made her feel positively shivery at the time and still did in recollection. And Alex had seemed somehow arrested as he held her, as though his attention had been caught. Probably by a smudge on her nose, or him wondering why she was so very clumsy, Jessica thought gloomily.

'Ah, there you are, my dear.' Her father lowered his newspaper and looked up from the depths of his armchair. It made her jump, she had been so absorbed in her thoughts.

'Papa.' She stooped to kiss the top of his balding head. 'I went to visit a friend and then walked in the park. And then I turned my ankle. Fortunately I remembered a recommendation from a friend for their doctor, Dr Chandler, so I went there. His wife looked after me admirably and I am told it is just a slight strain and will be well tomorrow.'

He nodded, clearly with something else on his mind, which surprised her. Usually he was inclined to fuss if she was unwell. 'I am glad to hear it is not serious, my dear, and that you have had a recommendation that proved so useful. I have had a very interesting visit while you were out, Jessica.'

'That's nice,' she said vaguely, dropping bonnet and reticule on to a side table and beginning to draw off her gloves.

'From the Earl of Branscombe, no less.'

'Who? Oh, yes, I recall him now. I danced with him a night or so ago, I think. Just the one dance.' Tall, dark and handsome. Very pleasant, not overly talkative. Quite restful, in fact. Jessica unbuttoned her pelisse and wriggled out of its tight sleeves.

'He came to ask my permission to pay court to you.' Her father was beaming now. 'Of course, he is not a duke or a marquis, but an earl's not to be sneezed at, now, is he?'

'No, absolutely not,' Jessica agreed. She had dropped her coat and knew now that she was making too much of a business of picking it up, folding it and laying it neatly over a chair back. 'Did he say why?'

Other than a desire for my dowry, of course.

'He said he greatly admired your charming character, your poise and your amiable nature. Apparently you befriended a young relative of his who was feeling very shy at Lady Ambleside's musicale the other evening and he was much struck by that. He observed how much kindness is to be valued in the wife of a nobleman who has to consider not only the welfare of his tenants and dependents, but also the upbringing of his children.'

Well, she must award Branscombe points for coming up with some personalised compliments and managing not to mention her dowry while he was about it. The thought of him did not set her heart aflutter, however.

Jessica sat down, assumed her best dutiful daughter expression and enquired, 'And what did you say to Lord Branscombe, Papa?'

'That I had no objection—mind you, I will have him investigated, never you fear—but that it is entirely up to you who you accept, my dear.'

'Thank you, Papa.' Jessica regarded the toes of her slightly grass-stained half-boots and tried to work out just how she felt.

It was a proposal from a nobleman likely to meet Papa's

stiff criteria for lineage and character, a handsome man who seemed intelligent and pleasant, even if he was a trifle stiff and reticent. A man showing a degree of thoughtfulness in presenting himself to her father and, she suspected, a rather conventional man as well.

Did that add up to the makings of a good husband? Probably. But did it make him the right husband for her?

He is not Alex Demeral.

But what if she had never met the Duke? Then Lord Branscombe would have seemed a very suitable match and she would have been interested in knowing him better, discovering if he would make the kind of husband she had decided was for her. Intelligent, considerate, a man with depth of character.

But now she had met Alex and every gentleman she encountered from now on was going to be measured against him, she admitted to herself. And that was setting the bar high.

'I would like to become better acquainted with the Earl,' she said firmly, as much to herself as to her father. After all, she had no desire to end her days a spinster. Papa would become anxious if she did not show signs of being serious about matrimony very soon and that was bad for his health. Daydreaming about a pair of fathomless dark eyes and a pair of broad shoulders was not going to get her anything but heartache.

'Excellent. He mentioned that he would be at Lady Outram's ball next week and I believe you are attending that. There is no need to mention that you know of his call on me, of course. Meanwhile I will have the usual checks made. I want to make certain there are no skeletons in his cupboards.'

By the time Papa's London lawyers and his men of business had finished there would be little they did not know about the Earl of Branscombe, from his debts to his choice of tea and probably the name of his first pony and his first mistress. Certainly any skeletons would be taken out, dusted down and thoroughly inspected. Not that any of that would be for her eyes, of course. Either Papa would approve or he would not. But she knew where he kept the keys to his desk and she would read the report, too: after all, she would be the one who had to live with the man.

It ought to be exciting, the prospect of a personable new suitor. Jessica fixed a smile on her lips and stood up. 'I shall take special care in choosing my gown for the ball, Papa.'

His look of pleasure went some way to lightening her mood. Bless him, he wanted only the best for her.

Over the next week the society columns in the news sheets heralded the arrival in town of several families joining the Season. They were the ones whose country seats were furthest from London, even some from Scotland, and they had wisely avoided an early journey, fraught with the increased risk of snow and heavy rain.

Alex scanned the columns before he looked at the post that had arrived after luncheon. Perhaps there was a young lady newly arrived from the West Country or the Borders who would be the one for him. For some reason the thought did not lighten his spirits as it usually did. He must be getting jaded with London life. He certainly missed Longstone where Demeral Castle sat in a wide bend in the river, brooding over the surrounding lands as it had done for centuries.

But if it were to brood for another few hundred years

he needed to return to it with money. He tossed the papers aside and went to shuffle through the pile of invitations on his desk. The Outrams' ball that evening would be one of the biggest squeezes of the Season and he should not miss that.

Would Jessica be there? He had restrained himself from calling to ask about her foot, knowing it would only excite her father unfairly. Perhaps she would not be dancing if the sprain was still painful, but even if she was there only to sit out, he would enjoy the pleasure of relaxed conversation with someone who seemed to find the same things interesting or amusing.

Yes, he would attend the Outram ball and perhaps a miracle would occur and he would find the One. And if it did not, then perhaps he and Jessica would have the interest of watching their friends' romances flourish.

Lady Outram had the reputation of one of the best hostesses in town and the house just off Grosvenor Square was ablaze with light, inside and out, when Alex arrived at eleven.

Crowds lined the pavements to stare at the stream of fashionables making their way along the red carpet that had been run from the front door, down the steps and across the pavement. Burly footmen in livery kept the onlookers back and supervised the flow of carriages which crawled along at a snail's pace before they reached the carpet.

It would never do to be seen actually *walking*, even if one lived two houses down, Alex though with a grin as he jumped down from his humble hackney carriage well back in the queue and made his way past to fall in behind the Dowager Marchioness of Witherby as she shepherd her three granddaughters ahead of her to the steps.

She had the reputation for being insufferably stiff-rumped but she condescended to talk to him as they ascended the stairs to the receiving line. He was, after all, a duke.

One step, pause, wait with one's nose a few inches from the spine of the person in front. Another step…

Alex looked around while maintaining his end of the dialogue, nodding to acquaintances, bowing to ladies. No sign of Jessica, but there was Lady Anthea and Lady Lucinda with Percy Rowlands between them as escort.

'Indeed,' he agreed, listening to Lady Witherby with half an ear. 'We have been fortunate with the weather so far this month.'

'Girls, do not fidget,' she admonished her charges, releasing him again to scan the guests.

Then he saw Jessica just a few steps ahead and to the right. She, too, was looking around her and, after a moment, saw him.

She inclined her head formally, making the small ostrich feathers set in her hair bob and flutter, but the smile she sent him made his heart give that strange little kick again.

Alex was still puzzling over it when he reached the landing and began to move along the receiving line, shaking hands, greeting his host and hostess before he could escape into the ballroom and look for Jessica again. She would be sitting down, surely?

He had arrived as partners were walking on to the dance floor for the new set and there was Jessica, saucy plumes nodding over her smooth coiffure, her hand in that of the Earl of Branscombe as he led her out and not a hint of hesitation in her walk.

Chapter Fourteen

It was foolish of Jessica to be exerting herself, Alex thought. He must keep an eye on her and insist she sit out for several sets to rest. He was certain Anna had not expected her to go throwing herself into vigorous country dances after only a few days' rest. Even as he thought it he recognised that as merely a distraction for a flash of jealousy.

It was too late to find a partner for this set, so he strolled around the room, chatting to acquaintances until he found Lady Lucinda in conversation with a rather earnest young woman wearing pince-nez on the end of her nose.

'Lady Lucinda, ma'am.' He bowed; they curtsied.

'Your Grace, allow me to name Miss Worthing. Miss Worthing, the Duke of Malvern. Miss Worthing is a keen student of the Italian Masters and we were just discussing the exhibition at Somerset House. Are you interested in art, Your Grace?'

'Appreciative, but woefully ignorant, I fear. Might I solicit a dance, ladies?'

Miss Worthing, it seemed, did not dance. 'I came this evening in the hope of viewing the Outrams' gallery,' she confessed.

Lady Lucinda granted him the next set and he moved on, his gaze roaming over the dancers. There was Lady

Anthea, talking earnestly to Percy as they processed down the line of dancers. And just behind them, Jessica, laughing at something Branscombe had said to her.

She did not seem to be in any discomfort, which was good. And she appeared to be enjoying herself which was, of course, excellent. There were new faces among the guests, many of them families he was acquainted with, but who must have recently arrived in London to launch their daughters into society.

Alex stopped to exchange greetings with several, asked for dances and was met with smiles and blushes and acceptances. All very pleasant young ladies, he was sure, but there was no spark. He found himself curiously distanced from what was going on around him.

Should I give this up, go back home and sell some land? he found himself thinking.

Then he realised the last dance of the set had come to an end and went in search of Lady Lucinda.

Four sets later as he was talking to an acquaintance about selling his phaeton and pair, he noticed that Branscombe was leading Jessica out again. Two sets, when there were so many partners to choose from this evening? It was not outside the bounds of convention, of course, but it made him wonder. Branscombe was a decent fellow. Rather a cold fish, Alex had always thought, but there was no reason to be concerned if he was paying his attentions to Jessica. None in the world.

Lord Branscombe was a very pleasant partner, Jessica decided. He danced well and maintained a flow of intelligent conversation.

His manner was somewhat formal and she had to suppress a smile when he said that he felt it would draw untoward attention if he asked her to dance a third time, but would she allow him to escort her in to supper?

Yes, she agreed, that would be very agreeable. It meant, of course, that she would have to make her excuses if anyone asked her for the supper dance, but as her ankle was beginning to ache a little that could be done with a truthful explanation.

She mentioned the sprain to Lady Cassington, who tutted, but suggested that she sat out all three sets before supper in order to rest it.

Jessica agreed and made her way to some vacant seats beside an array of potted palms where her chaperon could join her when she had finished talking to the Dowager Lady Troughton who was in full flow about her rheumatics, her unsatisfactory nephew and the horrors of finding a decent cook. Jessica felt there was little of value she could contribute.

She took her seat, turned down two offers to dance immediately, but sent the gentlemen away happy with the promise of resuming the floor after supper.

Alex was present; she had seen him several times, on and off the floor, but he had not approached her for a dance. She wondered why. Had he heard of Lord Branscombe's interest or was he assuming she would not want to dance with her sore ankle?

There he was, dancing rather slowly with a very young lady Jessica had not seen before and who was clearly concentrating fiercely on her steps. Alex caught her eye and they exchanged smiles, amused on hers, somewhat rueful on his.

They passed on and Jessica shifted on her seat, conscious of a draught behind her. The great room was becoming hot, but not yet so warm that it was pleasant to have cooler air stirring the hair on the back of her neck. She turned and saw it was coming from a jib door, almost concealed in the panelling, that was just ajar.

There were no footmen nearby so Jessica got up and went to push it closed.

'Let me go now, please,' someone said from the room beyond. It was a woman and she sounded young and uneasy. 'I want to go back.'

A male voice answered, the tone low and with an edge to it that Jessica did not like. She hesitated, her fingers resting on the door handle. She had no wish to walk in on a tryst, but on the other hand, if an inexperienced debutante was in an uncomfortable situation, then she could not simply ignore it.

She pushed the door half open and stepped inside. 'Oh, do forgive me, I did not realise this room was occupied.' Yes, something was very wrong here.

A girl she did not recognise—very young, very pretty—was pulling away from a man who had hold of her wrist. She was in tears.

He turned, an unpleasant look on his face. 'Well, it *is* occupied, so you can take yourself off, Miss Iron Smelter.'

She might not know the girl, but she knew who this was. Sir Matthew Hobson had an unpleasant reputation with women and she been forced to dodge when he had tried to push her into a corner in a deserted corridor at the theatre several weeks previously. The memory of the brush of his groping hands still made her shudder.

'I do not think so, not without this lady. Do you wish to leave, my dear?'

'Oh, yes, please.' The girl tugged against his hold.

'Then let her go this instant or I shall fetch some footmen and have you removed.'

'I do not think so.' He mimicked her voice unpleasantly. 'Miss Fawcett is my fiancée, or she will be before this night is out. Think of the scandal if she is discovered here alone with me.'

'But she is not alone with you, is she? I am here. You do not wish to marry this person, do you, Miss Fawcett?'

'No, of course not. I was hot and I wanted to sit down after we had danced and he said it would be cool in here and then… Then he…' Miss Fawcett burst into loud sobs.

Jessica took the two steps to bring her to them. 'Let her go.'

Sir Matthew pushed her away, his hand landing on her breast. It was not by accident, she was sure.

Jessica slapped him, hard. It stung, but it felt good. The girl screamed and began to struggle wildly. A chair fell over against an ornamental plant stand which fell with a crash. Jessica stabbed at his hand with her folded fan and then suddenly there was someone beside her.

She was aware of movement, decisive and powerful, and Sir Matthew reeled backwards to land sprawled over the plant stand. Jessica dodged aside and caught hold of Miss Fawcett, turning her away into the shelter of her arms. Over her shoulder she saw Alex rubbing his knuckles and looming over the fallen man.

Alex. Thank goodness.

The door opened again and there was Lord Branscombe.

'Miss Danby? Are you all right? I was coming over to speak to you and I heard a scream.'

'Let me past, sir! Jessica? What is going on?' Lady Cassington swept past the Earl and closed the door behind her. 'Keep your voices down, all of you. Do you want a scandal?'

The room was now decidedly overcrowded with Sir Matthew still on the floor, two large, angry men looming over him, a sobbing debutante, Jessica and now an indignant chaperon.

'Everything is under control,' Alex said without looking around.

Lord Branscombe stepped over the man on the floor and, for a moment, Jessica thought he was reaching for her. Then he said, 'Miss Fawcett! I had not realised your family had arrived in London. Good friends and neighbours of mine, you know,' he added to Jessica as Miss Fawcett threw herself on his chest.

'Oh, George, thank heavens. That horrible man—and then this lady tried to help and he pushed her and then this gentleman came in and hit him. Take me to Mama, please, George.'

'Here, wipe your eyes and blow your nose before you go out.' Jessica handed her a handkerchief, then pushed them both towards the door. 'By the sound of it people are going through to supper, you should be able to find Mrs Fawcett without attracting too much attention.'

They went out, both thanking her distractedly. Jessica shut the door after them and leaned against it. 'What are we going to do with him?'

'We must leave immediately,' Lady Cassington declared, loftily ignoring both her question and Sir Matthew who was trying to disentangle himself from the plant stand. 'I can only hope nobody saw you slip in here in that furtive way as I did, Miss Danby.'

'I was not being furtive,' she said indignantly. 'I was closing the door because of a draught and then I heard Miss Fawcett. She was clearly in distress. I could hardly walk away, now could I?'

She turned to Alex. 'What shall we do with him?'

'I am waiting until he stands up so I can hit him again,' Alex said. 'Did he touch you?'

She could almost feel the impression of one large hand on her left breast, but Jessica had no desire to provoke Alex into killing the man, which, from the look on his face, he very much wanted to.

'He pushed me. He was holding Miss Fawcett, poor girl. I slapped him.'

'Good.'

Hobson made no move to get up, so Alex leant down and hauled him to his feet, holding him upright with one hand clenched in his shirtfront.

'If I ever find you within half a mile of this lady, or of the one you have just so grievously insulted, I will take a horsewhip to you. I would call a gentleman out, but you clearly have no claim to the rank.'

Sir Matthew made vague gobbling noises.

'He is turning very red,' Lady Cassington said. She was quivering with indignation, the bugle beads embroidered around the hem and bodice of her gown shimmering in response. 'I suggest we leave him to make his way out, Your Grace. Your warning, in addition to the fact that I shall inform every chaperon and the Patronesses of his behaviour, will ensure he has little opportunity for this kind of outrage again.'

Jessica saw a door in the far wall and went to investigate. It opened on to some kind of service corridor. Alex let go of Hobson and pushed him that direction. 'Out.'

As the door closed behind him Lady Cassington sank down on the sofa. 'Well! It appears we have much to thank you for, Your Grace.'

'How did you realise what was happening?' Jessica asked, finding that she, too, needed to sit down.

'I happened to notice where you were sitting and then I saw you go to that door, which seemed strange. When you did not come out again I was concerned.' Alex appeared more focused on his bloodied knuckles which he dabbed with a handkerchief. He put it back in his pocket and looked across at Jessica and she realised that he was very aware of her indeed. 'I heard a scream as I got near. I thought it was you.'

'And as I was leaving the Dowager to join you I encountered Lord Branscombe who was seeking you to take you in to supper,' Lady Cassington explained. 'We heard sounds from this room and the rest you know.'

'Well,' Jessica said, striving for a lighter note, 'I appear to have lost my supper partner. I rather think that the Earl has realised that he had feelings for his neighbour Miss Fawcett that he had not been aware of. They appear to be reciprocated.'

'He was certainly struck, was he not?' Lady Cassington said. 'I have seen it before. A man grows up with a neighbour and never notices her, never sees she is now a young woman. Then she comes out, all grown up, and he has a revelation.'

Alex muttered something that sounded like, 'Not just neighbours.' He tugged his cuffs into order. 'I will leave you, unless there is anything else I can do, ladies? It might be more discreet if you wait a few moments.' With an abrupt bow he was gone.

'I do think he might have taken us in for super,' Lady Cassington said. 'Men can be so thoughtless. No doubt he does not wish to appear with broken knuckles. You appear to have lost your suitor, my dear.'

'Papa has told you about Lord Branscombe?'

'He has.' Her chaperon sighed. 'I did have hopes of Malvern as well but, for all his gallantry just now, he could not remove himself fast enough, could he?'

'He has never spoken to Papa about me,' Jessica said carefully. She was still feeling somewhat breathless, not so much from the encounter with the odious Sir Matthew, she suspected, more from witnessing the ruthlessly effective manner Alex had dealt with the man.

My hero. Oh, dear, this is not going to help me put him out of my mind.

'Let us take ourselves in to supper, Lady Cassington. I have to admit that I will feel very much better after a glass of champagne.'

Chapter Fifteen

Alex stood to one side of the dance floor watching the room. Branscombe was deep in conversation with Miss Fawcett and a lady he imagined must be her mother. By the look of it the young lady was rapidly recovering herself after her ordeal, helped, he had no doubt, by Branscombe's reassuring presence.

The man had been knocked into as much of a heap as Hobson, at least mentally, Alex thought with a wry smile. There would be a marriage agreed before very much longer.

As for himself, his hand throbbed and the anger he had felt flood through him when he had seen Hobson with Jessica was still churning unpleasantly, but the real facer was the revelation that scene had brought.

The possessiveness had hit him like an opponent's fist. *Mine,* he had thought through the red anger when he saw Jessica struggling with the man. Mine.

When had that happened? How had it happened? He had gone from regarding her as a friend, as an unconventional, intelligent companion, to wanting her as his. It was not physical allure, he thought, trying to get his feelings into some kind of order. Yes, he found her attractive and arousing, but not to the point where he thought her perfection, or could not sleep for thinking erotic thoughts of her.

He hadn't fallen in love. Again, he felt quite rational about this, not ecstatic, not dizzy with romance. This was not at all what he had expected and yet… Was this the revelation he had been waiting for and he had now found the bride he had told himself it was his duty to marry?

He liked Jessica a great deal. He admired her, thought her intelligent, honest, attractive and courageous. He had just discovered that he felt protective towards her. She was someone he could rely upon to work with him to make a marriage a success, raise children, care for the estate and its people.

Marriage. It was time to accept that he had a chance of real happiness and could rescue his estates, if he could only grasp it. The sense of relief was almost tangible, as though he had laid down a heavy burden he had been carrying for years.

Tomorrow he was going to call on the house in Adam Street and ask the iron founder for his daughter's hand in marriage.

But would Jessica accept him after all the things he had said to her when they had first met? She would think him a hypocrite and somehow he must overcome that.

Alex pushed away from the wall against which he had been leaning and made for the double doors. Miss Fawcett was in good hands, Jessica and Lady Cassington had passed him by on their way to the supper room without seeing him and Sir Matthew showed no sign of returning. He could safely go home and find the right words.

He would not need them for Danby, he was sure, but what was he going to say to Jessica to convince her of his sincerity?

* * *

'The Duke of Malvern!' Trotter, all pretence of being the superior lady's maid abandoned, rushed into Jessica's little sitting room.

Jessica dropped her pen, splattering a list of *Things To Be Done For May Day* with black ink. 'What? Where? Trotter, please calm down.'

'He called just now, Miss Jessica. Handed his card to Alfred and asked for Mr Danby, cool as you like.'

'He asked for Papa?' Surely he had not come to… No. Impossible.

Her father was in no very good mood, having received over breakfast a very formal note from Lord Branscombe withdrawing his request to pay his attentions to Miss Danby on the grounds that he did not feel it fair to her, given that he had realised his affections were engaged elsewhere.

Jessica had received a rather less stilted note, warm in its thanks for her help the previous evening, expressing the hope that she had not been too distressed by the incident and admitting very openly that he had realised that his heart was with Miss Fawcett. He apologised, with more humour than she had previously detected in him, for being so blind to his own emotions.

'He's fortunate not to receive a suit for breach of promise,' her father had huffed angrily over his sirloin steak.

'He made no promises, no proposals, Papa,' Jessica said soothingly. 'He was quite open about wishing to explore whether we were mutually compatible. I thought that very sensible—it would have been quite dreadful if he had proposed and then discovered that his heart was engaged elsewhere.'

Her father growled something about modern manners and nonsense about love. 'All this foolishness about romanticism and sensibility. Grown men not embarrassed to be moved to tears over some sunset or picturesque ruin. The awful majesty of the ocean and mountains, for goodness sake! Stuff and nonsense, I call it.'

'Papa, you know perfectly well that you and Mama made a love match,' Jessica had said with a smile and he had stopped grumbling and smiled sheepishly.

She told him what had occurred at the ball, judging it was better that he heard it from her rather than perhaps pick up some gossip if someone had seen something amiss.

'Good for you, my girl,' he'd said. She was not surprised: he had always been very frank about the dangers that some men posed and the actions a woman could take to defend herself. A pity the daughters of the *haut ton* were not so frankly advised.

'Swine like that should never be allowed near respectable ladies. I am glad the Duke came to your rescue.' He had looked at her hopefully and she had smiled.

'He happened to be passing and heard Miss Fawcett cry out,' she had explained, disappointing him again.

Now what could Alex be doing calling at two in the afternoon? Perhaps, she thought, blotting her ruined page, he had come to set Papa's mind at rest over the scene last night.

She should wait up here, of course, and Papa would tell her about it in due course. Or she could go downstairs into the breakfast room which adjoined Papa's study and apply her ear to the panelling. She knew it was thin, because her father had complained about the staff clattering dishes when clearing after the morning meal. 'Slipshod work,' he had said, rapping the wall with his knuckles. 'Simply battens with panelling nailed over.'

'Thank you, Trotter,' she said now calmly. 'Perhaps he has come to ask me to drive out. Please go and make sure a suitable walking dress is ready.'

She counted to ten when the maid had gone, then slipped out and ran, silent in her light shoes, down the stairs. She tiptoed past the study with its murmur of deep male voices muffled by the heavy door and gained the empty breakfast room.

The voices were much more audible now and, when she pressed her ear against the wall, they were startlingly clear.

'...think any more trouble from Hobson,' Alex said. 'I am glad to hear Miss Danby has recovered from the unpleasant experience. She showed great spirit.'

'She's no shrinking violet, my girl. I taught her how to deal with menaces of that kind. But I must thank you,' Papa said.

Alex replied with something inaudible, then said clearly, 'I have come to request your permission to ask Miss Danby for her hand in marriage, sir.'

Jessica sat down abruptly on the chair next to her.

He is proposing? After what he had said about falling in love? He has said nothing to me.

Jessica leaned close to the wall again.

'...have to say I am delighted to agree.'

That was Papa.

Of *course* he was. A duke was the summit of his ambition for her. She was suddenly very angry.

Both men got to their feet when she swept in to the study after a perfunctory tap on the door. 'Papa— Oh, forgive me, I did not realise you had company,' she said, hardly troubling to make that sound credible.

Her father would probably not notice at that moment if she had appeared with a peacock on her head, let alone sense her mood. Alex, however, raised one dark brow, looking more than ever like his cynical royal ancestor.

'Perhaps you could take the Duke through to the drawing room,' her father said, beaming. 'I believe you have much to talk about.'

'Yes, Papa, if you say so. Please come this way, Your Grace.'

'You were eavesdropping,' Alex said the moment the door was closed behind them.

'Yes, I was.' Jessica took several agitated paces down the length of the Chinese carpet. 'And I am now wondering just what has changed in the last month. You are not going to tell me that you looked at me last night, the scales fell from your eyes and you recognised your one true love, are you? Because I can tell you now, I will not believe a word of it.'

'No,' Alex said bluntly. 'I am not going to tell you that.'

'I see.' That took the wind out of her sails a little, but she rallied. 'So you have now had the opportunity to meet all the available young ladies, found none of them was the one and decided that my dowry made up for the lack of romance after all?'

'No,' he said, equally flatly. 'Not that either.'

His firmness took some of the heat from her anger and she stared at him, confused and strangely hurt.

'Please sit down, Jessica. Let me explain.' Alex did not sound as though he was going to move even if she started throwing the ornaments at his head, so she sat, hands folded in her lap, in a semblance of ladylike calm.

She thought he would pace up and down as Papa or her brothers did when they wishing to make a point, but instead Alex dragged a stool away from the wall, put it in front of her and sat down facing her, eye to eye.

'I know what I said and I believed it. I still do believe that there is such a thing as an instant attraction, a meeting of souls. But I have come to think there are other ways in which a happy marriage can be founded. There is friendship, mutual respect and liking. An attraction.' He must have seen her blush. 'We share those things, I believe. Am I wrong about that?'

'No,' Jessica admitted. 'I agree we have all those feelings. But you will always be wondering where your soulmate is, looking at every woman you meet. *Is it you? Or you?* And what if you meet her?'

'It is a risk that every marriage faces, surely?' he asked. 'That is where honour and loyalty come in. And trust.'

'Trust is important to me,' she confessed. 'Perhaps it is because I come from a background of commerce where so much relies upon accepting the word of the person you are dealing with. Where a handshake and a promise are as good as a legal contract.'

Alex sat back a little. 'That was how you saw this from the beginning, was it not? A business transaction, a merger of two firms? Your dowry for my title. You trusted me when you came to my house with your proposal.'

'I did not know then that I was dealing with a romantic,' she said. 'I thought I was proposing an exchange of assets between people who would deal fairly with each other.'

I did not know then how much I would come to yearn for

you. I did not know how much it would hurt if you looked elsewhere for something you needed in a marriage.

'Are you now saying that your feelings for me make the question of my dowry irrelevant?' she asked, steadying her voice with an effort. That was the crucial question: a great deal depended on how Alex answered it.

'No. No, I cannot in all honesty say so, because I cannot afford to make a marriage without that,' he admitted.

Thank goodness, he had not lied, not prevaricated. He was being honest with her.

'So, why have you changed your mind now?'

'Because now I know you. Now you have come to mean something to me. When I saw Hobson manhandling you I experienced more than the anger I would feel at seeing a man assault any woman. I felt that it was an attack on someone personal, someone who mattered to me. I knew then that I had to ask you to marry me.'

Her pulse thudded and she felt a little dizzy. Jessica wanted to say *yes*, to snatch at this offer. 'You have made this more difficult,' she confessed. 'Before, it was clearcut and straightforward. You say I matter to you. And I feel the same way. You are more than my friend, you matter to me, too. It may not be love, but now there are feelings involved this becomes a greater risk, for both of us.'

Alex reached out and took her hands in his. Now she did not know whose pulse it was that beat so strongly. His dark eyes were full of understanding. 'I know. Trust me.'

There was something else that she thought she knew the answer to, but could not be certain. 'Marriage is more than an exchange of vows. There's—' She broke off, blushing.

'I think I understand. May I kiss you?' Alex said. He held out his hands to her.

There were no words she could find, her tongue seemed incapable of moving. Jessica fell into his embrace, felt his arms around her. Safe. Then his lips found hers and all thoughts of safety vanished. This was not safe. This was dangerous, wild, a joining with another being that felt earthy and elemental. This was not something for two well-dressed people in an elegant drawing room with satin-covered sofas and Wedgwood vases. This was something that belonged under the open sky with bare skin against bare skin.

There was heat and moisture and the taste of a man and her tongue that had refused to speak was twining with his in a way that felt quite wonderfully wicked.

Then the heat and the touch of him left her and Jessica blinked up from the depths of the sofa cushions to find Alex kneeling beside her.

'I think, after that, we need have no concerns about any lack of mutual desire,' he said, his voice hoarse.

'Yes,' Jessica agreed, amazed to discover that she could speak. She sat up, tugged her gown into some kind of order and pushed back a lock of hair that had fallen into her eyes.

Alex. She reached out and clung to his hands as though she stood on the edge of a chasm and he would help her across. She closed her eyes for a second, then opened them and leapt. 'Yes. Yes, I do. I will marry you.'

'I swear you will not regret this, Jessica.'

'I think we should go and tell your father—'

'The devil!' The roar of fury from outside the door silenced Alex and brought Jessica to her feet.

'Papa?' She scrambled from the sofa, flung open the door and found her parent, red in the face, standing in the hallway and brandishing a letter in one hand. Both footmen came running and skidded to a halt at the sight of them.

Chapter Sixteen

'The stupid idiot!' her father spluttered. 'The fool. He'll be the ruin of me.'

'Come and sit down, Papa. You will make yourself ill.' Jessica tried to steer him into the drawing room, certain he was about to have a seizure at any moment. 'Alfred, fetch water. Henry, go to Dr Chandler at once. His Grace will give you the direction.'

Behind her she heard Alex say, 'Take my carriage, the driver knows the address. Tell the doctor that I think it urgent.'

Between them they managed to get her furious father seated. Jessica loosened his neckcloth and unbuttoned his waistcoat. 'Sit back, Papa. Put your feet up.' She added some brandy to the glass of water Alfred brought. 'Sip this slowly.'

When he finally did as she said she took the letter from his hand and read it.

'It's from my elder brother Ethan. He is writing to inform Papa that he is on the point of concluding an agreement with Bracegirdle and Sons—they are iron founders, too—to jointly buy the Fosdyke Works. And to seal the deal he is intending to marry Jane Bracegirdle.'

Her father sat up and slammed the glass down on a side

table, sending brandy and water sloshing over the finely polished surface. 'The Fosdyke Works are no use to us, but they will give Bracegirdle access to that watercourse he wants to divert to his foundry. And Jane Bracegirdle hasn't the brains of a peahen. She's not the wife a man of business needs. Bracegirdle must be beside himself, thinking he's got behind my back on this.'

'If your son has already offered for Miss Bracegirdle, it could be a problem,' Alex said.

'No,' Jessica said. 'At least he hasn't done that. He is writing to obtain Papa's blessing first. I can only hope he hasn't led her to believe a proposal is inevitable. But if he has entered into an agreement over the works...'

'He cannot. I did not give him control over enough funds.' Her father was slightly less puce in the face now and, to her relief his breathing seemed easier. 'He wants me to direct Earnshaw's Bank to release the money. The young fool seems to think he has managed a coup.'

'What does Joshua say?' Jessica scanned to the end of the letter. 'Oh, he opposes it, which Ethan says shows his lack of vision.'

'Good lad,' her father muttered. 'Good lad. I must return, fast as may be before Ethan lands us in a mess of broken promises and lawsuits. I should never have taken my eye off the business. Never.'

'Well, Papa, you will be glad to hear that some good has come of our trip to London,' Jessica said brightly, in an effort to distract him from his woes.

'Very much so,' Alex said. 'Sir, I am happy to tell you that Jessica has honoured me by accepting my proposal of marriage.'

To her alarm her father greeted this news by slumping back against the sofa cushions, eyes closed.

'Papa!' Was that the final shock that had been too much for him?

She reached for his wrist and then sank back in relief as his eyes snapped open again and he sat up, beaming. 'Wonderful. I am delighted, my dear. Everything your dear mama and I would have wanted for you.' He got to his feet with a grunt of effort and held out his hand to Alex, who shook it.

'Thank you, sir.'

'Well, don't hang about. Send your lawyer around at once and I'll get mine in. Then you must sort out the special licence as soon as possible. You had best get around to the Faculty Office if we're to have a wedding tomorrow. I can only hope the Archbishop is in residence at Lambeth Palace.'

'*Tomorrow?*'

'Of course, if I am to see you wed and get up to Long Welling as soon as may be. I'll send a letter off to Ethan now, express, and one to Joshua, too. Tell them to do nothing, agree nothing—sign nothing—until I get there.' He strode towards the door. 'Alfred!'

'Sir, I do not see how you expect us to be in a position to marry tomorrow,' Alex protested.

'You certainly won't be if you dally around here, lad. Er, Your Grace.'

Alex turned to her. 'Jessica, is this what you want?' he asked over the sound of her father's study door banging and the footsteps of Alfred hurrying along the hall.

The front door opened and Alfred came in, Robert Chandler, medical bag in hand, on his heels.

'In there.' Alex pointed at the study door. 'But I think the danger is past.'

Jessica found herself standing in the drawing room feeling as though she was on the edge of a precipice with seconds to decide whether to jump forward or backwards.

Should she marry Alex tomorrow? Or step back, say it was too soon, that she needed time. This gave her no room for second thoughts, but was that such a bad thing?

'Yes,' Jessica said. 'If it can be done, I will marry you tomorrow. Papa wants me settled and he will not be easy until I am, especially with this upset at home, and he has made up his mind you are the very best choice for me. There's the title and then he will have had you investigated—I am sorry,' she added as Alex's brows drew together in a dark line. 'He will have done that to every single nobleman in London between the ages of twenty and fifty, I'm sure.

'I will feel easier about him,' she confessed. 'He worries so much, for all that bluff exterior. I want him to have this positive thing, this marriage he desires so much for me. He will be calmer when it comes to dealing with matters at home. And, I confess, I have no yearning for some great society wedding.'

'Nor I,' Alex agreed. 'Mr Danby is a man who likes to tie up the ends and to draw a line under one matter before he tackles another, I perceive.' To her relief he did not seem too put out by her father's demands now. 'I do not know whether we can manage this for tomorrow, but I will try. It might help that the Archbishop is a cousin of sorts. I had best be off.' He bent and pressed a kiss on her cheek, then a fleeting brush of his lips on hers and he was gone.

Jessica sat down on the nearest chair with a bump, her fingers pressed to her lips. What had she done? She was going to marry Alex, perhaps tomorrow, certainly the day after. None of this seemed real.

The sound of the front door closing and the sight of both footmen out on the pavement hailing hackneys brought her to herself. Tomorrow she might be the Duchess of Malvern and she had not a single thing that might be described as bride clothes. Well, he would have to take her as she was and she could shop afterwards.

Jessica took two long steadying breaths then jumped to her feet and made for the stairs.

'Trotter, I am marrying the Duke tomorrow,' she announced as the maid came in to the bedchamber in reply to her ring.

'Lawks.' Mouth open, Trotter sat down on the end of the bed and stared at her. 'The Duke? Tomorrow? Does your father know?'

'Of course he knows, Trotter. Now, there is no time for shopping, so we must find the best gown we can for the wedding. I have no idea where we are going afterwards—His Grace's town house or the castle in Herefordshire, or somewhere else entirely, so you must pack bearing that in mind.'

'Castle,' Trotter repeated faintly.

'*Gown*, Trotter.'

'Oh, yes, Miss Jessica. The new rose pink, don't you think? Thank goodness we had the silk slippers dyed to match. And your mama's pearls and the little silver and pearl tiara for your hair—that will set off the silver embroidery on the hem and at the neck of the gown. And then a travelling outfit... My goodness, we will need all your trunks down from the attic.'

'That will have to wait until the footmen have come back. Papa sent them on errands. Oh, and then I will need one of them to deliver invitations to my friends. But I cannot write those until His Grace returns with news of the licence.'

She flopped down on the bed beside Trotter who, suddenly realising that she was not only sitting in her mistress's presence, but on her bed, stood up and bustled to the wardrobe, covering her embarrassment by pulling out hatboxes.

'I do not know whether I am on my head or my heels,' Jessica confessed. 'People spend months preparing for weddings.'

'If you ask me, Miss Jessica, this might not be such a bad way of doing things.' Trotter sounded more herself now. 'Saves a lot of time and worry, now I come to think on it. And what's a big society wedding for? Just give all those people who've turned up their noses a good meal and the opportunity to gossip about you,' she added with a sniff. 'And if you love him, you want to be with him, not waiting about buying stuff.'

For Trotter that was an amazing descent into sentimentality, but Jessica hardly noticed.

Do I love *him?* she wondered.

It was an uncomfortable idea. Loving someone meant you could be hurt by them and this was a man who confessed he thought his true soulmate was out there somewhere in the world.

She liked Alex, desired him, trusted him, but love was another step. A step too far. That was not what she had been looking for when she had begun to assess the eligible bachelors. Falling in love seemed too much of a lottery to be relied upon, she had told herself. True, her parents had loved each other, but she had seen so many marriages where cool indifference, or even polite toleration, seemed the overriding emotion.

Far safer to look for liking and compatibility and respect—those were qualities that lasted.

'Someone's at the door,' Trotter said, cocking her head at the sound of the knocker.

'That will be Papa's lawyers, I expect.'

It was, as she discovered by hanging over the banisters in a most unladylike manner. They were followed soon after by another two gentlemen in sombre black who looked much the same: Alex's representatives. The legal affairs were being looked after, now she just had to wait and see what luck he had had with the clerical matters.

It had seemed a long wait. The lawyers emerged from her father's study after two hours and were shown into the breakfast room where refreshments were brought to them while, presumably, they dotted I's and crossed T's. Papa, she knew, would have already drafted her settlement with his legal advisors, but the ducal pair had to agree and their proposals must also be scrutinised. It felt uncomfortably like a business merger was being arranged.

But that is what you wanted, she reminded herself.

Jessica fidgeted about the house from bedchamber to dressing room to her own sitting room and then back to the bedchamber where she fingered the hem of the pink and silver gown. Was she making the biggest mistake of her life or were those first instincts, that she could be happy with the Duke, that she trusted him, correct?

Finally, at six o'clock, Alex returned carrying a flat box. 'I have it and I persuaded a clergyman who was at the Faculty Office to come and preside. You and I, Miss Danby, are getting married in the morning.'

He laid the box on the table and opened the top to reveal a large document written on parchment with a big red seal at its foot. Jessica read the heading.

Charles Manners-Sutton By Divine Providence, Archbishop of Canterbury...

There were their names in flowing script. They were apparently 'well-beloved' of the Archbishop, which felt alarmingly personal, and it seemed that they could marry anywhere, at any time, provided the ceremony was conducted by a minister of the church.

'Well done,' she said faintly. 'Was it very difficult?'

'It would have been impossible if I was merely Mr Demeral, or even the Viscount Demeral. Dukes, however, are another matter.' He took her hand and drew her close, not quite touching. His fingers were chill from the outside air and she could smell damp wool from his greatcoat and the faint tang of citrus, perhaps his soap.

'It doesn't have to be tomorrow, Jessica. There is no date on this. This will reassure your father if you need to take more time. After all, I am asking you to trust me with your heart and your whole being. You must be certain.'

Was he looking for a way out, hoping perhaps, after all, that she would think twice about this? Jessica gave herself a mental shake. He had proposed, she had accepted. Either she went through with this now—or never.

'I trust you, with everything I have and I am,' she said and it felt like a vow. One that should be sealed with a kiss. She put her hands on his shoulders and he drew her closer.

'I am cold and damp,' Alex warned.

'And I am warm.'

His lips were chill, but his mouth was hot and she could feel the heat of his body because he held her so close. There was an urgency, an intimacy that she had not sensed before from him and, she realised with a shock, from her. This was something different from her awareness that he was an attractive man and she was drawn to him. This was something far more primitive, more physical.

As his mouth moved slowly over hers, drawing her tongue in to meet his, his hands held her, close and possessive.

Tomorrow I will be in his bed, she thought as she sank into the embrace.

Somewhere, at the back of her mind, she was surprised at her own lack of apprehension.

'I think it will be all right, don't you?' Alex said and she came to herself to find her cheek pressed against his chest. She could feel the reassuring beat of his heart.

She tried again. 'Yes. Yes, it will.'

Chapter Seventeen

'Here comes your papa, if I am not mistaken,' Alex said. 'Shall we sit chastely on the sofa and discuss tomorrow?'

Her mind was so full of imaginings of the night that would follow their wedding that it took Jessica a moment to realise what Alex was discussing. 'Yes, of course. We will be married here, I assume, but then what? I did not know what to tell Trotter to pack.'

'I have requested the clergyman—the Reverend Dixon—to attend at eleven. Then we can have a substantial luncheon and set out for Herefordshire in the early afternoon. I suggest we stop for the night at the Angel in Oxford, a six-hour journey, provided the weather holds. There has been no chance to reserve rooms, of course, but Oxford has many decent inns if we cannot be housed at that one.'

Jessica was agreeing to this—really, she had no alternative suggestions, even if she had been unhappy—when her father came in followed by two of the lawyers.

One for each side, she thought with a twinge of amusement.

'You have the licence? Excellent.' Papa listened to Alex repeating what he had just said to her, then handed him a sheaf of papers. 'All agreed and awaiting your approval.'

'Thank you. Excuse me, my dear.'

It was the first time he had used any form of endearment to her and Jessica found it rather disconcerting. 'Yes, of course.'

Alex settled down to read, his lawyer standing beside him and occasionally leaning over to point something out and murmur a few words.

Jessica took the opportunity to ask, low-voiced, what Dr Chandler had said.

'Told me not to drink so much port, eat smaller meals and not let my sons throw me into a rage,' he said with a snort. 'I could have told him that. At least he did not quack me with some expensive potion.'

Jessica patted his hand soothingly and he subsided with a grunt into the nearest chair.

After some time Alex stood up. 'Very satisfactory, provided you are satisfied, sir.'

'I am.' Her father snapped his fingers and Henry put an inkstand and pens on the table. They signed, shook hands and the lawyers took themselves off with the document, promising copies within days.

'I want to invite my particular friends,' Jessica said. 'I will write now.'

'And I will invite mine, which should please some of yours,' Alex said with a grin. 'Is there anything I can do to assist further, sir? I intend asking five guests, if that is agreeable.'

'And five for me, Papa. I think we should include Lady Cassington. So that is ten, plus us, plus you. Oh, thirteen.'

'Ominous,' Alex agreed. 'I shall invite Locksley, thus pleasing Miss Beech and evening the numbers. And now I must go. There is a great deal to arrange.'

He took Jessica's right hand and raised it to his lips.

'But I must not leave without doing this.' From his pocket he took a small leather box and handed it to her. 'By tradition this was presented to my ancestress by King Charles II. Rather a risqué origin for a betrothal ring, but it has served as such for every Demeral bride since then. Does it please you?'

Jessica opened the lid and stared at the domed ruby glowing on its velvet nest, surrounded by diamonds. It was an old-fashioned setting, but no less lovely for that and something deep in the red heart of the stone seemed to call to her.

'It pleases me very much. It has a personality, if that is not too fanciful a thing to say about a jewel.'

'It is not, but I suspect that it needs a wearer of equal distinction to see that,' Alex said as he took the ring from its case and slid it on to her finger. 'A good fit, I think.'

'A perfect fit.'

His hand tightened on hers and she looked up, met his steady, dark gaze. Yes, this was a fit and not only the gold band of the ruby on her finger, but this match with the man who had just given it to her.

Even her father, not a man of great sensitivity about emotions, seemed to sense something. He cleared his throat and turned away.

'And now there are letters to write and a wedding breakfast to order,' she said brightly, not certain she knew how to cope with all this. It was too soon, too unsettling. 'And there will be fifteen, now I think about it—we must invite the clergyman, must we not? Oh, and packing. So much packing!'

'Only take what you need for the first week,' Alex said, standing up and pocketing the empty ring box. 'The rest can come by carrier and we will not be entertaining or going out immediately. Pack plenty of warm clothes. Castles might seem romantic, but they are cold places.' She nodded. 'I will be here before eleven tomorrow. *À bientôt*, Jessica.'

And then he was gone. Jessica stared at the closed door for half a minute and then reached for the bell. 'Wedding breakfast, invitations, packing for both of us. Papa, I do not know whether I am on my head or my heels.'

'You will manage, my dear. My daughter, the Duchess. Now here's Henry—send my valet to my room, lad, and Miss Jessica's woman to here, and get down the trunks and tell Alfred to stand by to deliver messages. And send up Cook.'

Alex strode in through his front door. 'Pitwick, I am getting married in the morning. Tell James to be ready to take messages and then he's to pack my things. I need a valet, Pitwick, but I'll have to take him for now.'

'And you require a secretary, Your Grace. And several more staff in all departments.' Nothing, it seemed, shook the butler's composure. 'May I offer my respectful felicitations on behalf of the household? And ask who is the lady in question?'

'Miss Danby,' Alex said over his shoulder on his way to the study.

'Ah,' was all the butler said, but there was a wealth of relief and satisfaction in the soft sound. Then he hastened down the hall after Alex. 'Several letters have arrived from Longstone this morning, Your Grace.'

'I've no time for them now. I will read them on the journey. I'll be able to deal with whatever they are about in three days' time in any case.'

Alex scrawled notes of invitation to his close friends and sent the footman off with them with orders to call at the florist on his way back and have flowers dispatched to Adam Street. Then he swept the correspondence from the desk into a valise, added the various papers and ledgers that always travelled with him and put it in the hallway with the portable writing slope.

From below stairs he could hear Pitwick setting the remainder of the staff to work. Pitwick would follow them with the heavy luggage. Cook and the scullery maid would stay behind and keep the house secure.

'Pitwick!'

'Your Grace?' The butler, his black apron tied on over his dark suit and striped waistcoat, appeared through the baize door.

'We need to hire a carriage for you and all the trunks.'

'That is all in hand, Your Grace. I will take charge of your dressing case and the silver.'

'Thank you. You think of everything, Pitwick.' There was not much silver remaining and what there was travelled with him, so at least he could set a respectable dining table when he was entertaining.

'I endeavour to, Your Grace. I will supervise James with your packing when he returns. I have ventured to set out a decanter of the ninety-five port in the drawing room: I thought the occasion merited it.'

It took a glass of the dark red liquid before Alex could stop making mental lists and relax. He had done it. He had found a wealthy bride and had saved the estates. Now all the people who were his responsibility would be well housed and gainfully employed. The castle would be rescued from dereliction. He could hope to father children and provide them with security and education. The line of the Dukes of Malvern would continue, but the Pinchpenny Dukes could be consigned to history.

And in return for all this he simply had to be a decent husband. A faithful, concerned husband who would ensure Jessica's happiness and allow her to enjoy the status the title would give her. Used to the rank all his life, he could not but think he had the best of the bargain and that increased his responsibility to his new wife.

He had promised himself a love match and he had compromised. Now he swore to himself that, whatever happened, Jessica would never have cause to regret her decision. They might not be in love, but he had asked her to trust him and, for him as a man of honour, that was as binding as a declaration could be.

He had arrived too early. Nerves, he supposed, although he felt oddly calm. Alex was politely shown in to Mr Danby's study with the unspoken comment that bridegrooms were of little importance and were expected to stay well out of the way.

The sound of guests laughing and talking in the drawing room, and the chink of tea cups in saucers, penetrated the closed study door every time someone went in or out of the other rooms and servants were scurrying back and forth along the hallway. There was no sign of his future father-in-law and, naturally, none of Jessica.

He looked at the clock on the mantelshelf. Ten-fifteen. He should have brought a newspaper to occupy him until Robert Chandler, his best man, arrived. But he did have the valise with his correspondence, because that also had the special licence in it. He dug into the depths, came up with that morning's post and the unread letters from the day before and began to sort through them.

There were three in handwriting he recognised: his steward's. That must be the two that Pitwick had mentioned the day before and another that had been delivered that morning. What the devil was concerning Paulson so much that he had set pen to paper three times in two days? Usually he was as sparing with the written word as he was terse with the spoken.

Alex cracked the seal on the most recent one.

> *Old Mrs Jenkins died last night. The Williams child is still very poorly and little hope is held for him. The others, whose injuries are not so severe, seem likely to recover.*

The words seemed to swim in front of his eyes. Deaths? Injuries? What the devil was this?

> *I have housed the twelve homeless families and those injured in the castle. We are working first on making the less damaged homes weathertight. I hope this meets with your approval and that I will hear from you soon, Your Grace. The expense is considerable, but I felt you would agree it.*

Alex dropped the letter back into the valise and opened the others, a hard lump of dread in his gut as he read. A fire had started in the thatch of Widow Jenkins's cottage in the small hours. Neighbours thought she must have overturned a candle or lantern in her attic room. By the time it was discovered, the fire had spread and taken hold and hers, and twelve other cottages, had been destroyed or rendered uninhabitable. Injuries ranged from burns to broken limbs as people had jumped to safety and all were coughing badly. The unseasonably dry spell that had made the thatch and kindling stacks more vulnerable to fire had now been succeeded by torrential rain. Paulson had brought all the homeless families into the castle for shelter.

The pages crumpled in his hands as he sat staring at them. Old Mrs Jenkins, an infallible source of jam tarts for a small boy. Michael and Jenny Bond's new baby. More than half the little hamlet destroyed. Somehow he had to rebuild an entire community.

And then it hit him. Now he could. Now he could create a new village, build a school. Now he was a rich man, or he would be by the time he reached home.

But he had to be married first. He could hardly ruin Jessica's day by informing her that he would be taking her, not on a honeymoon, but to the scene of tragedy and devastation. He would have to break it to her on the journey.

Tomorrow, he told himself.

By then he would have plans made. Rapidly he scribbled a note to Paulson.

Spend what you have to. Spare no expense. Will be with you in two days with my Duchess.

Alex sealed it with a wafer and had just written the address and scrawled his name and title to ensure free delivery when a footman showed in Robert, his best man, and the Reverend Dixon. He handed the man the letter and told him to despatch it urgently, then, with what seemed like a physical effort, smiled at the new arrivals and put some warmth into his voice as he greeted them.

Somehow he had to get through this and reach home and he had to do it without causing Jessica any distress. He had thought all his troubles were over. He should have known better: Fate was not going to loosen her hold on the Penniless Dukes that easily.

Chapter Eighteen

'I wish your dear mama was here to see you now.' Her father unashamedly wiped a tear from his eye before settling Jessica's hand on his arm.

'So do I. But I have you, the best of fathers.' She gave the superfine suiting a comforting squeeze. 'You do like him, do you not, Papa? It isn't just the title?'

'If he were a rogue, he'd not get my blessing, duke or not,' her father said. 'Yes, I like him. He's honest and all the reports I've had are that he's a worker, a man with a sense of his responsibilities for those dependent on him. That's more than I expected from a lofty nob like him.'

They began to walk along the passageway leading to the head of the stairs, then he stopped. 'I've not tied the money up too tight. I trust him and it does a man no good not to be master of his own money. But I've set you up a nice little allowance as well, all of your own. There are all the details packed away in your luggage. I don't want him spending it all on that castle of his and you wanting for pretty dresses.'

'Thank you, Papa,' Jessica said and kissed his cheek.

'And very fine you look, too,' her father said as they began walking again. 'You'll make His Grace's jaw drop, see if you don't.'

Jessica hoped so. The gown was certainly charming,

Trotter had worked marvels with her hair and she had daringly allowed the merest touch of lamp black on her lashes and powder on her cheeks after the maid had pinched them ruthlessly to bring their colour up.

But did she look like a fit bride for a duke? At least this was no great society wedding with accounts of everyone's outfits in the Court pages of the newssheets and rows of critical matrons assessing everything from the length of her hem to the colour of her bouquet.

And she had Alex to thank for that. Hothouse roses of every shade had arrived that morning with a note.

I thought perhaps you would not have time to order these.

From them she and Trotter had created an arrangement of varying shades of pink with asparagus fern and silver ribbon. As she held it the great ruby glowed like a heart amid the pink petals. Looking down at it now carried her over the last few nervous steps to the head of the stairs.

Down they went and Alfred, who had been standing in the hall, darted in to the drawing room. Immediately there was the sound of the piano and of chairs being moved as people rose to their feet. It isn't even twenty people, she thought, concentrating on keeping her chin up and her shoulders back.

Trotter hurried down behind her. 'Veil, Miss Jessica.' The maid arranged the Valenciennes lace to cover her face and she breathed in the scent of lavender and dried rose petals that it had lain folded among since her own mother's wedding day. It brushed against her cheek like a kiss from long ago and she swallowed hard against the tears.

But now they were through the door and there was a clergyman in black cassock and white bands, standing at the table that had been draped in white with flowers and candlesticks as an altar. And there was the stocky figure of Dr Chandler, solid in well-tailored black with a cheerful red waistcoat.

And next to him… She made her eyes focus through the intricate mesh of the veil. There was the man who, very soon, would be her husband. Alex seemed very pale and very serious. Perhaps he was as nervous as she was. That was a strangely reassuring thought.

The rest of the room came clearer. Belinda seated at the pianoforte, her friends and Alex's mingled among the seating and not divided into bride and groom's sides. Lady Cassington half turned, beaming. Anna Chandler nodded encouragingly as she passed and then, in only a few steps, she was standing beside Alex.

Was his heart beating as fast as hers? Was his mind as suddenly and completely clear of doubts as hers was?

This was the man she wanted to marry. Not to satisfy Papa's ambitions, not to secure a place in society, but because she wanted very much to be his wife.

The Reverend Dixon was speaking and she realised that the service had begun. Nothing more important was ever going to happen to her, she must be aware of every moment.

'Who giveth this woman?' Papa lifted her hand and offered it to Alex and then stepped back, taking her old life with him.

There was no hesitation in Alex's voice as he took his vows, only an exciting urgency as though he could not wait to make her his.

Jessica had expected to be nervous, but when it was her turn she found the words came easily to her tongue and she could speak her vows clearly.

And finally, 'I pronounce them man and wife together...'

Alex put back her veil, lifted her hand with its new plain gold band next to the smouldering ruby and kissed her fingers. He still looked pale and serious, but there was a smile in his eyes for her.

'Is all well, Your Grace?' he asked her.

'All is very well, Your Grace,' she replied and laughed out loud with sheer happiness.

'Then let us go and greet our guests.' Alex placed her hand on his arm and walked down between the rows of seats and their friends stood and clustered around them, not waiting for the formality of a receiving line to offer kisses and handshakes and the warmth of their congratulations.

It seemed to Jessica, admittedly through a happy haze, that Alex was eager to draw everyone into the dining room. It must be because he wanted them to set off as soon as possible, to be alone with her.

For the first time the thought of that made her feel shy. This was real now, even though it had all the makings of a dream. She was the Duchess of Malvern—at least ten people had already greeted her by her title, the staff were saying *Your Grace* with every sentence.

Doctor Chandler rose to make a toast once the party was seated. 'To my old friend Alex Demeral and to my new friend, his wife: long life, happiness and every blessing.'

The Reverend Dixon said grace and there she was, Alex on her right hand, her father on her left, presiding for the first time as a hostess and married lady.

'This is the most elegant gathering you are likely to experience for some time, I fear,' Alex said as he raised his glass to tap against hers. 'Not only is local society in the immediate area somewhat limited, but our reception rooms are sadly lacking.' He sounded concerned about her reaction.

'We will have all the fun of renovating and then we can hold house parties and bring society to us,' she said. The idea of restoring a castle back to life and making it fit for a family in a new century was very appealing.

'Yes. That might take some time,' he said, rather flatly.

Had she blundered? Been tactless about the fact that it would be her dowry that would be paying for the renovations?

'I have concerns about the tenants and the estate,' Alex said. 'Those must take priority.'

'Yes, of course.' So it was not so much the money, she guessed, it was the fact that she had not comprehended the importance of his role as landowner and his responsibilities to the people who depended on the estate for their livelihood. 'You are going to have to teach me my duties in regard to the tenants,' she said. 'And the other villagers, too, I suppose. My family has never owned land as such, so I have a great deal to learn.'

'I imagine industrial employees have a different relationship with their employers.'

'It varies a great deal,' Jessica said carefully. It was certainly nothing like the feudal connection she sensed that landowners felt. Her father was considered soft by many of the neighbouring industrialists for providing a doctor for his workers and making sure they had time on Sundays to attend church and chapel. There was schooling of a sort for the children who were employed as well, but even so, she doubted her father knew the names of his workers below the rank of foreman, whereas she would wager her allowance for a year that Alex knew every one of his tenants and the local villagers by name.

But she had guests to attend to now and the problems of agricultural workers were for the future. The breakfast was becoming noisy with chatter and laughter. The Reverend was deep in conversation with Lady Cassington and her friends and Alex's were still showing the attraction for each other that she had seen from the start. How many more weddings were to be expected in the near future? She looked around the table, plotting where to throw her bouquet to best effect.

The last of the desserts had been reduced to crumbs and scrapes of cream. 'I think we should leave soon,' Alex said.

'Yes, of course, I will go and change at once.'

All the female guests came with her, descending on her bedchamber like a flock of gaily coloured birds while Trotter had her out of the pink silk and into her newest carriage dress with a smart bonnet, trimmed in blue velvet, and a matching blue redingote.

'That will keep you snug however draughty the carriage,' Trotter announced, standing well back to survey the results.

The others flocked out to assemble in the hall, but Anna Chandler remained behind. 'You love him, don't you?'

'I do not know,' Jessica confessed. 'I think I could, very easily. I do not know whether I dare let myself.' Even saying it gave her a little ache in her heart.

'It is a risk,' Anna agreed. 'But I think you have the courage.' And then she was gone, too, and there was nothing for it but to make her way down the stairs, leaving her girlhood behind, stepping into the unknown future.

She was passed from person to person, kissed by everyone—except the Reverend Dixon—and found herself out on the pavement with Alex waiting by the open carriage door. A second vehicle for the luggage, Trotter and one of Alex's footmen who was acting as his valet, stood behind.

There was nothing left to do but wave to the assembled staff, kiss Papa and pretend they were not both weeping, and toss her bouquet over her shoulder.

It found its mark, as she had intended, in Lady Anthea's hands. She blushed and glanced at Major Rowlands and said something about, 'Such nonsense', but her cheeks were a very pretty shade of pink and his ears had turned red.

Jessica was not conscious of climbing the step into the carriage or of sitting down, but there she was and Alex was next to her, leaning over to drop the window strap so she could lean out and wave.

When they turned the corner into the Strand he closed it again and handed her a handkerchief. 'It is quite clean. James is taking his duties as temporary valet very seriously.'

'Thank you.' She dried her eyes and folded the linen square neatly. 'I am not crying because I am sad, you understand. Just...' She waved a hand vaguely.

'It is a very big step,' Alex agreed. 'And a very abrupt one.'

'Yes, I am sorry about that. It has meant you have had no time to hire a valet or do any of the things I am sure you wanted to do in London before you left.'

'As it happens—' He broke off abruptly, then said, 'As it happens, I am not sorry to be returning to Herefordshire at this time.'

After that they settled down to watching the passing scene from the window. It proved less awkward than Jessica had feared—she had been rather dreading making conversation for almost twenty hours. They had never seemed to have any shortage of things to talk about before, but now she felt almost shy. Perhaps it was the thought of the wedding night ahead.

Now they could find plenty of interest to comment on and, when the light began to fail, Alex suggested that she remove her bonnet, gloves and coat and wrap a travelling rug around her legs.

'I have a basket of cakes and some lemonade. Have something to eat and drink—I noticed you did not manage a great deal at the breakfast.'

To her surprise Jessica found she was both hungry and thirsty and the refreshments were welcome, although she felt slight surprise and, if she was honest with herself, disappointment that Alex had shown no signs of amorousness. Clearly, as a gentleman, he would not attempt full lovemaking in a moving carriage in broad daylight, but perhaps a kiss…

Alex packed away the picnic basket and moved to the seat facing her. 'Try to sleep,' he suggested. 'It has been a long and tiring day.' He tucked her up warmly under the blanket when she stretched out on the seat and folded another blanket under her head.

Jessica closed her eyes and felt the brush of his lips on her cheek, the weight of his hand on her hair for a moment, then heard the sounds of him settling in the corner opposite her feet. He was clearly being considerate of her weariness and that accounted for his restraint.

There was the sharp click of a steel striking flint, a glow against her closed lids and the faint odour of warm oil. He had lit one of the lamps that were fitted against the bulkhead of the coach. There was a rustle of paper. It was curiously comforting and domestic, despite the jolting of the coach. Even that was not so bad. The road to Oxford must be one much travelled by the Mail as well as the stage-coaches, and the Royal Mail let very little stand in the way of their schedules, certainly not potholed roads.

She would just doze a little, then she would be bright and alert when they arrived at the Angel Inn, ready for her wedding night. Jessica found she was looking forward to it now, the apprehension and shyness had somehow disappeared.

The carriage slowed, stopped, there was the bustle of horses being changed, but she ignored it and slipped down into sleep.

Chapter Nineteen

She was in a garden, a large, wild, overgrown garden full of roses and ferns, tangles of brambles and clumps of nettles. Someone was blowing a horn, summoning her. A herald at the castle gate? A sentry on the battlements?

Jessica gathered up her trailing skirts and began to run towards the sound, but the thorns caught at the veils trailing from her wimple and tree roots tried to trip her. And then she came out into the open and found herself on the banks of a moat. The water was sparkling and swans were swimming and across it was a castle, white and perfect with turrets and banners. If she could only get there in time—

The horn blew again and she jerked awake out of her dream into faint light. She was stretched out on a bench of some kind that was moving and the room was swaying.

Of course—the carriage. And this was the nineteenth century, not the Middle Ages. That horn was the groom blowing for a toll gate to open or for a change of horses. She had fallen deeply asleep. Jessica sat up rubbing her eyes. Strange that she should feel so stiff after such a short nap, but it was not yet full dark.

It was difficult to see properly because the lamp had gone out, but she could make out the still figure of Alex in the corner diagonally across from her.

'You are awake,' he said.

'Yes.' She yawned and rubbed her eyes. 'Goodness, what a deep sleep. I was dreaming about a castle and a moat with swans and someone blowing a trumpet—but it was the horn, of course. Are we nearly at Oxford?'

'We passed Oxford long since.'

'We drove through the night? We haven't stopped?' No wonder she felt stiff and hungry and in need of a nice inn and its facilities.

'You were completely sunk in sleep. Exhausted. I thought it best to simply keep going.' Alex did not sound like his usual amiable self and he was staring out of the window.

Jessica bit back the retort that he might at least have discussed it with her, then decided that starting an argument when half awake, on the first day of their married life, was not a good idea.

It was daylight now, a misty March morning with a distinctly damp chill in the air. Jessica sat as the carriage slowed, turned, lurched over a hump-backed bridge. She glimpsed water foaming over rocks below. Then she glanced up and saw the castle. Her castle.

Three towers built of a reddish stone, slate roofs, a curtain wall linking the towers, punctuated with what must be arrow slits. No flag flew to welcome its master home and she could see no sign of the moat.

'I should have woken, you, warned you. I kept putting off waking you,' Alex said, his voice choked with some emotion she had never heard before. 'I am sorry.'

Then Alex threw open the door and jumped down, not waiting for the coach to stop. When it did, after a few more yards, Jessica leaned further out, completely confused by his words. Perhaps she was still only half awake.

She was not certain what she had expected to see. A pleasant village with friendly inhabitants coming out to greet their lord, she had hoped. Rather tumbledown, of course—Alex had spoken feelingly about the need for repairs and improvements and this was not the prosperous countryside surrounding London, after all—but a community. Children and old people, ducks on the pond and perhaps a goat on the green. A little church, an ale house, no doubt.

It was the smell that hit her first, before what she was looking at made any sense. There was the unmistakeable stench of burning, of wet ashes, the foul smell from still-smouldering old thatch. Then she saw the shells of cottages, most with the roofs completely gone, some with tumbled gable ends, others with their stone and plaster blackened by tongues of smoke. Charred timbers were everywhere, some sticking up like the skeleton of a long-beached whale, others jumbled on the ground.

The short tower of the church was visible behind, halfway to the castle. A cottage near the river bank was intact, but the bush hanging over its door—the sign of an ale house—was charred. There were no children, no animals, to be seen.

Men and women were working in the trampled mud that surrounded each pathetic wreck. Jessica clutched at the doorframe as she tried to count. Ten at least, perhaps more. Half of this little settlement gone. Even she could tell there was no hope of repairing these. Those poor people.

Alex was striding across the battered grass—the green she had imagined with playing children and a goat. He called out and the workers turned and flocked to him. She saw him put his arms around two weeping women, the men clustered close and from the direction of the church a clergyman hurried down, his hands held out, in greeting, blessing or in supplication, she could not tell.

When had this happened? Faint wisps of smoke still rose from some of the buildings, but she knew that thatch and wood could smoulder for days, she had seen it when one of the casting sheds at the works had burned down, taking a neighbouring thatched hovel with it.

Alex had known about this. He had made no exclamation of horror or surprise, but had been tensed to leap from the carriage the moment they arrived. No wonder he had been sleepless and drawn on the journey. He must have known before the wedding, even—there had been no messages delivered for him once he had reached the house.

The groom climbed down to unfold the step for her and she descended on unsteady legs. This was a crisis and there were far more important things to think about than her own anxieties. But she had to know.

Alex had gone to look at one of the cottages with a small group of people, so she walked across the green to where the vicar stood. He was drawn and unshaven and his cassock, which was filthy around the hem, had been buttoned incorrectly.

'Vicar?'

He turned to look at her uncomprehendingly. 'Madam?'

'I am the Duke's wife. We were married yesterday. Can you tell me when this happened, please?'

'Your Grace? When? Three days past, in the night. His Grace's steward wrote—'

'Yes, of course. His Grace did not want to worry me with details, but I need to be sure I understand everything.'

He nodded as though that made sense. 'Forgive me,

Your Grace. I am Harold Goodson, the Vicar here. I should welcome you to Longstone, but it hardly seems…'

'Please, do not concern yourself with me. Was anyone hurt?'

'Several people—burns, of course. Some were hit by falling beams and most inhaled smoke. We lost Widow Jenkins and the Bonds' baby died this morning.'

'A baby? Oh, *no*.' The scene in front of her seemed to tilt and sway so that she held on to the side of the coach. 'The poor parents. I can't imagine…' Mr Goodson took a step forward, concern on his face. She took a deep breath. She must not distract him with her distress, he had an entire village to comfort. And so, she realised, had she. 'Where is everyone? These cottages must be uninhabitable.'

'In the castle, Your Grace. There was nowhere else for them to go. The church is too small.'

'Your Grace!' That was Trotter, stumbling across the grass, batting away James's attempts to help her. 'What has happened?'

'As you can see,' Jessica said with a snap, 'most of the village has burned down. We must go up to the castle: there are people who need help. James, go to His Grace, see what he wants you and the others to do.' She managed a smile for the Vicar, then hurried back to the carriages.

The two vehicles bumped up the track, across a drawbridge—there was a moat, of sorts as Anna had described—and through an arch. The sound of the carriage wheels echoed and bounced off stone in the deep shadow and then they were through and into an internal courtyard.

It might have been a scene from the Middle Ages. Children played in corners, women stood around the well, waiting their turn as a man drew up bucket after bucket of water for them to carry inside. Plough horses were tethered against one wall and sheep and goats bleated from a pen.

'Your Grace?'

'Wait. Wait a moment.' Jessica sat and fought for composure. Alex had known about this when he proposed to her and he had offered because he desperately needed the money. Yes, this was a crisis and, yes, these people needed help urgently—but why had he not been honest with her? She had agreed to marry because she trusted him and, it seemed, she had been wrong.

Had he thought she would refuse? But she had known all along that he needed money, had known it when she had made him that audacious offer. Why had he not come to her and told her what had happened, told her that she had been right, that they could make a good marriage and that he had been too optimistic in thinking he could find romantic love.

Instead he had said nothing about that critical need for money. Why not? Because he did not believe she would accept him, she supposed. He had been very fortunate that the crisis at home meant that Papa insisted on a hasty wedding. But then, simply letting it be known that they were betrothed would have meant that lines of credit would suddenly open up for the Pinchpenny Duke. He could have waited months, if that had been what she had asked.

She supposed he had wanted to make sure. Sure of his bride, sure of her fortune.

Chapter Twenty

Jessica's bitter thoughts had not taken long. A man was hurrying across the courtyard towards them, chickens and ducks scattering before him. He opened the door, his expression one of profound relief. 'Your Grace!' When he saw her it changed to a look that would have been comical, if only she had been in the mood to appreciate it.

'The Duke and I married before we left London,' she said. 'I am the Duchess. And you are?'

'Paulson, Your Grace. Steward here. The Duke is with you?'

'He is down in the village. If someone can show my woman where my rooms are and take up our luggage, then perhaps you can show me the arrangements here for these unfortunate people.'

'Certainly, Your Grace. Chris! Billy!'

Two young men hurried forward, were given instructions and, hoisting the first of the luggage on to their shoulders, led Trotter away through the great double doors into the depths of the castle.

'This way, Your Grace. I will summon the housekeeper and arrange for refreshments for you.'

'I have just breakfasted, thank you, and I am sure she has many urgent matters to attend to. And I think that *ma'am*

will do, Mr Paulson. This is no situation for formalities.'
She took off her bonnet and coat and tossed them into the
carriage.

'No, indeed. Now, if you will allow me, I will show
where we have housed the displaced families. Oh, do mind
your footing, ma'am. The geese make such a mess.'

An hour later Jessica sat at the kitchen table, drinking
tea in company with a weary steward and a somewhat
flustered housekeeper.

'If we'd only known to expect you, Your Grace... His
Grace's letter said something about a duchess, but we could
make no sense of it and thought he must have written the
wrong thing in haste. And your suite hasn't been aired out
and the bed isn't made up.'

'The wedding was brought forward because my father
had to return home to deal with an urgent matter. As for
the room, if you can spare a housemaid, Mrs Black, then
she and my maid Trotter can make up the bed and do whatever else is necessary.'

There had been no sign of Trotter, which meant that either she had found a maid herself and was dealing with the
room or she had thrown up her hands in horror and was
even now composing a letter of resignation.

'My rooms are not a priority. I am full of admiration
for the way in which you have managed to accommodate
the families.'

A range of ground-floor rooms had been cleared of the
stored lumber, barrels and stacks of kindling they had been
used for, swept and scrubbed and furnished with whatever furniture the families had managed to save, supple-
mented by a motley collection of items taken from around

the castle. All the families had two rooms each, the single men were sharing and the elderly and frail were in guest bedchambers.

'And we've dug a row of latrine pits, if you'll excuse me mentioning the matter, ma'am,' Mr Paulson said.

'But it's feeding them, Your Grace,' Mrs Black said. She was a thin woman with greying hair and frown lines which spoke of habitual worrying. 'It's not that they're fussy— they're used to good plain food, all of them, but most have lost what stores they had and there's only a dozen of us here, so Cook hasn't that much laid by.'

The cook, Mrs Brightwell, nodded agreement and went on stirring what smelled to Jessica like a vat of porridge.

'Make a list of what you need. Not just food. Mattresses, bedding, clothes—whatever is lacking—and then send staff into the nearest large town and buy it all.'

'Ma'am?' They stared at her.

'Money will not be a problem.' Jessica opened her reticule where she had stowed the roll of banknotes her father had given her just before she left.

'It might take a while to set up the bank accounts and so forth,' he had said vaguely.

She hadn't counted it, but now she put it on the table and the notes curled across the scrubbed pine. Paulson, Mrs Black and Cook stared.

'Yes, Mrs Black, money will no longer be a problem,' said Alex from the doorway. He was still drawn, but the pallor had left him and he looked alert and grimly determined.

Jessica looked across the table and their gazes locked. She held the look for a moment, then glanced down at the money and back up. Now was not the time or the place for recriminations or explanations, but if her husband thought she was accepting the situation passively, he was much mistaken.

The staff who had been reticent about accepting the invitation to sit with Jessica at the kitchen table were far more at their ease with Alex, she realised.

They all leapt to their feet, of course, and there were respectful greetings of 'Your Grace' from all of them, but their smiles spoke of affection and relief, not servility.

'Thank you for all your work,' he said. 'Everything that could be done has and with real thought to what the displaced families need. I have spoken to the Vicar and the funerals will be tomorrow morning. Mrs Jenkins first and then the child.'

Jessica wondered whether she should go to the bereaved parents. She felt that she should and yet they did not know her—they might feel they had to somehow be on their best behaviour with her, which was the last thing they needed at this time. Perhaps she should go after the funeral.

'The place is in a right mess, Your Grace,' Mrs Black said. 'We haven't touched the family rooms since this happened, none of the fires have been lit for days up there and everywhere smells of the smoke from the village.'

'That does not matter,' Alex said.

'Indeed it does not,' Jessica added, cutting across what he was going to say next. She was mistress of this household now and instinct told her to take a firm grip now or she would find it harder later. 'Looking after the displaced people and the staff who are all working so hard must take priority. His Grace and I both have our personal servants with us—between the four of us we can make our beds and light our fires. Perhaps we can all have some breakfast now, then we can make lists and plans.' She had an instinct that if they did not have a second breakfast now it might be evening before they ate again.

'Of course, ma'am. You'll be more comfortable in the small drawing room, I'll be bound, and you can send your people down here, we will look after them.'

Jessica interpreted that as the staff feeling more comfortable if she and Alex removed themselves and she did not argue. She needed to speak to her husband alone. Soon.

He led the way up the back stairs and into the hall, or rather the Great Hall—the capital letters were quite audible. It was vast, with a table to match in the middle, fireplaces that could roast an ox, and probably had in the past, and a vaulted ceiling vanishing into cobwebbed gloom.

They met Trotter and James halfway across the stone-flagged floor.

'We've made up the beds, Your Grace,' Trotter said. 'And lit fires in both bedchambers and put the bedding to air. It all needs a good dusting, but it is comfortable enough. I have unpacked what I think you will need for today and tonight, Your Grace, and the girl showed us our accommodation.'

'Is it suitable, Trotter?' Jessica was conscious of Alex beside her, but she was not concerned with his reaction to her doubts. Trotter was a London-trained upper servant. She was entitled to a good bedchamber and was quite within her rights to take herself back to London if she did not have one.

'Perfectly, Your Grace, thank you.'

'Ma'am will do, Trotter,' Jessica said, not for the first time. 'If you go down to the kitchen they will make you your breakfast.'

That was one thing she had learnt about housekeeping very early—make sure the staff were comfortable. Jessica followed Alex through into a room that, to put it politely, seemed to have been lived in. It was a quarter of the size of the Great Hall and it was filled with a hotchpotch of furniture, some very ancient, some relatively modern. All of it looked well-worn but comfortable. This was no formal reception room, this was a room where you could kick off your shoes and curl up on a sofa to read a book, although most of the sofas appeared to have welcomed dogs as well as humans.

Alex closed the door behind him and faced her. 'You want to know why I did not warn you about the fire,' he said bluntly.

'Yes, I do.' Jessica sat down cautiously on the edge of the sofa that looked least likely to swallow her up in its mounds of cushions and sagging webbing. She folded her hands neatly in her lap, took a deep breath and told herself to say calm. She would not allow him to see how hurt she was feeling.

'I could think of no way to tell you, under the circumstances.'

'*Circumstances?*' Her resolution to stay in control vanished in a burst of anger. Jessica found she was on her feet, confronting him.

'You proposed to me because now you need my money and that overrides your romantic desire to seek your true love and everything you said to me about friendship and trust is so much flummery. If nothing else, surely I deserve your honesty? Could you not have said that your circumstances had changed for the worst and that you now find my practical proposal for a marriage of mutual convenience is acceptable if I am still of the same mind? At least that would have been honest. Instead,' she concluded on a sob she could not quite control, 'you lied to me by omission, let me believe that we might have…have something that had a meaning, that was built on trust.'

Her words rocked Alex back on his heels as though she had hit him. 'You are telling me that you thought that I proposed to you knowing this?' He swept his hand towards the window where she could see thin trails of smoke rising upwards.

'Yes. Of course. I know your steward wrote to you at once.'

'Of course,' he echoed. 'You think you cannot trust me now? It seems I never could believe in your professions of faith in me.' His face was set in anger, his voice bitter. 'I did not know about the fire until an hour before the wedding ceremony. I had not opened my post the day before because I was too distracted with thoughts of all we had to plan, to do.'

Alex turned from her, rested his hands on the windowsill and stared out. 'I had not opened it the day before that because I was nerving myself to propose to you. I do not have a secretary—it cannot have escaped your notice that I could not afford one.'

Jessica sat down again. The fire of her anger had left her feeling sick. 'Yet on the journey, you knew. You did not tell me. You let me think we would break the journey, yet you drove on. You could have explained—did you think I would refuse to come?'

'If I had, then I would have been right. You refused to believe in me when you descended from the carriage this morning,' he said over his shoulder.

'I was tired, half awake and taken utterly by surprise. What did you expect?'

'Trust—the quality you seem to set so much store by,' he said, turning to face her. 'If you can allow yourself to believe that I did not know until I opened my letters while I waited in your father's study, then perhaps you can believe that I was shocked, desperately anxious—and faced with telling my new bride that, far from spending the first weeks of her marriage in peace and tranquillity she would be pitchforked into tragedy and chaos. I judged it best to wait until you were rested before telling you. Clearly, I was wrong.'

Was this *her* fault? Is that what Alex was saying? That she should have believed in him and not judged without giving him the chance to explain?

She was angry and hurt and had been feeling a fool for believing in the honesty of his proposal. Jessica picked her way through her emotions.

'I assumed, when Mr Paulson told me when he had written, that you would have seen the letter when you proposed to me. If you tell me that was not the case, then, of course, I accept your word and I apologise.'

She meant the apology, but at the same time, she deeply resented it. The world was full of deceived wives who blindly put their faith in husbands who betrayed them, cheated them, deceived them. She had always thought herself too clever to be taken in by such a man and now she was being asked to apologise for perfectly natural suspicions. A lady was expected to meekly accept whatever her husband decreed, but she was not surrendering without some semblance of fight.

'Even so, I still think that you should have told me on the journey before I went to sleep,' she said as calmly as she could. 'You showed no faith in my willingness to put this disaster above my personal comfort and convenience.'

Silence. They stared at each other, Alex stony-faced, Jessica biting her lip. Then he said, 'That is true. I also apologise. I suppose we are having our first married argument.'

'Technically, I believe we are not actually married,' she countered.

'Because the union has not been consummated?' Strangely, this appeared to amuse Alex, or at least he seemed to relax a little. One dark eyebrow quirked. 'Am I to conclude that this is unlikely to occur?'

'No, of course not.' Jessica, who had spoken without really thinking, felt decidedly flustered. 'I mean... Oh, I do not know what I mean! I am upset, I am appalled by what we have found here, I feel sick that our trust in each other seems to have such shaky foundations, I am very well aware that to the villagers I am a complete stranger and one who does not understand their lives or their world. And I suppose I am feeling all the emotions of any inexperienced woman at the prospect of the wedding bed, and— Are you laughing at me? Because if you are, I am never going to speak to you again, Alex Demeral.'

'No, I am not.' He came across the room, knelt in front of her with head bent and took her unresisting hands in his cold ones. 'I am bone weary. Like you, I am appalled at those shaky foundations. I know these people, but I fear that whatever I can do for them might not be enough. I am feeling all the emotions of a man facing the prospect of lying with a virgin and dreading getting that wrong. And if you wish to laugh at me, you may.'

Chapter Twenty-One

Alex felt the touch of Jessica's hand on his hair, fleeting, tentative. They had made such a mull of this between them, he wondered if it was possible to find their way back to solid ground again.

Then Jessica's touch became a caress and he looked up and found she was smiling at him. It was a cautious smile, but it held hope and affection. She swayed forward, he leaned in to meet her and he felt that smile against his own lips and answered it.

It felt as though a boulder had been lifted from his chest. When he put his arms around her she slid from the sofa and curled against him with a soft sigh.

With an effort he kept the kiss gentle, slow. It was not what he wanted and, he suspected, if he had obeyed his instincts and made love to his wife there on the floor, she would have made no protest. But this was too important to get right and he broke the kiss and lifted her back on to the seat.

'Later,' he promised and this time her answering smile held certainty.

'Yes, we must think what is most important to do now.'

He sat down a little way from her and she asked, 'Where is the nearest town?'

'Hereford.'

'Then I suggest I go in with one of the carriages with a driver and groom from here who know their way around. I will ask Cook for a list and we will buy food and medical supplies. Plenty of both and blankets. The other things are important, but if people are well fed, warm and their hurts are taken care of, then I think they will feel more positive. Perhaps after the funerals I could visit each family and find out what they need to be comfortable in their temporary accommodation and then we can have another expedition with wagons to bring things like mattresses back.'

'Yes, I agree. I will make certain we have enough fuel in to keep everybody warm.'

'I will go as soon as we have eaten,' Jessica said. 'Can you find a driver and groom who know the town and a footman to help me? There are footmen, aren't there?' she asked.

'Two. One rather doddery. You take Sim.'

Alex was beginning to become concerned when dusk began to gather and Jessica had still not returned. He went up on to the battlements, warily skirting the more crumbling sections, looked out and sighed with relief as he saw the carriage making its way slowly along the potholed road.

Had she managed to get credit? he wondered. The local shopkeepers understandably wanted cash in hand from the castle—they knew the financial position as well as he did. But there had been that roll of banknotes, of course. It was still hard to accept that money was no longer a problem.

As the carriage drew up in the courtyard he came down the worn old steps. Jessica climbed out, saw him and gave him a triumphant grin.

'We are loaded! I defy you to find a space to squeeze in another potato.'

Even as she spoke, people began to emerge from the building to carry the stores in. Cook came to stand on the steps and beam at the procession and Mrs Black seized the package that Jessica gave her.

'Salves and bandages and willow bark powder. I explained to the apothecary what sort of injuries there are and he says this should all help,' Jessica explained.

'There was no trouble with paying?' Alex asked, leading her aside.

'No, I went to the bank first and gave them the letter of credit and introduction from Papa's bank. I paid in cash in the shops, but I told them where I was banking. I have no doubt they'll all be making enquiries and we will not have difficulty setting up accounts now.'

Alex watched the purchases being unloaded, conscious of an odd feeling of surprise. It took him a moment to identify it: he was not feeling the discomfort he knew some men would experience at having their wives pay for all this. It had not occurred to him before because he knew his duty was plain—what he had struggled with was trying to find both a woman to love and a wealthy one.

Now, he accepted, he had made a fair exchange. Jessica would not have married him if she had not wanted to. Despite what she said about pleasing her father, she was too intelligent and too independent to condemn herself to a miserable marriage. Nor was she a woman whose head was turned by the prospect of becoming a duchess and who would have married him whatever his character.

And a fair exchange is no robbery, ran the old saying—provided it *was* fair. And that was where his duty lay, to ensure that Jessica became fully his Duchess in every sense and was happy. He had never been responsible for another person's happiness before; it felt a daunting responsibility.

Dinner was excellent, even if the wine glasses were cloudy with age and the china plain and the crests on the cutlery worn by years of polishing.

They ate at one end of the great table as close to a fireplace as possible. Even with both fires lit, the Hall seemed to suck heat upwards and replace it with insidious little draughts around their ankles.

Jessica wondered how to tactfully discover what improvements would be acceptable and then decided as Alex passed her bread rolls that it was better just to ask.

'You said that the castle needs structural work,' she said, watching Alex. He seemed to be savouring the vegetable soup and a well-fed man was usually an amiable one in her experience. 'What about the interior?'

'The interior has hardly been touched for two hundred years and it needs dragging into the nineteenth century,' he said. 'It will not be easy. I suspect the draughts will be a lot worse when all the cobwebs and starlings' nests are removed.'

'One would not want to harm all the original features, though,' she said, ladling out more soup for both of them. It had been a long, tiring day and the hot food seemed to be doing them both good. 'How old is it?'

'The centre is the keep which was built in about 1390, then it was added to until Henry VII made it clear he did not appreciate local lords maintaining highly fortified castles. It has been gently mouldering ever since then—'

He broke off as the elderly footman whose name Jes-

sica had not yet learned came in with a roast, followed by
Sim with platters of vegetables. 'Pork? That smells magnificent. My compliments to Cook.'

Dinner, then, was a success, which was a good start,
Jessica decided. Not that she had anything to do with the
cooking of it, but she thought that she had bought well.

Now, as she scraped the last delicious traces of posset
from the dish, she realised that there was not a great deal
to do except think about what happened next. Should she
retire to the drawing room and sit alone while Alex drank
port, then joined her for conversation before she rang for
the tea tray to be brought in and then...?

No. Better to get it over with, although she was not at all
sure whether the butterflies in her stomach were entirely
agitated by dread. Some, at least, were excited anticipation.

'It has been a long day,' she said. 'I think I will retire now.
If, of course, I can find my way to my bedchamber.'

'Allow me to escort you.' Alex was on his feet before
the footman could step forward to pull back her chair.

Jessica swallowed. 'Oh. Thank you.' This was not what
she had anticipated. 'But I would not want to keep you
from your port.'

'I doubt there is a drinkable bottle in the place,' he said
ruefully. 'Brendon, see to it that hot water is sent up to Her
Grace's chamber.'

Another name to remember. Jessica focused on that and
then on following the twists and turns that led her from the
head of the massive oak staircase along corridors, through
a door and up a short flight of curving steps.

'You have your own turret and it is one of those still se-
curely attached to the main building, I promise.'

It was not as much a turret as a tower, she realised, stepping into a large room that would have been circular if a partition had not been built across the inner side to cut off a curved slice. A dressing room, she supposed.

'I see Trotter is here. I will leave you.' He bent and kissed her cheek. 'May I return later?' he murmured in her ear.

'Yes,' she whispered, suddenly very shy. It was difficult to remember now that she had summoned up the courage to propose to this man.

Jessica sat up in the big bed and hugged her knees. It must have been like this for countless brides in this chamber. There was little that she could see in her surroundings that reminded her of what century she was in.

At least she was warm and bathed and could expect an equally warm clean man to enter through the archway, not some unwashed, hairy fighting man with very definite ideas on the place of women—under him in all senses— and of his rights in a marriage.

The door opened with a creak and closed with a disconcertingly final thud. Then Alex stepped out of the shadowed archway and she stopped tormenting herself with Gothic imaginings and felt those fluttering butterflies of desire again.

He was wearing a heavy robe of some dark red material and his hair was ruffled, dark and shining with damp. A very clean husband, then, even if he did look disconcertingly like his regal ancestor.

She was bathed, too, although the tub had been small. Trotter had brushed her hair dry in front of the fire, dressed her in the very plain and very thin silk nightgown that had been carefully packed in dried rose petals and Jessica had dabbed rosewater behind her ears and, daringly, between her breasts.

The old, tarnished, mirror on the dressing table showed a figure that was hazy in the candlelight. Was this how a bride was supposed to look—ethereal and pale? Trotter appeared to think not and produced a rouge pot. Jessica had waved it away. No pretence tonight. She knew herself to be passably pretty, not a great beauty. Alex had seen her waking after a night in a coach, wan, heavy-eyed and slightly dishevelled, so he was not going to be fooled now by a display of artifice. Besides, this had gone beyond batting lamp-blacked eyelashes to seduce a man.

'May I come in?' He took her nod for assent and came quietly across the stone floor to the sheepskin rug by her bed where he kicked off leather slippers. 'I have done my best to keep my feet warm for you,' he said with a smile. 'My father always used to offer guests a choice of dog to sleep on their bed to help prevent frozen toes.'

'Then in the absence of a wolfhound, perhaps you should get into bed before you freeze.' It was hardly a romantic conversation, but she found she had relaxed a little. This was her friend Alex as well as her husband. She could trust him to take care of her now.

'You are sure about this?' he asked, one hand just touching the bedcovers. 'You have had a difficult few days. I can leave you to sleep if you are tired.'

'No,' Jessica said firmly, wondering if he could feel the vibrations through his fingertips. It felt as though her whole body was shivering in anticipation of his touch.

'Candles alight? Or not?' Still he did not move.

She had seen statues, of course, and not all of them had fig leaves. Besides, the fashion was for very tight knitted evening breeches and a lady could not keep her eye line at collarbone level for an entire evening. She had seen how the male body was different from the female in other ways: the muscles, the triangle of shoulders and narrow hips, unlike the feminine hourglass. She was ready to see the reality in flesh tones and not cold white marble. But, somehow, she had never thought about his gaze on her. Darkness felt safe, but it also felt cowardly.

'Leave them,' she decided, wondering as she spoke just how much of her thoughts were showing on her face. If she was being transparent with her doubts and fears, at least Alex had the courtesy to remain unamused by her bashfulness.

He was tactful, too, in the way that he put back the bed-clothes before shrugging out of his robe and getting in to bed beside her. Even so she was startled. This was what it meant when men were said to be aroused, she realised.

Oh, my goodness.

Chapter Twenty-Two

Jessica braced herself for what was to come, but Alex appeared to be in no hurry. He came up on one elbow, leaning over her, and kissed her, gently, softly, then more firmly as she found herself reacting, opening to him and the caress of his tongue, the little nips of his teeth. She found when she responded he made sounds deep in his throat, encouraging, responsive noises. It was arousing. He liked kissing her and, she realised, she liked kissing him. It was hot and intimate and more than a little moist and she became aware that her whole body was involved.

There were interesting aches and she was certain her breasts were somehow larger and between her legs she was damp, which should be embarrassing, but which somehow wasn't.

She wriggled, which didn't help at all, but it made Alex growl, so it must have been the right thing to do. Emboldened, Jessica began to explore with her fingertips. Damp hair, springing under her touch, the shorter hairs prickling on the nape of his neck, the smooth skin over his shoulders and the muscles tensing in response to her moving hand.

Alex was exploring, too, one hand skimming down over her silk-covered flank, rucking up the long skirts of her nightgown. She lifted her hips as he pulled it upwards and that pressed her closer to him, which was exciting and made him tighten his hold, then the gown was over her head and gone and they were skin to skin.

No smooth marble here. Her breasts and thighs encountered rough hair, but she had no time to savour that sensation before Alex had begun caressing her breasts which, she realised, were thrusting shamelessly into his hands, then against his mouth as he took one nipple between his lips.

She might be an innocent, but it seemed her body knew exactly what was happening and what it wanted. He rolled the other nipple between finger and thumb and she moaned, twisting against the sensation building there and in her belly and lower, between her legs. She pressed them together, but that gave no relief and she almost sobbed when Alex slid one hand between her thighs and touched her there.

'Gently.' He lifted his mouth from her nipple and moved up the bed to kiss her again. 'Softly,' he said, pressing her thighs apart. 'Trust me.'

He shifted his weight over her and instinctively she moved until he was lodged between her thighs, pressing against the needy, aching core of her. She arched up against him and he thrust, slowly but steadily.

Jessica heard her own little cry, then he had covered her mouth with his again as he moved inexorably deeper.

It hurts, she thought, almost indignantly. *I do not like this.*

And then her body, ignoring soreness, ignoring her efforts to tense against the invasion, caught the rhythm of his thrusts and began to move, too, and either the discomfort vanished or it was swallowed up in wave after wave of pleasure. She had lost the power to tell.

She clung to the broad shoulders sheltering her, surrendered to the possession that seemed to be an equal thing—he was hers as she was his. If only this tightening, spiralling intensity would give her some relief.

And then the knot snapped and she heard herself cry out as Alex surged within her once more, and again, then he, too, went rigid. Then she was limp in his arms as he collapsed on to her and she stopped thinking and simply existed.

'Jessica?' She blinked awake out of a dream so intense, so startling, that for a moment she had no idea where she was. Then she saw Alex's face as he bent over her and remembered. And it had been no dream, it had been reality and now she was truly his wife. She smiled at him.

'Are you well?'

She considered the question. *'Well'* hardly seemed to cover it, but she did not have the vocabulary for all the things she felt, so she nodded. 'Yes, very well.' There was one question and she must ask it now while she was still half awake and had the courage. 'Is it always like that?'

'I hope so,' Alex said.

Now, what does that mean? she wondered as she pulled herself up against the pillows, aware that she was sore and rather sticky. This seemed to be a process where one simply had to leave inhibitions and embarrassment behind. He was not a virgin, she felt certain. Did it mean that it had been very good for him, too, and better than some experiences he had had? Perhaps it was because she was a virgin, though. Men appeared to set great store on virginity. Still, she would take reassurance from the compliment.

'What time is it?'

In answer the clock she had seen at the foot of the spiral stairs struck two, its echoes reverberating up the stone walls and through the heavy door.

'That clock will have to go,' Alex said as he got out of bed and shrugged on his robe. He did not bother to fasten it, although she noticed that he slid his feet into the leather slippers before venturing out on to the cold floor. He went into the dressing room and Jessica could hear him moving about and the splash of water. The partition wall, against which the bed head stood, was clearly only thin wood. Dressing rooms were apparently not a medieval luxury.

Alex came back holding a basin and set it down on the bedside table, then wrung out a cloth that was in it. 'Only just warm, I'm afraid,' he said, then threw back the covers and gently washed away the stickiness from her skin.

He had covered her before she had the chance to feel shy and, before she had the chance to say anything, he had carried the basin back and reappeared tying the belt of his robe. Lifting one candlestick from the chest against the wall, he blew out another, leaving her in the light of the one beside the bed.

'Sleep now.' He bent, kissed her forehead and was gone, leaving her wondering again if it had all been a dream.

But the disorder of the bedclothes on both sides, the dent in the mattress next to her, the lingering scent of citrus and warm man on the pillows and the unfamiliar aches in her body told her that this had been reality—the pain, the pleasure, the startling intimacy. The Duke of Malvern had finally made her his Duchess in every way.

The candle flame was flickering in the draughts that made layers of blankets necessary. Jessica blew it out, then snuggled down, pulling the covers high over her shoulders to cover her ears. She wished Alex had stayed, but fashionable husbands and wives slept apart, just as they tended to live their own separate lives, coming together to entertain or be entertained, to eat and to have sex.

It felt rather a lonely prospect, but she would adapt, she resolved as she began to drift down into sleep.

I wonder where Alex's rooms are?

Down the spiral steps of the turret, along a short passageway—cold radiating from its stone floor and walls—through a door so studded with metal that it seemed designed to hold out an army and into the room he had taken as his own when he had inherited the title.

Traditionally the Duke occupied the turret opposite the Duchess's tower, but Alex put comfort over tradition and had chosen this chamber. It was conveniently rectangular, the walls were panelled, the fireplace was of a medium size and the window was large. Once hung with tapestries and heavy curtains, the draughts had almost been vanquished. He could do something about finding Jessica a bedchamber as comfortable before she succumbed to a cold.

As he shed his robe he wondered whether it would be best if she moved in here with him while another room was prepared. Or he could offer to exchange rooms with her. Best to ask what she wanted, tempting though the thought was of a shared bed. He must remember that this was a marriage of mutual convenience, not a love match. Despite the wonderful surprise of Jessica's passionate response to his caresses, that was no reason to suppose that she would welcome the intimacy of shared rooms.

Clearly he had married a woman of natural sensuality and that was a true gift, but he must not presume on it, he reminded himself. How she would feel, and what she would think, tomorrow morning when she woke, sore and shy, remained to be seen. Even so, he was aware of an overwhelming sense of relief mingling with the lingering pleasure of their joining.

Tomorrow would bring the grief of funerals and the prospect of unremitting hard work, but now he knew he had a wife by his side who would support him with strength, intelligence and loyalty. Providing she felt she could trust him—and that morning had shown just how fragile that trust was.

As his body slipped into sleep Alex tried to clear his mind of the vague, unsettling doubts that lurked in its shadows. Tonight he would dream only good dreams.

She had fallen asleep wishing that Alex had stayed with her. Now, waking in the unfamiliar room, Jessica was glad that he had not.

Had they really done those things, felt those things? She huddled the bedcovers around her shoulders as she sat up, wondering where her nightgown had gone. Not that fine silk would be much help against the chill of a stone turret on a March morning in the Welsh Marches. Unattractive flannel seemed infinitely more attractive.

At breakfast she would have to preside over the table, pour tea and coffee, instruct the servants to replenish the toast and face her husband, all with the memory of their naked bodies intertwined, joined. And, of course, everyone in the castle would know what had happened last night.

The door opened to reveal Trotter. Someone else who knew, who might be speculating on how it had been. 'Good morning, Your Grace. I have brought hot chocolate.' She placed the tray next to the bed and fetched a folding screen that she set up between bed and door. 'The footmen are bringing the water for your bath, ma'am.'

Jessica murmured her thanks and sipped her chocolate while Trotter bustled around, just as she did every morning. She retrieved the nightgown from the floor, shook it out and laid it over her arm, quite as though finding garments scattered across the room was normal.

There was the sound of feet on the stairs, heavy breathing and considerable sloshing. It obviously took several trips to fill her bath.

Trotter produced her wrap and Jessica scurried into the dressing room. At least there the walls were panelled, the tiny window reduced the draughts and steam was rising from the bath.

The warm water was soothing, the fragrance of jasmine from the salts delicious, but Jessica felt a fleeting reluctance to wash the scent of last night from her skin.

Think about the day, not the night, or you will never be able to face him.

And today held funerals.

'Blacks this morning, Trotter. I hope we have something suitable in the luggage.'

'Yes, ma'am. The heavy luggage arrived in the early evening. Everything is pressed and I have laid out your jet parure.'

'Excellent. You will attend the services, I hope, and the other staff who came with us as well.'

'Certainly, ma'am. And I have ironed all the black neckcloths for the men and they have armbands as well.'

'Thank you, Trotter. I knew I could rely on you.'

'Yes, Your Grace. This might not be what we're used to, but we're all determined to stand by you.'

That sounded ominous, but Jessica told herself that if things seemed primitive above stairs, below they were probably medieval. That was all Trotter had meant.

Several years of managing her father's household stood her in good stead when Jessica sat down at the breakfast table.

The meal was served in a small room off the Great Hall, to her relief. It was shabby but comfortable and she was not surprised when Alex confessed that it was where he always ate unless he was entertaining.

He had risen and come to greet her with a kiss on the cheek when she had entered and pulled out her chair himself.

Jessica plunged into the familiar morning ritual and hoped that the colour on her cheeks would seem to be the result of entering a warm room, rather than shyness at confronting her husband.

'Tea or coffee?' she asked, trying not to recall what he looked like naked. What was she supposed to call him? Many of the married ladies she knew addressed their husband as Mr X or Sir Y, but surely she was not expected to call him *Your Grace* over the marmalade? *My dear*, at the other end of the spectrum of formality, seemed equally difficult.

Until Alex said, 'Coffee, if you please, my dear. Black.'

She managed that without splashing and Footman Two, the elderly one—she really must make an effort with everyone's names—carried it to the other end of the mercifully short table.

Food had been set out under covers on the sideboard. Pewter, she noticed, not silver.

'May I serve you, Your Grace?'

Brendon, that was it. 'Thank you, Peter. Some scrambled eggs and a rasher of bacon, please.'

Alex went to the sideboard himself and returned with a heaped plate of bacon, kidneys, eggs and fried potatoes. 'Your shopping expedition was clearly a success with Cook,' he remarked as he picked up his cutlery. 'James tells me that the staff are also very pleased with their provisions.'

'I am glad. At what time is the first service?' Jessica asked.

'At ten. Widow Jenkins had no family, so it will be followed immediately with that for the Bonds' baby.'

'Poor mite. Did it have a name?'

'It would have been baptised today. Michael Alexander. The second son. He had three sisters as well and fortunately all are safe and unharmed. I do not think that will make the family's grief any less, however.'

So often Jessica had heard people remark that the children of the working classes were so numerous that the parents could lose one or two without undue distress, as though poverty somehow dulled parental love. Some people spoke as though the poor had coarser feelings, felt less refined emotions than the upper classes. She was glad Alex did not share that unthinking prejudice and smiled at him warmly.

He returned the smile and she found her shyness lifting a little. 'Some more coffee, my dear?' she managed to say with what she felt was a perfectly steady voice.

Chapter Twenty-Three

It was a beautiful March morning when both coffins, one very light, the other very small, were carried together to the church with the mourners following on foot behind, the Widow Jenkins's old friends supporting the bereaved parents.

All the servants from the castle came, too, bringing up the rear, with Alex and Jessica walking in the middle of them.

'I hope you do not mind,' Alex said as they walked across the drawbridge and waited as those villagers who still had homes standing joined their disposed neighbours.

'No, of course not. This is the villagers' occasion. It would not be right to distract the Vicar from greeting them.'

Thank goodness it is not raining, she thought as they passed the sad ruins. *This is a dismal enough day as it is.*

Jessica was touched by the services, the Vicar's gentle sermon and the warmth the villagers showed to the bereaved and to each other. This had been a happy community and it would be again, she was certain, watching people. They were sad, but they were determined. When this day was over they would work to build again and they were clearly confident that they could rely on the Duke to help them do it.

* * *

Everyone had been invited back to the castle for the funeral meats and Jessica judged it time to take her courage in both hands and start introducing herself.

She joined Alex as he spoke gently to the bereaved parents and added her own quiet words to his, but did not linger. She did not want them to feel they had to be polite to the new Duchess.

It was easier mingling with the other villagers. They knew who she was by now, of course and she was taken aback by their warmth and the fact that they kept apologising for spoiling her honeymoon.

That was difficult to answer—she could hardly say she was enjoying herself—so she smiled and plunged into conversation, desperately trying to remember names and who did what. They were curious about her, too, and quite ready to ask questions, exclaiming in wonder at the news that her father was an ironmaster and that she came from Shropshire.

'Why, that's just next door,' one man said. 'I'm the smith and we use good Shropshire iron in the forge. Jeffrey Caudle.' He held out a gnarled hand, its scars and lines engraved with black despite its scrubbed cleanliness.

Jessica took it. 'It is good to shake the hand of a worker in iron, Mr Caudle. I have no doubt we will be calling on your skills once you are free to work on the castle.'

That was an important point, she remarked to Alex as they met at the long table serving food. 'My head is spinning with ideas for the castle that I would like to put to you, but we cannot take any resources away from the village.'

'I was thinking of establishing a group of parishioners so we can decide fairly on who has priority for the new housing as it is built and how they would like to see the village planned. And, even with all our skilled craftsmen employed, we will still need outside workers if we are to get this done quickly,' Alex said. 'All this means I need a secretary. Soon. The Vicar's eldest son is a possibility. He was employed by Lord Arnside, but he died recently so Goodson is out of a place. I will ask if he has accepted another position.'

'I need a secretary, too,' Jessica agreed. 'I will ask Papa if he knows of anyone. You need someone who has an understanding of society, I need one who is a down-to-earth practical man!'

Alex took her by the elbow and steered her towards a narrow arched doorway she had not noticed before. 'Give me your plate and glass and climb the stairs.'

They proved to be a short flight of spiral steps. Jessica emerged on to a wide ledge with a stone balustrade, with a view over the Great Hall below.

'The minstrels' gallery,' Alex said emerging, cautiously balancing two plates and both glasses. 'Shall we sit a while and eat our luncheon? There is something I want to say to you.'

'That sounds ominous,' she said, not entirely in jest. But she sat on a stone bench topped with a moth-eaten cushion.

'Not at all.' Alex looked out over the crowded room below and then back at her. 'I simply wanted to tell you that I cannot imagine that any woman I might have married could make a more ideal lady of the manor for this place than you, Jessica.'

'Oh.' She found herself without words. That was a serious compliment and it gave her reassurance that she was not an outsider blundering in to a small community. But, of all the things she had dreamt of hearing from Alex's lips, that was not one of them.

I desire you. I am happy being with you. I love you...
No, that was a wish too far.

As she thought it Jessica looked at her husband, at his profile as he had turned to look out over the Great Hall again and the realisation hit her.

I do love him.

It wasn't simply desire, it wasn't just liking, or admiration for his care for the people who relied on him. It was love.

How ironic. Here she was, married to a man she loved, a man whose own dream had been to marry for love. In her, he had not found that, although he had just told her she fulfilled her duties well and, last night, had surely proved that he desired her.

She felt tears welling and blinked them away, finding a smile as he turned to look at her. Alex smiled back and hoped welled up as well. Love grew. It might sometimes be instant, as he thought so romantically, but it could also unfurl slowly, like a bud. It had happened to her and it might happen to him.

'Thank you,' she said. 'That means a great deal.' There was too much else that she feared to blurt out, so she turned the conversation deliberately. 'Hasn't Cook made a wonderful spread?'

'Wait until you witness her Harvest Suppers.' Alex took a mouthful of a raised pie and chewed with obvious enjoyment, then raised his glass of cider. 'To the future.'

Jessica clinked her own glass against his. 'To the future.'

And, although it felt as though she was holding her breath for most of the time, the future did seem to be holding the prospect of happiness.

To Jessica's relief her father wrote from the iron works

to tell her that the crisis had been averted and relations with the rival firm of Bracegirdle and Sons had returned to normal. Her brothers and her father were still renegotiating their relationship, she suspected, but Joshua wrote to tell her that he was courting Prunella Wilson, the eldest daughter of a family of whom their father greatly approved and, it seemed, Ethan was taking an interest in her younger sister, Naomi.

'I suspect we may be travelling to Shropshire for a double wedding in month or so,' she said, passing the letter to Alex.

They had their desks together in what Alex was planning to be the library. Their new secretaries shared a room next door—Adam Goodson, the Vicar's son, and Charles Fielding, the young man who had been working in the ironwork's office and whom her father had picked out for her. The architect Alex had hired to design the new village had his desk there, too.

Now, a month after their wedding, she and Alex had settled into a harmonious working relationship, although that could not always be said of the architect. Mr Phelps had produced an elegant design of cottages either side of a street leading up to the drawbridge. Jessica had pointed out that half the cottages would have gardens facing north and Alex had refused point blank to have an ornate new Gothic-style gatehouse built on the village side of the drawbridge.

Eventually they had compromised on a crescent that gave everyone a good aspect for their garden. It also provided a suitably picturesque prospect for the architect, although Jessica still treasured the memory of closeting him with a delegation of village housewives who left him in no doubt about what was needed in the way of accommodation, wash houses, bake houses and privies. He had retaliated with a Gothic style of pigsty which made Alex laugh so much that he signed off the drawings without a protest.

The first families would be moving out to their new homes very soon and Jessica finally felt she could turn her attention to the castle itself. Beginning with her bedchamber. She really could not inflict those stairs on the footmen every time she wanted a bath.

'I'm glad things are settling down with your brothers,' Alex said, passing the sheet back. 'It must have been a concern for your father.'

'Yes. And now he has started fretting about the May Day parade—I keep sending him pages of notes and there is plenty of time yet.' Jessica sealed the letters she had been writing. 'I will see you later, I have some housekeeping tasks to attend to.'

He looked up and smiled at her and, as always now, something inside her warmed and softened. Alex was affectionate, passionate in bed at night, generous in sharing his thoughts and asking for her opinions. He was always pleasant and attentive during the day, although he never seemed to share her thought that a kiss, and what might follow, might be desirable, even in broad daylight. On the surface it seemed an ideal marriage, only beneath the surface did she feel its foundations tremble.

And that was her own fault, she recognised that. She was constantly waiting for Alex to realise that he had found what he had always looked for—a true love. He would not act on it, she was confident of that, she told herself. He was an honourable man. But she loved him now and that made it a deep and gnawing fear.

In all the weeks she had lived there, Jessica realised, she

had explored no further than the rooms they used daily, below stairs in the kitchens and the temporary accommodation for the displaced villagers. It was time she took possession of her new kingdom.

She closed the door behind her and set off to explore the castle thoroughly, floor by floor, staircase by staircase, beginning at the very top. At one point she thought she was lost and should have taken a thread to guide her back, like Theseus in the Minotaur's lair, but she finally discovered a door behind a mouldering tapestry and found herself on the minstrels' gallery.

It was clear that only the rooms on the first floor held any hope of being comfortable until a great deal more work was done. She had worried about the servants, but when Pitwick had arrived from London, he and Mrs Black assured her that the servants' wing, being a newer part of the castle, was quite adequate and had been properly maintained. Alex had looked after his staff's needs, even while the castle crumbled around him. New mattresses, bedding, rugs and curtains were all that were needed there and those had been ordered.

Now she began to explore the first floor, passing the stairs that led to her own turret. The first door that she opened was clearly Alex's bedchamber. She had never been into it, he had always come to her. It struck her now that somehow symbolised their marriage—apparently open and shared and yet with hidden corners, unopened doors on to private worlds of thought.

Now she stood on the threshold and took in the dark panelling, the heavy draperies at the windows and around the bed, the old Oriental carpets on the floor, which was boarded, not stone. Similar carpets had appeared in her chamber after that first night without her having to ask. In the corner was an opening which she supposed led to a dressing room.

It was gloomy and worn, but it was comfortable, she thought. Perhaps the other chambers on this floor were as good. She closed the door without entering and walked on.

Alex found her in the room next door, standing in the middle of the floor and rotating slowly. 'What on earth are you doing?'

He came in and closed the door. Jessica found herself unaccountably breathless.

'Finding myself a new bedchamber,' she said, determined not to be defensive. This was her home, too.

But there was something about Alex's smile that made her put up her chin and give him back stare for stare.

Chapter Twenty-Four

'Are you not comfortable where you are now the floor is covered? That turret has always been the Duchess's room,' Alex said, mildly enough.

'I am comfortable, and that chamber can be made more so, but the unfortunate footmen have to negotiate those stairs every time I want hot water and I expect Trotter to break her neck on them at any moment,' Jessica said. She spotted another door and went to open it, glad of something to break this odd tension. 'Oh, good, a dressing room.'

'It connects to mine next door.' Alex had followed her. She could not read his mood at all.

'I like this room,' Jessica said. 'But would you prefer that I choose another?' She meant it as a challenge and it sounded like one to her own ears. 'Does it bring me too close, liable to invade your privacy?'

'Not at all.' He sounded surprised that she might have thought so. 'It was simply that I did not want to treat you any differently from your predecessors. And this suite is even shabbier than mine.'

'Where did *your* predecessors sleep?' she asked.

'In the other turret—the one that is threatening to fall down.'

'Ah. Yes, I can see why you moved. I am afraid I put

comfort and convenience over centuries of tradition in this case. May I have this chamber, or shall I look for another?'

'I would very much like you to sleep here.' Alex backed out of the dressing room, drawing her with him. Now she had no difficulty understanding his thoughts. 'It is undoubtedly convenient—for many things.' He kept going, without looking back, until his legs met the edge of the bed and he fell back on to it, pulling Jessica with him so that she landed on top of him.

There was an ominous cracking sound, a cloud of dust and feathers and they sank deeply into the musty bedding, sneezing violently.

Jessica scrambled free and staggered off the bed. Alex was coughing and laughing too much to lever himself out, so she held out her hand and helped him to his feet.

'The webbing and base boards must have gone,' she said, fanning away the dust. 'Never mind, the frame is marvellous. Look at that carving, it must be very old. I'm sure it can be—'

She did not finish the sentence. Alex lifted her in his arms and backed her against the wall. 'We do not need a bed.'

Instinctively Jessica wrapped her legs around his hips and put her hands on his shoulders. She was not at all certain that one could make love standing up, but she was definitely willing to try and clung on. With his hands free, Alex was raising her skirts, tearing at the falls of his breeches.

It was inelegant, shocking, excitingly urgent. Jessica felt the familiar heat and knew her body was ready for him. More than ready and he knew it. There were none of the careful, considerate preparations that she was used to; this was a different man, one whose impatient desire for her was thrilling.

As Alex sheathed himself she heard her own cry, not of pain but of triumph. This was no mild, polite marital bedding, this was raw craving for *her*, the woman, not the wife.

It was untidy, uncomfortable, noisy and ended far too quickly. Jessica felt her own peak cresting as Alex surged deeply within her and his shout of triumph mingled with her own scream of pleasure.

Alex slumped against her, his whole body pinning hers to the panelling, his forehead resting against hers as they panted in unison.

'Bed,' he managed to mutter after a minute.

'But—'

'Mine.' With her still clinging to him, Alex shouldered open the dressing room door, then the connecting one into his and finally through into his bedchamber. They collapsed on to the bed in an intertwined, overheated sprawl.

'Should I apologise for that?' Alex asked when they finally found the strength to disentangle themselves and lie together against the pillows.

'Oh, no. It was wonderful.' Jessica rolled her shoulders experimentally. 'I do not think we should do that every day, but perhaps once a week? That would be very invigorating.'

'You might be invigorated, Wife. I am a shattered man,' Alex complained, but his look of smug masculine contentment gave the lie to his complaint.

'We were so loud, though,' Jessica said worriedly as she snuggled up against his shoulder. She ought to get up. Her stays were digging in, one garter seemed to have worked its way down to her ankle, and her skirts were rucked up beneath her in a way that would create frightful creases. 'Whatever will the servants think?'

'That we are newly wedded and some exuberance is to be expected.'

'We aren't *that* newly wedded,' Jessica protested. 'It is at least five weeks. Why, we are almost an old married couple.'

'That would explain my aching legs.' Alex finally got off the bed and began to strip off his disordered clothing. Then, naked, he started on hers. 'I am old and frail and therefore need reminding how to make love to my wife in a sedate and respectable manner.'

'Oh, you ridiculous man,' she said, laughing up at him as she pulled him down to the bed. 'You may make love to me in any manner you choose, provided you release me from this infernal corset.'

Alex did both in a manner that left Jessica limp with pleasure. Even the embarrassment of climbing into her crumpled gown and having to retreat to her turret and ring for Trotter did not dampen the warm glow that lingered.

It was sensual satisfaction, of course, but it was also hope. Alex was so affectionate, so passionate. Surely love was beginning to creep up on him, just as it had ambushed her?

Chapter Twenty-Five

'This is not April Fools' Day, is it?' Jessica demanded, waving a letter at Alex across the breakfast table.

'That was a week ago. Why, is someone playing a trick on you?' He put down his coffee cup and reached to take the letter from her. 'It appears to be from Miss Beech—or, no. Mrs Locksley, I see she is styling herself.' He glanced at the top of the sheet. 'In Edinburgh, no less.'

'I never thought they would do it,' Jessica said, twitching the letter back from his hand. 'I really thought that her nervousness and his respectability would put an end to that romance, especially when I have heard virtually nothing from her for weeks. So how did they manage it?'

She read the letter through. 'Oh, they were very clever. Jane enlisted the support of her aunt, who lives in Bath. The lady wrote to Mr Beech to say she was feeling unwell and begging for Jane's company. She would, she said, send her own travelling chaise to collect her. But how clever! Jane was collected with her luggage and without raising a whisper of suspicion. Locksley was waiting around the corner with his own bags, got in and they headed north.

'They married just north of Berwick at the toll booth… Staying with Locksley's cousin who is an Edinburgh lawyer… Expecting to return to London later this month so that he can take up a position as secretary with Lord Want-age who has shown great interest in promoting his ca-reer...' Jessica read out the highlights as she went. 'And Mr Beech promptly disinherited her, went down to Bath where he had a blazing row with his sister who promptly changed her own will to leave everything to Jane and not to her unsatisfactory nephew, who is the son of their other sis-ter and who happens to be a great favourite of Mr Beech.'

'Good for them,' Alex said, apparently losing interest in the Locksleys in favour of his sirloin steak and eggs.

'Which reminds me,' Jessica said. 'I must go up to Lon-don myself in two weeks, otherwise Papa is going to wear himself to a thread worrying about this May Day celebra-tion.'

That did catch Alex's attention again. 'I thought every-thing was organised. Why do you need to go? You have put in a great deal of work on this already.'

'It *is* organised, on paper. And my friends have been helping as well, but Papa has a touching faith in my abil-ity to ensure everything will go smoothly.'

'And so you will stay in London until May Day?'

'Yes, of course—I have not done all that work not to enjoy the results! Why, do you object?' Surely he was not going to prove to be the kind of husband who expected their wife to mind hearth and home and never venture out without him?

'Besides, everything is under control here,' she said. 'The building works are going well, almost all the villag-ers can expect to be rehoused by next month and there are no more decisions to be made about the rooms in the castle that we have agreed should be renovated first.'

'It is simply that I will miss you,' Alex said. 'I agree,

all is going well, but I do not think that both of us should be absent for several weeks until everyone is resettled and that wretched turret is finally stabilised. I have every expectation of it falling down the moment my back is turned.'

Jessica puzzled over his words. He would miss her—but for herself or because of her role in the work here?

'You could come up to town for a few days at the end of the month,' she suggested. 'Stay for May Day and then we can travel home together.' *Home.* That was another thing that gave her a warm glow of hope, the fact that she instinctively referred to the castle as her home now and that Alex treated her as an equal partner when decisions about it had to be made.

He nodded now as he finished his food and reached for his own post. 'Yes, that sounds ideal.'

They sat for a while in a silence punctuated only by the crack of breaking seals or the rustle of paper as they opened letters. Jessica had plenty of tradesmen's accounts to scan and pass to Charles Fielding. There was news from all her London friends, some notes from Hereford dressmakers and milliners soliciting custom and several fashionable magazines.

Alex's pile looked equally mixed, but when he had finished sorting it he passed her a handful of gilt-edged cards. 'The London Season is drawing to a close and families are returning to the Marches. We can expect more invitations soon, but these will give you a start in getting to know our neighbours.'

Jessica shuffled through the cards. 'They are all for the evening. Are the distances very great?' She was still coming to terms with living in the country—and in hilly country with poor roads, at that.

'Ten miles or so for the nearest. They will all be timed to coincide with the next full moon—you'll see that the dates are close together. If the weather turns bad, then it is expected that the host puts people up for the night. In fact, that largest card is for a full dress ball and we will be staying.'

'We will? It does not say so on the invitation.'

'The Hawksmoors are very old friends. I always stay, even though it is one of the closest estates.'

'Are they so very grand then, that they hold full dress balls the moment they return from London?' The card was certainly of very heavy stock, the gilding extensive, and it was engraved, not simply printed.

Jessica read it again with more attention.

The Viscount and Lady Hawksmoor

'He is only a viscount,' she said, pretending haughtiness.

'A wealthy one with a large family and a disposition to hospitality. Our families have always been very close.'

'But a mere lodge?' Jessica said, smiling at herself. 'See how haughty living in a castle has made me,' she added with a laugh.

'You will be surprised when you see it,' was all Alex would say. 'But it will definitely be the occasion for your very best ball gown and your sapphires.'

'A week's time to the full moon.' Jessica looked at the other cards. 'It is going to be a very busy few days.'

The Hawksmoor ball was the first of the parties and, Jessica suspected, the other hosts had deferred to them in setting their own dates.

She had expected to find them stiff and formal, arrogant

even about their status locally, especially when she saw the sprawling mansion that someone with either a wicked wit or a very humble nature had named The Lodge. But she could not have been more wrong. Alex had insisted that they arrive early so they could settle into their rooms and it was clear from their welcome that this was expected.

The Viscount wrung Alex's hand and slapped him on the back, his wife stood on tiptoe to kiss his cheek, then descended on Jessica in a flurry of lace to embrace her. 'We are so delighted that Alex has finally brought his bride home,' she said. 'Welcome to Herefordshire, my dear.'

Half a dozen people ranging from a girl still in the schoolroom to a mature man who was clearly his father's heir were introduced as, 'Some of the children, the rest will be at the ball. Do not bother with names yet, Jessica—we may call you Jessica? You will see, Alex—we have the entire family here to celebrate your return.'

It was said jovially, but Jessica thought there was some restraint in Lady Hawksmoor's smile that had not been there before. But she did not know the woman and she must have a great deal on her mind with the ball to prepare for.

Another carriage was arriving, so Alex said that he knew the way to his usual suite perfectly well and guided Jessica upstairs, followed by Trotter clutching her dressing case and James, who had been promoted to valet after admitting that he much preferred it to being a footman.

'You have your bath now, Your Grace,' Trotter said, bustling about. 'Oh, my! Look, they have *running water* in the dressing room!'

Jessica and Alex joined her to marvel over this luxury. Trotter opened another door. 'And a water closet. Why, this is a palace. Madam, could we—?'

Jessica seeing mild panic in Alex's eyes, shook her head firmly. 'One day. The castle plumbing must wait for more urgent work, Trotter. But how lovely—we will certainly take advantage of this while we have it.'

Trotter shooed Alex out, saying firmly that her lady needed to bathe and then rest, then returned, clearly determined that Jessica was going to outshine every other lady present, however magnificent this house might be.

Jessica gave in to being fussed over with good grace. After weeks of constantly feeling dusty and having nothing more glamorous to think about than upholstery colours at best, and drains at worst, she was rather looking forward to this party. Although whether she would be able to conjure up any conversation that did not involve guttering, structural underpinning or the design of piggeries remained to be seen.

Jessica and Alex joined the family and the eight other house guests for the early dinner before the other guests arrived. There were twenty-two seated at the long table, she realised, trying to get everyone straight in her head.

Lord and Lady Hawksmoor were at the head and foot of the table with Jessica as the ranking lady on her host's right and Alex by his hostess. Lord and Lady Henderson, The Right Reverend and Mrs Pomfret, Sir Aubrey and Lady Tanner and Mr and Mrs McDonald, she had managed to commit to memory. The family were more difficult. There were five unmarried siblings—three men and two young ladies and four married couples. There was also one empty seat in the middle of the side opposite her.

The family seemed determined not to draw attention to it. She saw Lady Hawksmoor's gaze flicker to the butler who gave what, in a lesser servant, would have been a shrug and her smile became more fixed.

Finally, just as their hostess nodded to the butler for service to begin, the door opened and a slight figure hurried to the vacant place. A footman pulled out the chair for her and she slid into it, keeping her head down. Ringlets the colour of mahogany fell from a central knot and effectively veiled her face from Jessica. The substantial bulk of the Rural Dean on one side, and one of the middle Hawksmoor sons on the other, served to screen her from everyone except those sitting opposite. Jessica did not think that Alex had even noticed her entrance, it had been so discreet.

It was intriguing, but none of her business. She concentrated on Lord Hawksmoor and managed not to let her conversation stray into asking his opinion on the design of pigsties.

When Lady Hawksmoor nodded to the ladies at the end of the meal and rose to lead them out to the drawing room, the latecomer slipped out behind other guests, leaving Jessica increasingly curious about why she was so shy.

Lady Hawksmoor left the ladies with the tea tray, which they all ignored, and excused herself to go to attend to the last-minute preparations for the ball.

'I will send word when enough people have gathered to make it worth coming through,' she said. 'Meanwhile, do make yourselves comfortable.'

They sat, distributing themselves around the various sofas and chairs which had been arranged into conversation groups. The mysterious young woman—she *was* young, Jessica was certain—retreated to a corner and took an embroidery frame from a basket by the chair.

Definitely a daughter of the house then. Perhaps the poor girl was simply very timid. 'Who is that?' she asked Mrs Pomfret. 'The young lady over there with the embroidery.'

The Rural Dean's wife pinched her lips disapprovingly and lowered her voice. 'Helena, now Lady Charlton. The third daughter.'

'She seems very shy,' Jessica ventured.

'I am only amazed that she is permitted to show her face at a social gathering.'

Jessica blinked. 'Indeed? Why is that?' She did not care if she was being nosy; now she had to know.

'She has left her husband,' Mrs Pomfret said, almost in a whisper. 'Can you imagine!'

'Well, I can imagine that she must have had a very powerful motive,' Jessica retorted. 'After all, she is here and not with another man, is she not?'

That caused a sharp intake of breath. 'A wife's place is with her husband. Announcing after barely a year of marriage that he does not suit you is no excuse for such a lack of duty.'

'Perhaps he was a drunk. Or violent towards her.'

'Lord Charlton is a most sober and upright gentleman. And it is a husband's right to chastise his wife.'

'Only if he is a brute,' Jessica retorted, loudly enough that several heads turned. 'Her parents have accepted her back,' she added more quietly.

'Very lax of them.' It was clear that only her title was saving Jessica from a sharp lecture on wifely behaviour.

'But charitable, do you not think?' Jessica said with a sweet smile and turned to Lady Tanner on her other side before she said something regrettable.

It was brave of Lady Charlton to attend the ball at all, she thought. It was rather too pointed to go across and intrude on her self-imposed solitude, but she would see if she could find the opportunity for a word once the ball was underway.

A footman came in and bowed. 'Ladies, her ladyship asks me to say that you may wish to join the guests in the ballroom at your convenience.' He went through to the dining room and could be heard delivering a similar message.

'I am going up to tidy my hair,' Lady Tanner said. 'Come with me?' She offered her arm, Jessica linked hers through it and they walked companionably to the stairs. Below they could hear the sound of many voices. 'The ballroom is off to one side in an annexe built in the last century,' Lady Tanner said. 'This is such a rabbit warren!'

'I am still finding my way around my own, much dustier warren,' Jessica confessed and they went off laughing to find their rooms. She was going to enjoy herself, she realised. After so much hard work she was going to dance in her husband's arms and give herself up to pleasure.

Chapter Twenty-Six

'In London this would be called a frightful squeeze,' Alex remarked half an hour later as they surveyed the crowded ballroom from a position in one corner of the room. 'I think every family of note for miles around is here.' He smiled down at her. 'Too much? These country affairs are rather more lively than town balls and we are out of practice.'

'It is less lively than a masquerade at the Pantheon,' she retorted, teasing, and laughed when he shuddered theatrically.

'Although that evening did have its moments,' he said. 'I can recall a certain dark alleyway off the Strand…'

'I seem to have forgotten that,' Jessica said demurely as a set came to its end and couples began to come off the dance floor, opening up a view across the corner to the wall. 'Perhaps you can remind me later. Alex?'

She had expected a response, but when she glanced up he was staring across to where a slender young woman with dark hair in ringlets stood quietly behind a group of gilt chairs.

It must be the late arrival at the dinner table, Lady Charlton, Jessica realised and saw in the next moment that she was very beautiful indeed, with high cheekbones, dark eyes, a sensuous mouth and those glossy ringlets.

'That is Lady Charlton,' she said sharply, and Alex started, as though she had shaken him awake.

'Charlton? Little Nella?' He still had not taken his eyes off her.

'I thought you knew them all.'

'I do, but I do not think I have seen Helena since she was about sixteen—all eyes and mouth too large for her face and hair always in tangles and as skinny as a rake,' he said without looking away. 'They sent her off to look after her grandmother when the old lady had a stroke, I think.'

'Did you not attend her wedding?'

'No. That was last year and I was not here for some reason... I forget why now.'

He looked to Jessica as though he had probably forgotten his own name as well. She was beginning to have a very bad feeling about this.

'She has left her husband,' she said tartly.

She is a married woman.

That did get his attention. 'Do you know why?'

'No.' Why did she say that? Now he was bound to go and ask the woman. *Little Nella.* A girl he had known for years and had clearly been fond of. Surely that was why he looked poleaxed now—the discovery that the plain little chit was now a beauty. That was all it was. Nothing else. *Nothing else.*

'Excuse me,' Alex said vaguely and started to make his way around the corner of the dance floor to where Lady Charlton stood.

She could, of course, go with him, ask to be introduced to an old friend of the family. Or she could stand rooted to the spot while her husband reached Lady Charlton and spoke and she turned and reached out a hand to him. Alex took it in his and she clung to it, looking up into his face and talking rapidly and urgently.

Jessica watched as Alex lifted his free hand and touched Lady Charlton gently on the cheek, saw the other woman turn her face into his palm, caught the glint of a tear as Alex moved so that he was sheltering her from the room.

She is distressed...he has known her since she was a child...his instinct is to protect...

The excuses and explanations ran through her head and all the time the voice of cold reason said, *This is what he always expected and you always dreaded. This is the* coup de foudre. *He has fallen in love.*

'Are you quite well, Your Grace?'

Jessica turned, suddenly dizzy, and realised that she must have been holding her breath. Around her guests moved and talked and laughed and a new set was forming. She had been unaware of any of it.

A gentleman stood beside her, his expression concerned. She knew him, he had been at dinner. Her mind was blank.

'Just a little light-headed,' she managed. 'The heat, you know.'

'Allow me to find you a seat.' He took her by the arm and steered her towards the nearest chair. 'May I fetch you something to drink, Duchess?'

She remembered his name as she sat. Thank goodness, her wits were returning. 'Thank you so much, Lord Henderson. I will be quite myself in a moment,' she said firmly and smiled and he gave a little bow and, mercifully, went away.

Her fan, with its ebony sticks and its hand-painted leaf, gave her some privacy as she fluttered it, keeping it close to her face. She looked across and saw, through the weaving pattern of dancers, glimpses of Alex's back turned squarely to the room.

They would have a great deal to catch up on, she thought, striving to keep calm. And he would want to give Lady Charlton time to compose herself. She would sit here where he had left her while this set came to its conclusion. Alex had asked for the next one, teasing her as he had pencilled it in on her card—the first opportunity to waltz with his wife—so he would come back then.

The final dance ended and, as the dancers left the floor, going this way and that, stopping to chat, she lost sight of Alex. When she could see clearly, he had gone and so had Lady Charlton whose seat was occupied by a flushed young woman fanning herself vigorously and laughing rather too loudly with her companion.

There, she told herself. *He is coming to claim you for the next dance.*

Only, he did not. Everyone was on the floor, she could see the string players in the orchestra lifting their bows, and there was still no sign of Alex.

'May I have the pleasure, Duchess?' It was one of the older Hawksmoor sons.

'Of course. I would be delighted.'

Jessica wished she could recall his name, but he danced well, sweeping her elegantly around the room and maintaining just the right level of conversation. Years of training in deportment helped her outward composure and having to think about answering him, as well as minding her steps, was calming.

Then she saw them. Alex was waltzing with Lady Charlton, holding her close, his head bent to listen as she talked.

'Oh, I am so sorry. Did I step on your toe?' She had stumbled, but her partner held her firmly and kept the rhythm.

'Quite all right.'

'Is that your sister dancing with my…dancing with the Duke? Lady Charlton, is it not?'

He glanced across and frowned. 'Yes. She is not quite herself at the moment. I am glad Demeral has persuaded her to dance.'

'She is very beautiful.' A sweeping turn took them out of sight.

'Yes.' Mr Hawksmoor chuckled. 'Helena was rather a late developer.'

'And is she married?' Jessica persisted, striving to sound as though she was making polite conversation. 'I imagine she must have been a great success at her come-out.'

'To Viscount Charlton, the heir of the Earl of Strickland.' His smile was definitely forced as he spoke. No amusement now.

'I have never met him. Is he here tonight?'

'No.' That was curt.

'What a very fine ballroom this is,' Jessica said brightly. Clearly time for a change of subject and her spinning brain was incapable of coming up with anything more original.

'Indeed. We are most fortunate.' Mr Hawksmoor had relaxed again.

Somehow Jessica got though that set and the ones that followed. Alex reappeared—alone—to take her in to supper and she managed to smile brightly and not to make any mention of missed dances, or of Lady Charlton.

If she had not seen him with the other she would not have known anything was wrong, but now she was alert to the slightest change in him.

Eventually she could not bear it any longer. 'Lady Charlton appeared upset,' she remarked lightly, pretending indecision over the choice of savouries on her plate. 'But I saw you waltzing, so you obviously lifted her mood.'

'It is hardly a question of mood,' Alex said, lowering his voice. He looked sombre. 'She tells me that her husband is a brute, frequently in his cups and unfaithful into the bargain.'

'That is dreadful,' Jessica said and meant it. A married woman was, effectively, the property of her husband and had few rights. Lady Charlton's flight to her family might be frowned on by society, but was completely understandable. At least they had taken her in: Jessica had heard of families where the door could have been slammed in the face of a daughter trying to leave her husband.

But Helena had her large, wealthy and influential family. She did not need Jessica's husband, except as a friend.

'What will happen to her now?' Divorce was prohibitively expensive, involved an Act of Parliament and, as far as Jessica was aware, no woman had ever managed to divorce her husband. 'Are there children?' They would legally have to remain with their father, another crushing blow to the distressed wife.

'No, thank goodness. I assume she will stay here while her father negotiates a separation with Charlton who may, eventually, divorce her. But neither of them can remarry if that happens—this will deprive Charlton of an heir.'

'Serves him right,' Jessica muttered.

Alex gave a grunt of agreement. 'But it will not make him any easier to deal with. He will want her back.'

'A horrible situation. Still, I am sure the good wishes of old friends such as yourself will help raise her spirits,' she said with determined cheerfulness and swallowed her champagne.

Something in her tone must have struck him as false because Alex glanced at her, a slight frown on his face. 'I hope so.' His expression lightened. 'She is not the girl I recall from our childhood. Seeing Helena was quite a...a revelation.'

I could see that.

Jessica told herself that jealousy was unattractive, that it was feeble to feel so insecure and that it was simply Alex's gallant nature and warm heart that had drawn him to Lady Charlton.

'That was a deep sigh,' he remarked.

'I was simply making a resolution. Please pass me one of those cheesecakes.'

They retired well into the small hours, but Jessica lay awake, unable to sleep. It seemed Alex was not going to come to her bed. Was that because he was tired and was already sleeping or because he was lying awake thinking about the lovely Lady Charlton? Was he facing the fact that he had fallen in love, as he had always expected he would?

If he had, she was sure he would pretend it had not happened, would not let her see what had occurred. And he would not act on his feelings. At least, she was almost certain of that. Alex was a gentleman, a man of honour. And he was kind. He would not want to hurt her. He had been angry when he had realised she thought he had deceived her over the fire and the reason for his proposal. He had expected her trust and she had failed to give it. Now she must remember that. If only that small nagging ache of doubt would leave her.

* * *

There was no sign of Alex the next morning when she came down for breakfast to find the other house guests and the family as heavy-eyed as she was. But then, there were only half the places at the table occupied.

He might still be sleeping, or have ordered a tray in his room or gone out for a walk to clear his head. But that meant nothing. They were expected to remain for a light luncheon before travelling home, so there was really no need for Alex to be up and about yet.

There was no sign of Lady Charlton either.

After she had managed to finish a slice of toast and two cups of tea Jessica went upstairs. She would go for a walk, she decided, asking Trotter for a bonnet and warm cloak. But on her way out she would just look in on Alex.

His bedchamber was empty. She walked in to the dressing room and made James jump. 'I'm sorry, I was wondering whether His Grace was coming down for breakfast.'

'He was up at daybreak, Your Grace,' the valet said, his arms full of the previous night's clothing. 'I haven't seen him since.'

'I expect he has gone for a walk, which is what I am about to do.' She smiled and made her way downstairs. Alex was up early every morning at the castle and it had probably become such a habit that lying in bed once awake was not restful.

A footman directed her to the nearest door to reach the gardens and she stepped out into sunshine. It was cool and the air was damp, but there was a scent in the air that held the promise of spring and of growing things, of a brown world turning green again.

A lawn stretched out in front of her, ending in a ha-ha

which allowed the view to be open to the parkland beyond. Paths led off from the terrace left and right and on a whim she took the left-hand one. It led to a shrubbery, not so overgrown as to be dismal, and wound its way between artfully placed shrubs and small trees. In gaps between the branches she could see the roof of what must be a summerhouse of some kind and made her way towards it, walking quietly in the hope of seeing wildlife. Rabbits, perhaps, or a squirrel or even deer.

She was almost on the little building now. As she approached it from the side it appeared to be an open-fronted shelter. It was positioned so that it looked out over an open glade with a pond in the centre and would, once the weather was warm, be a charming place for a picnic.

The path led up to it and then turned to follow its wall around to the front. Jessica stopped and looked at how it had been built, thinking it would be simple enough to have one made for the castle grounds. There was a perfect spot—

'But he will find me if I go with you,' a woman said.

Jessica froze, her hand resting on the lapped boards of the hut.

'No one need know. I can get you away in secret, find you a house in some small town. You can become a widow.' That was Alex's voice. Jessica's fingers cramped on the rough wood. 'There are plenty of market towns near London where you could be quite unknown.'

'I would know nobody. I would be alone.' The woman's voice cracked. She was crying.

'You would have me,' Alex said, his voice warm. 'You would always have me, Helena.'

Chapter Twenty-Seven

'Swear you would tell nobody? Your wife will guess, surely?' the woman said.

'No,' Alex said. 'No, Jessica trusts me.' There was regret in his voice, she could hear it even through the buzzing in her head that warned her that any moment she might faint.

Jessica sat down abruptly on the damp ground, but Alex's voice went on relentlessly. 'Ours was not a love match for her, you see. And she believes that I had given up on my foolish dream of falling for someone, heart and soul, so she will not be suspicious.'

'But she was wrong.'

'She was wrong,' Alex said. 'But how can I tell her that?'

Silence, the sound of soft weeping. Then he said, 'Don't cry, Helena.'

'Then kiss me.'

'Oh, Helena.' There was a world of feeling in Alex's voice.

It brought Jessica to her feet. She took a step towards the front of the shelter. She would confront them…

But she had married Alex knowing this might happen one day. Many men kept their mistresses in a discreet house somewhere convenient and their wives never knew, or perhaps did and chose not to confront the situation.

She should never have agreed to marry him without deciding what she would do if this happened, and now it had and the man she loved...loved another.

How did one remain a complacent wife in the face of this? How did you welcome your husband into your bed knowing he might have lain with another woman, the one he loved, only hours before?

Walk away. Walk away now, before this can become any worse than it already is.

Jessica began to walk back the way she had come, dry-eyed, sick at heart, her mind in turmoil.

Alex shook his head ruefully. Kissing away tears as he had done when they were both children was not going to help now, however effective his old nanny's advice for soothing childish upsets had been.

But he dropped a kiss on to each of Helena's tear-soaked eyelids even so and tightened his arm around her shoulders in a fierce hug.

'You must stay here and decide what you will need to take with you,' he said when Helena's tears had finally dried and she was sitting upright, a look of determination replacing the hopelessness on her face. 'How likely is your husband to come and try to remove you, do you think?'

'He will not come. Papa wrote and told him that I am with the family and that I will stay under this roof for as long as I want. He is very upset, very disapproving but, when I told him that Charlton had struck me, he said nothing more about me returning to him. He will not hear of me living anywhere else, though. He thinks that by hiding me away here it will somehow hide the scandal, too.'

'In that case you are safe for a few weeks. It will take

me a while to find the right house for you.' And a while to raise the money for it. This was not something he could use Jessica's money for, even though she would never know.

'You must not pay for it,' Helena said, as though reading his thoughts. 'I have my diamonds, left to me by my great-aunt. They are worth a lot of money, enough for a house, I know, because Mama told me that when I inherited them. But they are quite hideous, I never wear them and they are here, in the safe in my dressing room.'

She broke off and sat, clearly thinking. 'I will not give them to you to sell, because they might be traced back to you and that could put you in a most difficult position. But Mr Evers, our Vicar, is travelling up to London next week. I will give them to him, parcelled up, and let him think it is some simple piece that I want Rundell, Bridge & Rundell to clean and reset.

'I will enclose a note saying that I want to sell them. They know they are mine because they cleaned them when I inherited the set.'

Planning had improved her spirits, Alex could see. She was determined now that she could see a way to escape and the means to do it.

'Then I will write when I have found a suitable house. I have to go up to London soon, so I can look at possibilities then. We can agree a date and I will send a hired carriage to collect you. But, Helena, I must tell Jessica about this, I cannot keep secrets from her. And I may have to tell Robert and Anna as the plan to get you away develops but you know you can trust them.' It would need more subterfuge than that, of course—several changes of vehicle, for a start. But that could be dealt with nearer the time.

'Oh, thank you. I understand about Jessica and of course

I know the Chandlers would help.' Helena's eyes were pink with weeping and so was her nose, but she was still the most beautiful woman he had ever seen.

And, he recognised very clearly, she meant nothing to him beyond an old friend who desperately needed help. She would never be more lovely to him than Jessica. Jessica, whom he loved and who gave him no hint that her feelings for him might be turning into love.

But she was his and they were together. There was always hope.

'You go back first,' he said to Helena. 'They will be wondering where you are. I will go for a walk and come back from a quite different direction.'

He sat for a while, wishing he could tell Jessica about this, ask for her help. But Helena had become almost hysterical when he had suggested it and he had sworn to tell no one else in order to calm her.

There were things he could do immediately, he decided. He would write to his London lawyers, tell them he had to find a home for a distant relative, respectable but in straitened circumstances. Then, when he joined Jessica in London for May Day, he would have time to inspect what they had found.

After a while he stood up and stretched and strolled out across the glade, following a winding path that, if he remembered rightly, led down to the river bank. From there he could cut across a meadow, circle around to the other side of the house and no one would know he had been with Helena.

Over an hour later Alex entered the hall through a side door and encountered his host.

'Ah, there you are, Demeral.' Lord Hawksmoor looked concerned.

'I went for a walk. Is there a problem?'

'Your wife has left—she said she must get back to the castle urgently.'

'Had a message come?'

'No, although that only struck us after she had left. Perhaps she had recalled something.'

'How strange.' Alex thought back to the previous evening. Now he came to think about it, Jessica had seemed somewhat subdued, brittle almost. He had put it down to tiredness and the impact of the Hawksmoors, who tended to be somewhat overwhelming until one got to know them. 'She will have taken the carriage, I suppose.'

'Yes. I must say she seemed rather distracted—I expect she intends to send it back for you. Or you can borrow a horse and gig from the stables if you don't want to wait.'

Odder and odder. 'Thank you, I'll do that. One of the grooms can return it tomorrow. Excuse me, I'll get my man to pack.'

There would be a good reason, of course. Jessica would not leave her hosts so abruptly, let alone him, without a word. Was she feeling unwell? An unpleasant sense of foreboding gripped him and he tried to shake it off as he walked into his bedchamber.

'We need to leave right away, James.' Then he saw the valet was just closing his valises.

'Yes, Your Grace. I intimated as much from the departure of Her Grace and Miss Trotter. Her Grace left a note.'

Good. That would explain everything. It was sealed with a wafer which Alex tore open. He read what it said, then sat down on the bed to read it again because his legs no longer seemed able to support him.

The second time the words sank in and made horrible sense.

I think I realised as soon as I saw you set eyes upon her that you recognised Lady Charlton as the one you had been waiting for, hoping for. I thought I was prepared for this, for you finding your true love, but it seems I need time to accustom myself.

Please do not come after me. I do not want this to become some hideous confrontation when we both will say things we will regret one day.

I married you knowing this might happen and knowing that, when it did, I must do my duty as Duchess of Malvern. I will return. Of course I will. I do not break my promises and I know, of course, that you can never marry her and nor can she give you an heir. But for now, do not ask it of me. I do not think I could bear it.

Jessica

The anger that flared through him shook Alex almost as much as the letter that he held crumpled in his hand.

On the evidence of his concern for Helena last night Jessica had decided that he had fallen in love with the woman? She had reacted to his distraction and his neglect of her by leaping to the conclusion that he would be unfaithful to her?

How could she have so little faith in him? But she had shown that she did not trust him when she had assumed that he had hidden the destruction at the castle from her in order to win her wealth.

It hurt this badly because he loved her; he retained enough control to recognise that. And she did not love him. She thought she was the injured party here when, in fact, he was the one who, because of his concern for an old friend, was the one who had been abandoned. Blamed.

Alex strode out of the room and into the bedchamber she had occupied, managing not to slam the door behind him. He could not let James see his emotions or sense that anything was amiss with the marriage.

He flung open the window and stood, hands on the sill, breathing in the cool air until his heart rate returned to something like normal and he could think straight.

I love her.

He loved his wife. This was not friendship, or desire or any other form of attraction that he could think of. He was in love and he loved. How had that happened? How could he have been so wrong about himself and his emotions? But this had to be love because, surely, nothing else could hurt so savagely?

He had been wrong all along—love *could* grow, slowly, subtly. It had developed as he learned to know Jessica, as she had become as essential to him as breathing. And, obsessed with the idea of recognising his one true love, he had not realised what the affection and desire and feelings of warmth and closeness meant as they wove their way into his heart and mind.

After a minute or so he found he could begin to think through what he must do. He would go back to the castle and he would wait. Wait until Jessica came back. She would do; he trusted her word, as, it seemed, she did not trust his. But he would not write—this was not something that could be mended with words on paper.

Then, somehow, they must make this marriage work, even if its public face was a mask fit for the Pantheon masquerade, because if she had so little trust in him, he would never believe protestations of love—not after this.

It was a plan, but one that held none of the hope he had experienced only a few hours before.

Jessica arrived back in London three days later. She had deliberately not forced the pace, not wanting Trotter, or the driver and grooms, to realise that she was leaving in such circumstances. They believed what she had told them, that her father needed her and she was concerned about him, so had decided to return a little earlier than planned. Also, she informed Trotter, as the work was proceeding so well on the castle, she thought that it was time to improve things at the town house.

Inside she felt as though she was bleeding. It was her own fault, of course. Once she realised that she loved Alex the last thing she should have done was to marry him, risking this heartbreak.

And somewhere beside the pain there was anger. He had been furious that she had not trusted him when they arrived at the castle to find the smoking ruins of the village and she had chastised herself for that lack of trust. She had believed that, even if he did fall in love with another woman he would be too much a gentleman to act on it.

Now she knew he would act. He would kiss his true love, he would plan to set her up in a convenient house where he could visit her. He would make her his mistress. Perhaps she already was. Perhaps on the night of the ball he had not come to his wife's bed because he was weary, but because he was in Lady Charlton's.

Why had she not read her own future in that moment when Miss Fawcett had thrown herself into the arms of Lord Branscombe and they had realised that a childhood friendship had blossomed into something else entirely?

Her father greeted her with delight, but expressed concern about the dark circles under her eyes. 'You have lost weight,' he accused, ringing for hot chocolate and cake.

'It is tiring, the work on the castle and village,' Jessica explained. 'I thought London would make a pleasant change. Alex, however, will probably be unable to spare the time. He takes his responsibilities very seriously.'

Except those to his wife.

Chapter Twenty-Eight

'I am so excited about May Day. Only a week left!' Belinda Newlyn was curled up in the corner of the sofa, nibbling biscuits. 'I can hardly wait to see the results of all our hard work. And our beaux have been a great help, too, of course.'

'And now we have decided on the final order of the floats, which is really the last major decision, I think,' Anthea said.

Jessica made herself sit up and pay attention. Nine days since she had overheard Alex and Helena in the shrubbery. A week in London presenting a cheerful face to her father and her friends. Thank heavens for the May Day planning: at least it gave her mind something to occupy it instead of spinning like a dog in a turnspit wheel.

'Oh, and we do need chimney sweeps after all, because the ironmongers decided to have a float with their various domestic equipment like dust pans and fire irons and coal scuttles, so there will be a float with a hearth and a sweep and some of the girls dressed as maids. But it is all right because our housekeeper asked our sweep and he is organising that.'

'The other floats will be as we agreed,' Lucinda chimed in, making check marks on a list. 'There's the tower of greenery with the maiden at the top and the knight in armour—signifying ironmongery generally—riding along-side and the one with flowers and our pretend milkmaids who will all have various metal items of equipment—cream skimmers and pails and bowls and so forth.'

'What about the apprentices?' Anthea asked. The management of a mob of over-excited youths had been worrying all of them. They were to be dressed as spirits of the forest and would caper alongside the floats with pipes and drums.

'Papa says that they will be supervised by the journey-men who, one can only hope, are old enough to keep some kind of order. The Ironmongers themselves, those who feel able to, will process behind.'

'Apparently the sweeps' boys run riot at May Day,' Belinda added. 'They dress up as girls, toss brick dust about and bang their brushes and shovels. We do not have to do anything about those—they will plague everyone equally, I believe!'

'I have a letter here to Papa from the Master of the Guild giving the time for everything to assemble in the yard at Ironmongers' Hall,' Jessica reported. 'Have you all decided whether you want to take part?'

'Goodness, yes,' Belinda said. 'We are all joining in as milkmaids and Major Rowlands has agreed to be the knight in armour because his horse is accustomed to bat-tle so will not be alarmed at the noise. Will you be with us on the float, Jessica? Or is it too much of a romp now you are a duchess?'

Jessica's stomach gave the unpleasant lurch that it pro-duced whenever she was reminded of her marriage. 'Um, I had not thought. No, I had better be with Papa—he wants to be in the yard to make certain everything sets off prop-erly and then we were going to take the carriage by back streets to where he is joining a party with a large balcony overlooking the route.'

'But you will join us in Green Park at dawn?' Lucinda asked. 'We are going to bathe our faces in the dew which, I am reliably informed by our housekeeper, will render us ravishingly beautiful.'

'You *are* ravishingly beautiful, dear,' Belinda teased. 'Or so a certain viscount believes.'

Lady Lucinda threw a cushion at her friend. 'And a certain baronet thinks the same about you.'

'Spring is in the air, two of us are married and we are all in love. Isn't it wonderful?' Belinda caught the cushion.

'Wonderful,' Jessica echoed, her smile fixed firmly in place. Where was Alex? There had been no reply to her note and there was no sign of him in London, certainly not at his town house. She had made quite certain that the staff there knew where she was and that they must send all post around to Adam Street the moment it arrived.

Was he with Lady Charlton, or had he simply stayed at the castle, too angry with her for leaving to communicate in any way? Or was he too ashamed of himself to face her? No, it could not be that. Whatever Alex's faults, cowardice was not one of them.

Had she done the right thing, leaving? It felt more and more difficult to contemplate returning with each day that passed. But she must, it was her duty. She was the Duchess, people depended on her and she had made vows which she took very seriously, even if her husband did not.

Alex paced along as much of the battlements as he could before the way was blocked with scaffolding poles, buckets of lime mortar and piles of stone. The masons had taken one look at his expression and had moved to the far end where they were working with none of their usual jests and whistling. Even the sharp orders thrown at the apprentices were muted.

One week until May Day. He should be travelling up to London today, as they had agreed. He had resolved not to go, but now he wondered. What would he find if he did? A wife consumed by jealousy? He wondered again how he could explain what had happened and be believed.

Yes, he had been taken aback at the sight of Helena, his childhood friend, grown up and beautiful, and he would have come back to Jessica immediately and apologised, laughing at himself for his instinctive male reaction.

But he had seen the misery in Helena's eyes and he could no more have walked away from that than he could from an animal lying injured in the road. Yes, he had been so absorbed in Helena's story and in trying to cheer her that he had forgotten a dance with Jessica—and had not remembered that until after he had read her letter—but surely husbands committed worse crimes than that, with only a china ornament thrown at their heads in retribution?

So was it jealousy? Or did Jessica, after all, care more for him than he thought? Had he been blind, or was this flickering flame of hope false?

He passed back, kicking shards of stone out of his path as he went. The masons' hammers were like an echo of his churning thoughts.

I love her. She has left me. She does not trust me. I love her. Could she possibly, after all, care for me?

There was no one he could talk to about this, because it would feel like a betrayal of Jessica. Even if he could, his closest friends were at the Lodge and the very nature of the split meant that any mention of it was impossible in the Hawksmoor household.

Robert and Anna were the only people he felt he could trust with this and they were in London. And so was Jessica.

The anger had left him now, replaced with confusion and a dull ache under his breastbone which, if he was a fanciful romantic, he might call a broken heart. But he was no longer a romantic, daydreaming of love. He was a man in love with his wife and, he realised suddenly, he would do anything to get her back.

To hell with his hurt feelings, with the feeling of betrayal that Jessica did not trust him, although that still stung. He was her husband and he loved her.

And I never told her.

Alex stopped dead, one hand on the ring handle of the tower door. He had never risked telling her he loved her. 'Coward,' he said now, out loud. What had stopped him? The fear that she would pity him and be kind about it? The risk of looking a fool for his romantic theories of love at first sight when it had happened to him so slowly, so gently, that he had hardly realised what was happening?

She did not know and all she had seen was what he had said he wanted to happen—a glimpse of someone across a room and, apparently, her husband falling for a lovely woman.

The handle turned in his hand and he was halfway down the spiral stairs before he realised what he was doing. 'James!' he yelled as he reached the first floor.

'Your Grace?' The valet shot out of the bedchamber, his hands full of neckcloths.

'Pack. I am going to London.'

'Now, Your Grace? Only it is three in the afternoon and—'

'Now.' Alex took the main stairs two at a time. 'Goodson!'

The secretary appeared. 'Sir?'

'We leave as soon as bags can be packed. Ah, Pitwick, have the carriage brought round. Two drivers, two grooms. I am leaving for London immediately.'

The staff scattered, leaving Alex standing in the middle of the Great Hall feeling, he realised, more like himself than he had since the morning after the ball. Was this what it was like going in to battle once the decision had been made to charge? Everything became quite clear-cut—live or die. Or, in this case, win or lose.

He was still standing there when Goodson came and deposited a portable writing slope and a portfolio of papers on the table, then ran for the stairs.

An hour later they were on the road, a large hamper of food on the seat beside James, Goodson sorting papers beside Alex and a spare driver and groom outside trying to snatch some rest before they took over for the next stage.

'I have brought the correspondence relating to that house you wished to acquire, sir. Do you wish to review it now?'

Alex stared at him, then realised what he was talking about. 'No, that doesn't matter now.' He would think about that later. Helena was safe where she was—all he had room to worry about was Jessica.

As Alex had expected, Jessica was not at the London house when they arrived fifteen hours after they had left. That did not prevent the sharp stab of disappointment.

'Her Grace is at her father's house, Your Grace,' Cook reported. She was more than a little flustered by the arrival on the doorstep of her employer, unannounced and unshaven. 'She is helping him with this May Day affair, sir, but she said to send all the post around to her.' She turned to shout down the back stairs. 'Milly! Hot water for His Grace and the gentleman.'

'Mr Goodson, my secretary,' Alex said, stripping off his greatcoat. 'James, you go and get some food and sleep. You, too, Goodson.' It was tempting to simply take the coach and driver to Adam Street, but he knew that would be a mistake.

A weary, dirty, unshaven husband arriving without warning and announcing that he loved her was no way to court a wife. He needed his wits about him, every single one that he could muster.

'I will bathe, shave and I would welcome some food, Mrs Dobson. Anything you can prepare easily. Then I shall rest. I shall be out this evening.' Not to Adam Street, but to the Chandlers' house and, he fervently hoped, the chance to work out just what had gone so very wrong with his marriage.

'Alex! What a lovely surprise. Come in.' Anna appeared in the hallway behind their footman and waved him through to the drawing room.

'Are you free this evening?' He kissed her cheek, then shook hands with Robert who had put down a book and got to his feet. It had only just occurred to him that they might be out, or entertaining.

'We are, unless a patient staggers thought the door,' Robert said. 'Sit down. You look as though you need a stiff drink.'

'Food, rather, I would say.' Anna tugged the bell pull and when the footman appeared, told him to tell Cook they had one more for dinner. 'Roast chicken,' she said when the man had left. 'That can stretch to any number of guests. What is wrong?' she added when they were all sitting down.

'I am tired. I did the journey from Herefordshire without stopping except to change horses.'

'I can see that.' Anna did not exactly roll her eyes, but it was close. 'Jessica is in town and has been for over a week. She has not called and when I saw her by chance in the street I thought she looked like a woman who was doing a great deal of weeping into her pillow, despite the very brave face she was showing to the friends who were with her. Now here you are. And you are with us, not at home, not at her father's house. You are looking, I have to say, like death warmed over.'

'Thank you for that description,' Alex said. 'It makes me feel so much better.'

'Then eat, drink a little and then talk,' Robert said as the door opened and dinner was announced.

Onion soup, roast chicken washed down with two glasses of good claret and lemon tart to follow certainly stopped him feeling quite so light-headed. Robert and Anna's questions when they were back in the drawing room were sufficiently sharp to complete his revival.

'What happened?' Anna asked.

'I encountered an old friend at a ball. She had…she was in considerable trouble. I was so absorbed in talking to her that I forgot a dance I had promised Jessica. She was very cool about it. I do not think it helped that Hel—that the old friend is very beautiful.'

'Lady Charlton,' Anna said. 'Of course I remember her,

we were always friendly, and we know about what has happened to her—her sister Marjorie and I correspond.'

'Go on,' said Robert.

'The next day Jessica had gone. To London. She left a letter that said she realised that I was in love with Helena, that it had struck me just as I had always thought it would, fool that I am. That she had to come to terms with it, but would come back when she had, because she recognises her duty.'

Robert said something short under his breath, then, 'Her duty.'

'What else happened?' Anna asked. 'Jessica is a sensible woman with feelings for you that go beyond duty. She might have lost her temper with you if you have been flirting with a beautiful young lady, but she is not going to react in such a dramatic manner as that.'

He shrugged. 'I met Helena the next morning and I promised her that I would find her a house near London and help her escape to it without anyone else knowing. By the time I got back to the house Jessica had left.'

'And since then the pair of you have been nursing your wounded feelings and misunderstandings at a distance of over a hundred miles and are both too proud to try to work out what has gone wrong?'

'Yes,' Alex admitted. 'I was angry. And hurt.'

'And had you told her that you love her?' Anna demanded. When he did not answer, she did roll her eyes. '*Men*. Sort out Helena's problem so that when you do work out what to tell your wife you can give her the facts. Find Helena a lawyer so you will not be involved so closely with her until you are sure Jessica accepts her as your friend.'

'I promised I would get her away from home.' He had

given his word, but he could see now that he must keep a distance, at least until Jessica's faith in him was restored. If it ever was.

'We will do that,' Robert said. 'Go home and sleep.'

He saw Alex to the door. 'Good luck.'

'Thank you, both. I think I will need it.'

The next day Alex approved the house Goodson had picked out. He found a lawyer to deal with matters and he wrote to Helena, telling her that the Chandlers would help her and that the lawyer would manage her affairs for her. And he told her frankly that their friendship had caused a misunderstanding with Jessica that he must put right.

The day after that he called at the house in Adam Street at two in the afternoon. The door was answered by Alfred. He did not step back to allow Alex to enter.

'Is Her Grace at home?'

Alfred went red, but said firmly, 'No, Your Grace.'

'Not at home or not receiving?'

'Not receiving, Your Grace.' Now even the tips of his ears were scarlet. 'I am sorry, Your Grace.'

Alex nodded and walked steadily the short distance to the junction with the Strand. A carriage passed him and he looked back. It drew up outside Mr Danby's house and Lady Anthea and Miss Newlyn got out. They were admitted immediately.

Chapter Twenty-Nine

May 1st, just before dawn

Alex set his booted toe into a crack in the brickwork, reached up, put his hat on top of the wall between the alleyway and the back yard of the Danbys' house and hauled himself up.

There were lights on in the kitchen and on the upper floor. So, the servants were about. He jumped down into the yard, retrieved his hat, then walked to the back door, not troubling to be quiet about it. His feet crunched on spilt coal and as he reached it the door opened to reveal a scullery maid clutching a coal scuttle and shovel on her way out to refill it.

She gave a shrill scream and dropped them both with a crash.

Alex lifted his hat. 'Good morning. I do apologise for alarming you.' He walked past into the kitchen to confront a woman in a vast apron, a kettle in one hand. 'Good morning,' he repeated. 'This way for the back stairs?' and was gone before she could speak.

He encountered Alfred just reaching the foot of the stairs. The footman opened his mouth, closed it again and said, 'Miss Jessica's gone out, Your Grace.'

'At quarter to five in the morning? You'll have to do better than that, Alfred.' Half expecting the man to try to stop him he stepped to one side, but Alfred just shook his head and let him pass. 'Miss Trotter'll tell you. Dabbling in the dew. My ma always used to do it and my sisters. Used to swear by it for their skin or some such.'

And so did the village girls on May Day, although more, Alex had always suspected, to meet their swains than for a beauty treatment. And where, exactly, would someone living off the Strand go for wholesome dew?

'Which door?'

'Second on the right.' Alfred caught the sovereign that Alex tossed him neatly in one hand. 'Thank you, Your Grace.'

Alex took the stairs with more care. He had no wish to come face to face with his father-in-law at this hour of the morning.

The second door on the right was ajar and he went in, closing it behind him.

Trotter, clad in a sensible flannel robe and with her hair in curl papers, gaped at him. 'Your Grace?'

'Indeed.'

Trotter sat down on the bed, threw up her hands and said, 'Thank goodness!' She bounced up again and Alex could see her blush in the candlelight. 'I beg Your Grace's pardon, I'm sure. She's gone to Green Park, Your Grace. Driving herself in the phaeton with a groom and off to meet friends. It is going to be all right, isn't it, Your Grace? Only I've been that worried.'

'If I can make it so, Trotter. I might make a mull of it yet because I feel I'm groping in one of London's famous fogs.'

Trotter's only answer was to produce a large handkerchief and burst into tears. Alex beat a hasty retreat, down the stairs, through the kitchen, out of the back gate that Alfred was obligingly holding open and up to where Will was waiting with the curricle.

'Green Park, Will. Go to Cleveland Row.' That was the most direct route, less than a mile and passing St James's Palace. He would leave the curricle there and cut through by foot.

Despite the hour there was enough traffic—and most of it heavy vehicles and delivery carts—to slow them. The clock over the great Tudor gatehouse of the Palace was chiming five as they passed it and the first glimmerings of dawn were breaking through the clouds.

It would be a fine day. Alex only hoped it would be a good omen as he strode out into the Park.

There was the holly bush they had hidden behind when they saw Anthea kissing Major Rowlands. How idiotic to feel sentimental about a small prickly shrub. Better that than a large, prickly husband, she supposed.

'David, stop here,' she told the groom. 'You go home and I will drive back with my friends. They are only over there—see?'

He looked across and, indeed, there were Belinda, Anthea and Lucinda, close enough that their laughter and shrieks as they patted their faces with cold dew was perfectly audible. 'If you're sure, Your Grace. There doesn't seem to be anyone else about...'

'Exactly, and they have their grooms with them. Off you go back to Adam Street.'

As he drove away Jessica walked over to the holly bush and sat down on a tree stump next to it. What on earth was she doing here? No amount of May Morning dew was going to make her beautiful. She would probably catch a cold on the chest and perish, which would leave Alex a wealthy widower. Then he could live in sin with Lady Charlton and they could have beautiful children together.

Oh, don't be such a feeble creature, she told herself savagely, brushing her hand across her cheeks, which were quite damp enough without any dew. *You agreed to be a duchess, now behave like one. You* will *make this marriage work, somehow. You will learn to pretend that there is nothing wrong. You will do your duty and keep your vows.*

'Jessica?'

She was so started that she reeled back and almost fell off the stump.

Alex—or this figment of her miserable imagination—went down on one knee on the wet grass and took her hand. 'Jessica. What are you doing here?'

'Dabbling in the dew,' she said defiantly. He was real, his bare hands warm on her chilly ones.

'That is not dew.' He raised one hand and brushed the pad of his thumb along under her eyes. 'I don't think that works. I mean, why are you in London? Not because I forgot one dance, surely?'

Of course, she realised, he did not know what she had overheard, she had been too distressed to put that in the note. She pushed his hand away. 'I was in the shrubbery the morning after the ball. I heard everything. About the house, about seeing her. I know you kissed her.'

That set him back on his heels. She took the chance and jumped to her feet, took two strides away until the holly bush was between them.

'You were in the shrubbery?' Alex got to his feet slowly.

Giving himself time to decide what to say, she thought miserably.

'I went for a walk after breakfast. I saw that little shelter in the glade and thought it might be nice to build one in the castle grounds. For…for picnics. I had no idea anyone was inside, but I was standing there and then I heard everything, very clearly indeed.'

He was watching her, his face very grave. 'So that explains it. I knew you were not a woman who would do something so drastic over a missed dance and the possibility that I was flirting with a pretty girl.'

'And you were quite correct,' she threw back at him. 'But I am a woman who finds it hard to come to terms with seeing my husband fall head over heels, to hear him making arrangements to set up his mistress close to London, to hear him kissing her.'

There was a long silence, then Alex said, 'When I was a small boy my old nurse's sovereign remedy for tears was to kiss the eyelids. I did it to Helena once when she fell over and grazed her knee. I think she was eight at the time. That was what she asked me to do, because she was weeping.' He watched her face in the growing light, his own tipped a little to one side. 'Did you leave at that point?'

'Of course.' Jessica sounded defiant, but there was doubt on her face now.

'If you had stayed, you would have heard me making practical arrangements about Helena's house. You would have heard that she is going to pay for it by selling jewellery, not from any money I might give her. I have found the house now and a lawyer to administer her affairs for her and Robert and Anna Chandler, who are old friends of her, will help her escape from home and settle there.

'I understand why you believed what you did, having overheard our conversation as far as that very innocent kiss, but I give you my word, Jessica, I have no desire to make Helena my mistress, although I hope she will always be my friend. I have no desire for any mistress.'

'You are not in love with her?'

'No. How could I be, when I am in love with another lady altogether?'

He couldn't mean… No, it could not be true. 'Who?' she managed to ask.

'You. My wife,' Alex said simply. 'I was quite wrong— I didn't fall in love at first sight, or even fifth or sixth or seventh sight. I fell in love slowly, so gradually that I did not realise what had happened to me.'

'But you didn't tell me. You said nothing.'

'Because you did not love me. I did not ask you to, I married you knowing why you agreed to wed me, just as you understood my motives. Only they changed. I changed. But I couldn't put that burden on your shoulders of having to be kind to your husband who loved you.'

'Oh.' It seemed her feet were rooted to the ground and then suddenly she could move, could rush into his arms and wrap her own around him. 'Oh, we have been so blind! I love you, Alex. I have loved you for so long and I couldn't tell you. Alex! What are you doing?'

He scooped her up in his arms and strode off towards the Palace. 'Taking you home.'

His groom looked bewildered, but touched his cap politely. 'Good morning, Your Grace.'

'Home, Will, and then go around to Mr Danby's house and tell him his daughter is with her husband and will doubtless see him later this morning.'

* * *

Alex carried her up the steps, over the threshold and up the stairs to the bedchamber she had never seen, passing poker-faced staff as he went. He turned the key in the lock and looked at her as she lay getting grass and mud from her shoes on the handsome blue coverlet.

'What time must you be at the Ironmongers' Hall?'

'Eight,' she said.

'Then we do not have much time.' He began to strip off his clothing, letting it fly anywhere. 'But first I fully intend to make love to my wife—whom I love—very thoroughly indeed.'

'Oh, yes, please.' Jessica began to struggle with pins and laces until he helped her. They tumbled together on the silk, laughing and kissing.

'If only your letter had told me that you had overheard us—'

'If only you had swallowed your pride and come to London to confront me—' She smiled up at him as he came over her, his weight on his elbows. 'If only we were perfect instead of two poor mortals in love and very insecure with it.'

'Just at this moment I do not feel in the slightest insecure,' Alex said as he took her slowly, inexorably sinking into her welcoming heat, and she closed around him, caressing him with the muscles she had discovered over weeks of intimacy, finding new pleasures in the emotion she could see in his eyes.

He had said there was not much time, but Jessica was unaware of it passing, only of the slow slide of skin against skin, the pressure of lip against lip, the strength of the body joined to hers and the spiralling pleasure his caresses brought.

She could say it now. 'I love you. I love you, Alex. Now and always.'

And the words she heard as everything broke and splintered into the intensity of pleasure, were his, gasped out as he came with her. 'I love you, Jessica. *Jessica.*'

Mr Danby's well-trained staff did not turn a hair at the return of the daughter of the house, dishevelled, creased, smiling and in a desperate hurry.

'Trotter, where is my gown and my garland? Trotter—I am going to be late. Oh, Papa, Alex is in London. Do you mind dreadfully if I see the parade with him?'

Her father in his Sunday best with a huge nosegay for a buttonhole, kissed her cheek and made for the front door. 'Of course not, my dear. Off you go and get changed.'

Trotter, who for some reason seemed rather red about the eyes, was ready with the leaf-green gown, the darker green slippers and the circlet of spring flowers. She thrust Jessica into the dressing room with a cry of, 'No time for a bath! The water's warm.' When she emerged after a hasty wash, Trotter got her into petticoats, stockings and gown before attacking her hair.

'Pearl and aquamarines, I think,' Jessica managed to say between yelps as the circlet was ruthlessly pinned into place. 'Papa has found all the staff a good place to view the celebrations from, hasn't he?'

'Oh, yes, ma'am. A lovely balcony and a hamper of food from Gunther's so Cook can come, too.' She pushed in the last pin. 'Oh, you look a picture. His Grace is going to be so proud of you.'

'You know he is in London?' Of course, Alex must have

come here first, no wonder he had known where to find her. 'Have a lovely day, Trotter.'

The yard of Ironmongers' Hall off Fenchurch Street was a scene of apparent chaos. Horses neighed, people, all draped in flowers and greenery, ran back and forth, everyone was shouting and the horses were neighing. Jessica almost panicked, then she saw that Major Percy, in armour on horseback, was directing the floats to line up in order and that Alex and his other friends were lifting the faux milkmaids on to the carts and marshalling the apprentices and journeymen.

The clock stuck the quarter-hour: it was almost time to leave. Then she saw that the float that had had the scene of housemaids and a chimney with a sweep by it had a large throne-like chair placed where it looked out from the back. It was covered in greenery and bunches of flowers.

'Here she is!' Alex fought his way towards her through the throng. 'Come along. You are to be the Queen of the May.'

Before she could protest he started unpinning her wreath, draped a vast fragile white silk veil over her head and replaced the coronet. Then he picked her up and lifted her on to the float, got up beside her and handed her on to her throne. 'Your sceptre, ma'am.' She took the wand decorated with flowers and trailing ivy.

'Here's your costume, Demeral.' Viscount Oakham, almost unrecognisable beneath green paint and a long green wig handed Alex a strange structure like a domed basket with a hole at the front. It was absolutely covered in foliage, but no flowers. 'And here's the mask,' he said as Alex upended the structure over his head.

'I am the Green Man,' said this rather scary apparition. 'Lord to the Queen of the May.'

There was a very military shout from Major Percy and suddenly they were in motion. The gates opened and the roar of the crowd greeted them. All around was music, singing, cheers, catcalls. Small boys—the sweeping lads—ran back and forth, hurling their brick dust, onlookers, many of them dressed in green, joined in, dancing along-side for a while before they fell back to greet the next float.

Following her, Jessica could see the maiden in her tower and catch a glimpse of cocked hats and gold chains as the Ironmongers fell in at the rear.

It was chaos, it was almost anarchy, but it was joyful. Spring had come, green shoots were bursting out between cracks in old paving, soot-laden plane trees were decked once more in fresh leaves. Everyone was having the most marvellous time. Small boys were everywhere, hands held out for money, calling, 'Sir, remember the Bough!'

She saw the crowded balconies, saw her father who was brandishing his hat and tossing coins to the lads and milkmaid.

Jessica waved and kissed her hand and was pelted with flowers, some money—which small dirty hands rapidly scooped up—and some brick dust.

Behind her Alex rested one hand on her shoulder, his fingers tracing caresses on her bare skin. He was laugh-ing, throwing back flowers as they hit him, but she could hear his voice, pitched to reach only her ears.

'Queen of the May, queen of my castle, queen of my heart. True love of my life.'

* * * * *

Author Note

Modern Ironmongers' Hall, rebuilt in 1922 after a bomb destroyed the building in 1917, is in Aldersgate. The Hall that Jessica knew was in Fenchurch Street and was built in 1745, replacing the medieval halls on that site.

Maypoles had disappeared from London by the Regency, although they persisted—and can still be seen—on village greens throughout the country.

Mr Brand, in his *Observations on Popular Antiquities... Vulgar Customs, Ceremonies and Superstitions* recorded:

> *In the* Morning Post, *Monday May 2nd, 1791, it was mentioned that yesterday, being the first of May, according to annual and superstitious custom, a number of persons went into the fields and bathed their faces with the dew on the grass, under the idea that it would render them beautiful... The Mayings are in some sort yet kept up by the milkmaids at London, who go about the streets with their garlands and musick, dancing...*

And as for the chimney sweeps' boys—those he describes as *'the most striking objects in the celebration of May Day in the streets of London'.*

If you enjoyed this story,
be sure to check out some of
Louise Allen's other great reads

The Duke's Counterfeit Wife
The Earl's Mysterious Lady
His Convenient Duchess
A Rogue for the Dutiful Duchess
Becoming the Earl's Convenient Wife

And why not pick up her
Liberated Ladies miniseries?

Least Likely to Marry a Duke
The Earl's Marriage Bargain
A Marquis in Want of a Wife
The Earl's Reluctant Proposal
A Proposal to Risk Their Friendship